INKED 8

A TATTOO SHOP REVERSE HAREM ROMANCE

STEPHANIE BROTHER

INKED 8 Copyright © 2022 STEPHANIE BROTHER

All Rights Reserved. This book or any portion thereof may not be reproduced or used in any manner whatsoever without the express permission of the publisher except for the use of brief quotations in a book review.

This book is a work of fiction. Any resemblance to persons, living or dead, or places, events or locations is purely coincidental. The characters are all productions of the author's imagination.

Please note that this work is intended only for adults over the age of 18 and all characters represented as 18 or over.

ISBN: 9798433805026

1

KYLA

"You have to apply for the job," Dawn says as she leans against the counter at the Daily Grind, my current miserable place of work.

"Sshhh," I say, glancing around and finding my manager safely out of earshot. Not that Dawn would care. She's been telling me to leave this place since I first secured the role. Admittedly, the pay sucks, and my manager works me until I'm broken and expects a smile to top it all off. Not only that, but I'm actually one of life's weirdos who doesn't have a hard-on for coffee. Give me a nice creamy hot chocolate every time. Or a glass of wine.

Going home every day with the smell of burnt coffee beans in my hair and clothes is just the icing on a hugely gross cake.

"I don't know anything about tattoos," I say. "How can I apply for a job in a tattoo parlor?"

"You don't need to know anything about tattoos," Dawn says. "It's an admin role. They need someone to organize them, and you are the queen of organization."

She's right. Just thinking about my pantry that's filled with labeled glass jars, and my color-coded closet fills me with peace and joy.

"How did you find out about it?"

Dawn grins and yanks down the back of her baggy boyfriend jeans, twisting her body around so she can show me the new ink she has on the small of her back and watch my expression at the same time. My expression of horror.

"YOLO?" I blink slowly, wondering why my friend would have a word that isn't even a word marked forever on her skin.

"Yeah. You know, you only live once."

"Oh, yeah. Of course." I paint on the best smile I can to conceal my shock. "Well, that certainly fits you."

"Exactly," she gushes. "And anyway, while I was getting this done, the boss over there was ranting about how he can never find anything, and one of the guys suggested they get someone in to do their admin. At that point, I told them I knew just the person. The role hasn't been advertised. You'll be the only one going for an interview."

"Until they meet me and realize that I'm not exactly Miss Cool."

"They're not looking for Miss Cool," Dawn says as her eyes drop to take in my light blue sweater and skinny jeans. I know they're not supposed to be fashionable anymore, but I can't seem to move on from their figure-hugging style. "They're looking for Miss Organized."

I catch my manager scowling in my direction from the corner of my eye. Dawn has been hanging around for too long, and I'm going to get warned about it any minute.

"When should I go in?"

"I told them you finish from here at five pm. They're

expecting you just after."

"Today!" I snort, a hot flush rising up my neck and burning my cheeks.

"Yes, today. Strike while the iron's burning, or whatever the saying is."

"Hot," I correct, because that's exactly what I am. Roasting with embarrassment and mortification. "I can't go dressed like this."

Dawn scans my attire again but dismisses my objection with a wave of her hand. "You'll be fine. Just talk up your admin experience, and everything will be great. Oh, and push them for a decent paycheck. You deserve at least twice what you're making here, and they can afford it. Ink Factor is a countrywide franchise. These guys started it, so they're loaded, but they still like to stay close to their craft."

"Twice? Are you sure?"

"Twice," she says firmly. Her hand goes to her earring, rolling the black beads between her fingers as she glances around the coffee shop. It's quiet today, which is the only reason I've had more than two seconds to talk to her. And the only reason my boss hasn't flipped out yet. "I'd better go. I'm picking up some seriously negative vibes from the dragon."

"She's going to breathe fire all over me," I whisper mournfully.

"Let her. And tomorrow, you'll be able to tell her to stick her job up her tight, scaly ass!"

"Sshhh," I say again as Dawn pivots daintily on her chunky black loafers.

"I'll sshh if you promise me that you'll go."

"Okay, I promise." I guess I have nothing to lose, except my dignity and my confidence and this job if Dawn doesn't make a sharp exit.

My bestie bows, giving me a wink. "From now on, you can call me your fairy godmother. Oh, and call me as soon as you're done." A sly smile creeps across her red lips as though there's something she's not telling me, but she's backing away before I get a chance to probe.

The bell on the door jangles loudly as she leaves, and my boss opens her thin lips to tell me that friends aren't supposed to keep us busy at work, but before she gets a chance, I make my excuses and dash to the toilet.

In the mirror, I find my disheveled self in all my glory. Why didn't I put on some make-up this morning? My hair looks like I've just got out of bed after some very vigorous sex. Splashing my face with some water, I pat it dry with a paper towel. At least my skin is clear, and after some finger combing, my hair is a little more presentable.

Posture, I remember my mom shouting at me every time I slouched as a teen. Rolling my shoulders back, I draw myself up to my full five-foot-six-inches and try to look like Miss Professional. It's going to take a seriously straight spine to pull this off, but I'm going to do it, just so I can see my boss's withered butthole of a mouth when I quit.

2

KYLA

Ink Factor is exactly as daunting as I pictured it would be. With blackened windows, a sign that is mostly graffiti, and pumping music pouring from inside, it's not the kind of place I would ever usually walk into.

I cross my arm over my chest, grabbing the brown leather handle of my purse and taking a deep breath. *You deserve to get paid twice what you're making,* I mutter under my breath. *You're an excellent administrator, and you're going to get this job. You can do this.*

Reaching my hand out to take ahold of the door handle, I jump, sensing someone behind me.

That someone is tall, gorgeous, and tattooed almost everywhere that there's skin on show.

"Sorry," I stutter. "Were you waiting to go inside?"

"I was." His deep voice rumbles, tickling my nipples and the place between my legs that has seen so little action that it doesn't know what to do in the presence of so much testosterone. He must be at least six-four of muscle and sex appeal, with a shaven head and eyes the color of honey. But it's the way he draws his bottom lip between his teeth as his eyes trail over me like maple syrup trickling over a pancake that has my heart beating triple time.

God, it should be illegal for one man to be so perfect. He should have a warning sign permanently pinned to his snug black shirt to let poor unsuspecting girls like me know just how dangerous it is to look at him.

The scene from the *Jungle Book* movie flashes through my mind where the snake's eyes begin to pulse in concentric circles, mesmerizing Mowgli. Poor thing never stood a chance, and neither do I!

"I'm sorry," I mumble again, all memory of my pep talk disappearing in a fog of sex and stupidity.

"Were you waiting to go in?" Cocking his head to the side, he rests his hand over mine on the door handle, making me jump.

"I'm here for a job interview." My voice is a husky croak as he eases open the door, controlling my hand with a firmness that I feel everywhere.

"A job interview," he repeats, nodding knowingly. I want to ask him what he knows, but I can barely breathe with his warm skin pressed against mine.

Touching hands shouldn't feel this forbidden.

"Yes. For an administrator."

He smiles at that. "Well, I didn't think you were an artist. Too much of a virgin."

"Virgin?" I stutter as he places his booted foot in front of the door to wedge it open.

"Yeah," he says with a smirk. His hand brushes my neck and over the pale skin of my shoulder that's peeking out where my sweater has slipped down on one side. "So much pretty virgin skin."

Oh God. My cheeks flame like a freaking gas explosion,

and a shiver sends a rush of goosebumps just about everywhere, all of which is completely obvious to this man. He bites his lip ring again, that slow smile easing over his perfect lips.

"Noah," a voice yells from the depths of the shop. "Your appointment is here. Quit stalling in the door."

He rolls his eyes, still in no rush to get inside. Dipping his head, he gets close enough that I can smell the lemony fresh scent of his skin. "You can do it," he murmurs. "You've got this." And with a wink, he adds. "You deserve twice what you're getting paid. Tell Carl. He'll give it to you if you ask nicely."

And with that, Noah rests his hand on the small of my back and ushers me inside.

Gazing around, I must look like a terrified raccoon caught in the beams of an eighteen-wheeler. The walls of the shop are a mixture of bare brick and graffiti-style art that reflects tattoo imagery, from dragons to pin-up girls. A huge messy desk dominates the front of the store, and behind it, a huge man, with broad shoulders and light blond hair tied back into what looks like a Viking style, frowns at some paperwork.

"Hey, Carl. This girl is here for the interview."

Carl lowers the paper slowly, his icy blue eyes rising to judge me. Noah makes what sounds like a derisive snort and disappears to one of the stations, shaking the hand of a bulky man in a leather vest waiting there.

"I'm Kyla," I say, stepping forward and holding out my hand. "My friend Dawn told me you're looking for an administrator. She told me to come for an interview."

Carl's eyes drift to my hand, and he stands, rising to a height that should be impossible. I thought Noah was tall, but Carl is more wall than man. When his hand envelopes mine in a brisk and firm shake, it's like a giant shaking hands with a child.

Clearing his throat, he draws his hand back. "You'd better come through to the back."

He turns before I have a chance to respond and makes his way deeper into the shop, leaving me with a view of his retreating form. And what a form it is.

In his snug gray shirt, the V of his back is like an ancient marble carving of Hercules. His powerful ass and thighs are almost fighting to get out of the confines of his jeans. And his arms…oh Lord, his arms. His biceps are bigger than the widest point of my leg.

As I finally find the brain cells to tell my body to move, I feel eyes on me. I don't turn to look at the other men who are staring at me with interest. They're supposed to be working, and I'm supposed to be making a way more professional impression than I'm making right now.

Carl disappears through a door, and I stumble to keep up, finally stepping into an office space that is nothing like the customer-facing side of the business. In here, it's sterile white, with a mishmash of generic office furniture and piles and piles of paperwork.

Two chairs are tucked under the desk, and Carl pulls one out, offering it to me before slumping into the other. When I take a seat, I find myself sitting really close to him without the protection of a table between us.

Awkward.

"So, Kyla?" He sounds uncertain that he's remembered my name correctly.

"Yes."

Carl nods, jotting my name down on a scrappy piece of paper. "Have you worked in a tattoo shop before?"

Shaking my head, I feel the dread of failure already creeping in, but I straighten my shoulders and channel Dawn's confidence. "I don't know anything about tattoos, but I do know admin. I have experience in organizing small businesses, and I can put in place systems for bookings, finances, and human resource admin. I know how to get you out of this mess."

My eyes drift over what is frankly disorganization and chaos.

"Do you have a résumé?"

"Not with me. This was kind of sprung on me this afternoon, but I can send it to you when I get home."

Carl studies me carefully, the ice blue of his eyes scanning me like an x-ray machine. What's he thinking right now? I'd love to know what's going on in his head. He's probably wondering why a scruffy woman has wasted his time without any evidence of being qualified.

"Well, you come very highly recommended," he says, leaning back in his chair.

"By Dawn," I smile. "She's always singing my praises, but she's not exactly a previous employer."

"And this isn't exactly a traditional small business. We're all here because we love our art. The business side is just taking over. All I want to be able to do is hand it over to someone and get on with what we started this business for in the first place."

"Well, I'm certainly happy to take it on." I scan the office again, already itching to order some pretty pastel-colored files and one of those machines that prints out labels. I'll have this place organized in no time if Carl will just see that I'm made for this job.

"One-week trial," he says with determination in his deep voice.

"I have a job," I say, "And I can't give it up for a trial."

"Can you stay now? Work three hours and take me through what you've done. I'll pay your rate for the time you spend, regardless of whether you get the job at the end.

"Three hours?" I'm already exhausted from a long

shift, but if that's what it's going to take for Carl to see my skills in all their glory, I'll do it.

I tell him my rate, and he doesn't even blink at the amount Dawn suggested. With a simple nod, he stands and stares at the worst pile. "It's all yours."

And then he's gone, and I'm left to sift through the worst disorganization I've ever seen in my life.

3

CARL

Kyla sorts through the surface mounds of paperwork for three hours, forming piles amongst the chaos. There's so much dust in that room that I almost head in there with a cloth for her to wipe her hands on but to be honest, I'm too embarrassed. It's not like me to let life get into a disorganized state, but I've just taken on too much that I don't enjoy, and I'm craving to get back to my passion.

As Kyla's three hours come to an end, I hang out in the doorway, watching her glancing around at the beginnings of the organization that she's created, probably wondering if she's done enough to get the job. She's barely scratched the surface, but I can see that she knows what she's doing and will have no problem tackling the worst.

Anyway, we can afford to make a mistake in hiring her. Business has been good. It's worth taking a chance if it gives me some breathing space. I'm an optimist and a realist.

When I knock on the open door, she almost jumps out

of her skin, and I have to swallow the smile that threatens, aiming to keep professional.

"How did you get on?" I ask.

"I've made a tiny dent in the surface paperwork. I've made date-ordered piles for paperwork for each of your other franchises. This pile is for bank statements, this one is for credit card bills. This pile is all your expenses, and this one is everything HR-related." She continues, pointing out all the categories, and then she shows me something that makes my jaw drop. "And these are the invoices I believe are overdue. You really need to pay them before the suppliers cut off your credit or start legal proceedings."

As I flick through the five overdue invoices, my eyebrows rise. "I didn't even know these were here."

"I'm not surprised. Look, I know there's a lot more to be done, but I hope you can see that I know what I'm doing. I can really help you."

"Send me through your résumé, and I'll send you a contract tomorrow. What's your notice period?"

"One week," she says. A slight flash of color spreads across her cheeks. Is she excited about this new role? Can she really see herself working in a place like this? She doesn't really fit in appearance-wise, but that doesn't matter to me. I've always loved girls with milky white unmarked skin, and anyway, no one knows what's under a person's clothes. She could have tattoos all over her butt, and no one would be able to tell.

"One week it is. Can I ask you something else?"

"Sure." Rising from the chair, Kyla smooths her hands over her jeans, hoping to dislodge any visible dust.

"Will you come out for a drink with us now? I want the rest of the team to meet you."

"Now?"

"Yeah." I glance at my watch, finding that it's only 8.30 pm. It's hardly the Cinderella pumpkin hour, but maybe

Kyla isn't a party girl.

"Err...okay. I guess."

"They're a good crowd," I say, my lips quirking slightly at her obvious uncertainty. "I promise I'll keep them under control."

"You make them sound like a pack of rabid dogs," she laughs nervously.

When I clear my throat, she shifts on her feet. "There's a bar around the corner. That's where we usually hang out to blow off some steam. Why don't you head over there while I get this place closed up? We'll join you in a few minutes."

"Sure, okay."

I direct Kyla to the Red Devil, which is primarily a hang-out place for the college kids in town. We know the manager, which is why we go out there. It's probably not the kind of place that Kyla would expect us to go to. It's not really a place I can see Kyla fitting into either. But they serve an awesome cocktail, which most of the girls drink. It's red and sticky and is what the bar is named after.

When I show Kyla to the door, she seems nervous. I guess it's to be expected. I hope she'll have more confidence once she starts, or the men in this place are going to eat her alive.

"She's cute," Noah says, emerging from his station and wiping his freshly washed hands on a towel.

"She is," I agree. "Something fascinatingly awkward about her."

"She was just nervous," Noah says, but the smile in his eyes tells me he knows what I'm thinking.

Inappropriate thoughts.

Fantasies of ordering Kyla to her knees with her hands behind her back, telling her to open her mouth for me, and forcing it open when she hesitates. Kyla would be perfectly submissive for me, at least in my dreams. You never can tell in real life.

"Did you hire her?" he asks.

"If her résumé checks out, then yes. And we're meeting her at the Red Devil to make sure you guys think she'll fit."

"Oh, she'll fit alright. There's not a man in this place who wouldn't love a pretty girl to work here. Plus, you've been walking around like a bear with a sore head for weeks. We need the help."

"Get the rest of these reprobates to hurry up so we can go and meet her. I don't want to keep her waiting too long."

The Red Devil isn't as busy as usual, but I guess it's still early. I spot Kyla easily, sitting in a booth that's side-on to the door. She's on the phone and not aware that we've arrived. "You guys wait here. I'll go see what Kyla's drinking. As I approach, I find Noah, and his triplet brothers, Niall and Nash behind me. In addition to their identical looks, they seem to have an identical inability to take instructions. I guess they're more than a little curious about our newest employee.

Kyla's talking loudly, and I don't want to interrupt.

"You are terrible," she says to whoever is on the other end of the call. "They're all strictly off-limits. This is a work arrangement, not a hook-up."

There's a pause, and then she adds. "I'm pretty sure they'll all be dating. I mean, the women of this town would have to be blind to have passed over the gods of Ink Factor."

"Gods?" Noah says. "We've been called many things over the years, but gods isn't one of them."

Kyla swivels her head so fast it must have jarred, finding Noah grinning wickedly at her, surrounded by his carbon copies and me. Her eyes widen, flicking back and forth as though she's worried if she's drunk so much, she's hallucinating. I guess identical triplets aren't the most common phenomenon. I forget that, having grown up with the Johnson brothers.

"I've got to go," she whispers into the phone, lowering it before the person on the other end would have a chance to respond.

She blinks slowly again as though she's attempting to clear her vision, but we're all still there when her eyes open. She must notice the differences between Noah and his brothers. Niall has tattoo sleeves, slashes through his eyebrows, and an eyebrow piercing, and Nash has tattoos peeking over the collar of his shirt and two sparkling diamond earrings.

Definitely triplets.

"Guys, this is Kyla. These two lesser versions of me are Niall and Nash," Noah says.

"Hi," she mumbles as they flash her with their matching smiles. *Gods*. Did she really just say that about us?

I shouldn't like the thought as much as I do. People worship gods. I'd love this girl to worship at my feet. I'd treat her strictly and reward her devotion.

"Another drink, Kyla," Noah asks, his honey eyes gleaming with mischief.

"I think I'm going to need one," she says, knocking back the last gulp of sweet alcohol in her drink. She's looking for some liquid confidence.

Noah nods toward the bar, a clear indication for his brothers to fetch the drink, and they leave without any objection as Noah slides into the booth opposite Kyla. I take a seat too, resting my arms on the cool table top.

"So, you got the job," Noah says. "All that pep-talking outside definitely did the trick."

I have no idea what he's talking about, but I make a note to ask him later.

"I think it was more the sheer desperation of your boss," she laughs, glancing at me out of the corner of her eyes.

"Carl doesn't do anything unless he's absolutely certain," Noah says. "He's a man of clear purpose."

"I am," I agree.

Nodding, Noah glances to where the rest of the team are gathered at the bar. "You'll learn that he likes things to be done a certain way."

"Well, I'll try to follow his orders," Kyla says, blushing in my direction.

Noah grins a little wider than fits with the conversation.

She flops back against the soft red booth. "So, how long have you been working together?"

"We're all neighborhood friends," I say. Beneath the table, my ankle brushes Kyla's, and I feel the sensation in totally unrelated places. "We grew up together and decided to start a business."

"Wow, that's awesome."

"It has its moments."

I glance back to the bar, finding a wall of men walking toward us, bearing drinks. Nash is first to reach the table and tells Noah to make room. We all slide further into the booth giving the rest of the Ink Factor team space to sit down. Kyla steals furtive glances at her future workmates.

"Everyone, this is Kyla. She's joining Ink Factor, and she's going to drag our disorganized asses into a new era of professionalism." I nod with purpose, as though by the very act of speaking, I can manifest my will.

"She's gonna need some super-strength," Kole says. Kyla's eyes drift over his tight black tight curls and cloud-gray eyes. He has a slightly crooked nose that was broken in a fight, and a faint scar that runs up his right cheek. She'd be right in thinking that he's the brawler of the group. There's always one who has a short fuse. When he rubs the side of his nose, his knuckles are latticed with thin white scars.

"She's going to get our help," I insist.

"Of course," Noah says. Kyla jumps as though Noah touched her beneath the table. Is he seriously already manhandling the new recruit? Maybe hiring a woman is a mistake, but there's no going back now.

"Right, let's do introductions." I nod to Dex, who's sitting next to me.

"I'm Dex, and this is Lex." He tips his head in his brother's direction, and they both grin. Unlike Noah and his brothers, Dex and Lex are so identical it's hard for even me to tell them apart.

"Show her your hands," Carl says.

They each hold up their right hand, revealing a difference that will help her in telling who is who. Dex has a large intricate D tattooed across the soft skin on the top of his hand, and Lex has a matching L.

"She knows us already," Noah says.

"Just us left then. I'm Kole, and this is Kase."

"I can introduce myself," Kase says, rolling his eyes. "He always does that. Thinks just because he was born a minute early that I'm incapable of speaking."

"On a daily basis, I regret becoming friends with so many fucking multiple births." I down a long pull of my beer and place it onto the table with a little too much force.

"Do you have brothers or sisters, Kyla?" Niall asks.

"Nah," she shrugs. "Just me, but my friend Dawn is like my sister. We've known each other since kindergarten."

"Is that Dawn with YOLO?" Niall asks.

"That's the one."

"So, who's going to pop your tattoo cherry?" Kole asks.

"No one," Kyla blurts. "Since I had a ruptured appendix as a teen, needles have become a whole lot more terrifying. There's no way I'll let anyone come near me with one unless it's life-or-death."

"Is it even a thing to have a tattoo-free person working in a tattoo parlor?" Dex asks. When he speaks, I catch a glint of the piercing in his tongue and wonder what Kyla thinks of us all with so many body modifications between us.

"Well, I guess I don't have to take the job if you have a problem with it," Kyla says.

"No problem," I say. "But if you do want a tattoo one day, I claim that first one."

"Why do you get to claim it?" Noah grumbles.

"Because I'm the boss."

"And do I get a say in the matter?" Kyla asks.

The stern look in my icy blue eyes should tell her absolutely not. When I say something, I mean it. No ifs. No buts.

Kyla only stays with us for one drink and then makes an excuse to leave. When she's gone, the team all give me the seal of approval. Their opinion is important to me, but I wouldn't have changed my mind about Kyla even if they didn't like her. We need the help too much. When she gets home, she forwards her résumé immediately, and within five minutes, I send her the contract. I imagine her reading through the great salary and awesome benefits and smiling that pretty smile.

I hope she's as happy about joining our team as I am to

welcome her.

Now all she has to do is quit her other job.

Fingers crossed that all goes off without a hitch.

4

KYLA

"What did she say?" Dawn whispers as I prepare her coffee. In the corner of the shop, my boss is currently grim-faced, her eyes glued to her computer.

"She looked so shocked. It's like she assumed I really like working here. Or should I say, working for her."

"I wish I could have been here." Dawn reaches out for the cardboard cup of her favorite Americano. "I'd have paid good money to see her expression."

"Well, it's done now. All I've got to do is get through the next few days."

"Just think about what it's going to be like being surrounded by all that sexy inked eye candy every day." The salacious wink Dawn gives me makes me snort with laughter.

"Yeah, I have a bone to pick with you. How come you failed to mention how gorgeous they all are?"

"Would you have gone for the interview if I shared that, or would you have been completely intimidated?"

"Intimidated," I muse. "Anyway, I didn't tell you who came in today?"

"Who?"

"Luna Evans."

Dawn's black-lined eyes widen. "The popstar? The one who's fucking seven sexy bodyguards?"

"Yep. She's in this group called The Reverse Harem Ladies Club."

"They have a club? Who's in the club? I want to be in the club!"

We both chuckle but this time, when my boss looks at me like she wants to melt my insides out of my eyeballs, I don't care one bit.

"There are five women. Natalie has three husbands, Connie has four. Melanie isn't married, but she's in a relationship with five cowboys, and Sandy is with six men. Luna's harem is the biggest."

"Go Luna!"

"They were joking that I should try for a harem of eight. Me!"

Dawn rests her hand on my arm, the way she always does when I'm putting myself down. "Why the hell not you? Those guys would be lucky to have someone as awesome as you."

"I couldn't handle one of them, let alone eight." It's true. I wouldn't have a clue how to go on a date with a man that good-looking. My two past boyfriends were nice guys but definitely not highly ranked on the sexy chart. I could think clearly when we were together, and I could also see when things weren't working out without being blinded by their looks.

Gorgeous men have a terrible effect on me. They shrivel my brain cells until I'm a blubbering, swooning mess of a person. They also shrivel my confidence, which is saying something because it's already microscopically small.

I wave my free hand to show Dawn that I'm not bothered either way. "Anyway, Luna wants a tattoo. She's going to wait until after she has the baby, but she wants to go to Ink Factor to speak to them and plan everything out."

"Seriously."

"Yep. I've booked her in for a consultation later."

"Your first customer is a celebrity. Those guys are going to love you!"

"Well, she's not paying yet, but if she likes what they suggest, I guess she will be."

"Can I come too?"

Oh my goodness. Dawn and Luna. I'm not sure what that combination will look like, but I can't say no to the girl who got me the job in the first place. "Of course. Just come back at five pm."

At 5 pm, I leave the store by the front door with my soon-to-be-ex manager still scowling. Dawn is leaning up against the wall outside, grinning at something on her phone, and perfectly on time, as a black limousine with heavily tinted windows pulls up at the curb. The front window lowers, and a man in dark glasses nods in my direction.

"My friend is coming with us," I say, waving to get Dawn's attention. This is all suddenly feeling really inappropriate, but I'm in too deep to reverse. The bodyguard throws open the door, drawing himself up to an impressive height, glancing up and down the street like he's expecting an ambush.

Another window lowers at the back, and Luna leans closer. "That's fine. Jump in."

"Oh my God," Dawn whispers, seriously star-struck for the first time in her life. I think it's because Luna's biggest hit came out when Dawn was going through a bad breakup and the words really resonated.

I pull open the door, finding Luna flanked by two bodyguards inside. There's another opposite and, thankfully, enough spare seats for Dawn and me.

When we're inside, the door slams behind us and locks click into place.

For a few seconds, while my eyes adjust to the low light, I gaze around. It's not just a car. It's a whole different world. Total luxury and anonymity rolled into one.

"Thank you so much for coming with me," Luna says. "I'm really nervous."

"Oh, don't worry," Dawn says, her voice suddenly a whole pitch higher than usual. "The guys are really nice, and they do exactly what you ask for."

"That's just it," Luna says, turning her hands over, so her palms face the sky. "I don't really have an idea of what I want."

"Why are you getting the tattoo, if you don't mind me asking?"

Luna blinks slowly, drawing in a deep breath as though she's trying to push down something painful. "My brother passed. I want something so that he's always with me."

I frown, wondering if I knew that about her. The news is always bubbling with celebrity gossip, but so much about Luna has been the narrative about her humble beginnings; a Cinderella story of sorts, and the rest has been about her unconventional relationship. "I'm sure if you talk to them about him, they'll be able to come up with lots of ideas." Dawn nods firmly, so confident that my new employers are going to come through. I wish I had the same certainty.

Before Luna has a chance to reply, we're already outside Ink Factor. She shuffles forward on the seat, leaning to look at the place, her rounded pregnant belly getting in the way. "I guess this is it."

"It'll be fine," one of the bodyguards says, but then he puts a hand on her knee, squeezing reassuringly, and it seems more intimate than professional.

Luna catches me staring and smiles. "This is Hudson. He's got more tattoo experience than me. He's come along to help me decide."

The door is pulled open from the outside, and Dawn and I escape its depths first, followed by the bodyguards, Luna, and then Hudson. I'm immediately struck by how tiny she is. There's definitely a larger-than-life persona that comes with being a celebrity.

"You ready?" I ask her.

"As I'll ever be."

I take the lead, opening the door to my new place of work, probably more nervous than Luna. The music is something heavy with lots of drums and rising guitar melodies. The sound of the tattoo machines is a low hum, and even lower are the deep voices of my coworkers as they talk to their clients. Carl is at the desk, clutching a handful of papers, the frown between his brows so deep that it would rival the Grand Canyon.

When his cool blue eyes flick up, he's quick to straighten at the sight of all the burly bodyguards. When his gaze lands on me, his shoulders sink with what looks like relief. "There you are, Kyla," he says. "Please tell me you've come to deal with this?"

"Not until next week," I say sweetly. "I'm here with Luna Evans. I called and booked her in earlier."

"Luna Evans." He uses his index finger to sweep down the messy appointments book, finding her name. Glancing up again, he surveys the group, and I see the moment he recognizes that the Luna Evans I'm talking about isn't just an ordinary client. "She's with Noah," Carl says. "But I'm free to assist in any way."

"I'm sure Noah will be fine."

The man of the hour pops his head around his booth. "Come on in," he calls, totally undaunted by the famous woman he's going to be talking to. I like that about him.

We all make our way over, and Luna perches on the reclined chair, her hands folded in her lap. Hudson watches everything with cool assessment, including the bodyguards.

Noah rests against the counter that runs down the side of his booth, folding his well-muscled arms across his broad chest. "So, you want a tattoo?" His soft, caramel eyes drop to Luna's swollen belly. "We wouldn't recommend it now, but when you've had the baby…"

"I'm not going to get it until after the birth," Luna says. "I just want to get an idea of what it will be like. I'm a planner."

Noah smiles. "Well, is there something in particular?"

"My brother's name," she says softly. "Jake."

"Okay," His expression softens. "So, something that reminds you of who he was?" Noah reaches for a pad and pencil, jotting and already sketching. "Do you just want his name in cursive, or with a photographic-style image of him, or an object or something that you associate with him?"

"I'm not really sure. This is my first tattoo."

"She likes mine," Hudson says. Without hesitation, he unbuttons his crisp white shirt, revealing an elaborate cursive name across his heart.

"That's great lettering," Noah says. "But I'm thinking something more illustrative for Luna. Tell me about Jake."

"He was always smiling like he had sunshine pouring

out of him. He loved running and being outdoors."

"I've got an idea," Noah says. Scribbling on the pad frantically, he draws his lip ring between his lips. Luna shuffles back a little, crossing her legs and shaking her black spike-heeled boot. I guess women who get chauffeur-driven around don't need to worry about inappropriate footwear. My worn Converse are hardly sexy, but who has time to worry about that when I'm on my feet all day.

Carl hangs around outside the booth as though he's worried that Noah will fuck things up, but when Noah tucks the pencil behind his ear and turns the pad to Luna, her reaction is extreme. Her hands fly to her mouth and her green eyes fill with tears.

The image is stunning. A sun rests in the protective crescent of the moon, with the lettering of Jake's name curled around the bottom. "You can have it in color or black, whichever you prefer."

"I love it like that." Luna brushes a tear from her eye, her hand going to gently touch the crescent moon at her throat. "Can I take that with me? I want to show it to Asher."

Noah nods, tearing it from the pad. With his phone, he snaps a quick picture. "I'll save it in case you lose it before you want to come back."

Luna presses the drawing to her chest, smiling sadly. "I won't lose it."

"Do you feel better now?" Hudson asks softly. When she nods, he rests his big hand on her shoulder.

"Wow," Dawn says. "I told you these guys are awesome."

Her comment is directed at me, and I nod, smiling at Noah, who winks with self-satisfaction. I guess there was no worry on his part about whether he could design something fitting. By the time I glance back to Carl, he's already disappeared.

Luna stands and holds out her hand for Noah to shake. "I'll be back in a few months when this one is safely in the world."

"Good luck with that," Noah smiles. "Getting a tattoo won't be half as painful."

Then Luna grimaces and then turns her attention to me, taking my hand and walking out of the booth. The bodyguards hustle around us as she leads me back to the sidewalk. "Thanks, Kyla," she says, pulling me into a gentle hug. "Oh, and if the other six are as gorgeous as the two I met, you should definitely go for it."

Her grin is just about as wicked as I have ever seen, and my blush feels like a raging inferno across my cheeks. "What should she go for?" Dawn asks, only hearing the tail end of the conversation.

"That would be telling," Luna says. Reaching out, she takes Hudson's hand. "Let's go home," she says. "The others will be wondering what's keeping us."

"Don't worry," Hudson smiles. "I already messaged them. Do you think Connor would expect anything less?"

As they disappear into the limousine, waving as it pulls away, I can't help but think about what Luna said. Eight men.

That little woman handles seven, but she's a firecracker. I'm just an ordinary girl. Seven might be lucky for a superstar, but eight would be impossible for little old me.

5

NOAH

I arrive at work earlier than usual, knowing that it's Kyla's first day. My brothers don't believe my excuse that I left my station in a mess. I'm meticulous when it comes to my art, and there has never been a day when I've left Ink Factor without getting everything clean and tidy.

Whatever.

I don't miss their shared glances, but I don't care about what they think anyway.

I hang around by the reception desk, making small talk with Carl. He seems happy to unload some of the business challenges, which is unusual for him. Or maybe it's just unusual for me to provide a listening ear.

Out of the corner of my eye, I see Kyla arrive outside, pausing to straighten her black slacks and a pink button-down shirt. She's curled her chestnut hair this morning, making it obvious that she wants to make a good impression on her first day.

What she doesn't realize is that she made a pretty big

impression the first time she came into this shop.

Kyla's nothing like the girls that usually hang around a place like this. My last girlfriend lived in band tees and ripped jeans. She wanted me to cover her in ink. By the time we broke up, there wasn't much virgin skin left.

Kyla, on the other hand, is all virgin territory. Her pretty pale skin is just begging for marks, but she doesn't want any. As she pushes open the door, I have to stifle a smile. It's good that she's kept true to herself and not tried to blend in with the shop and the rest of us. I like that she looks like a doctor's receptionist. It adds a certain professionalism to the place and shows me that Kyla has confidence in her own identity.

"Morning," she says brightly, her eyes scanning first over Carl, lingering on his long blond hair, which he has drawn into an elaborate braided style. He's channeling his Viking heritage and has the air of an ancient warrior. Today he's wearing a sleeveless shirt that shows off his elaborately tattooed forearms covered in a latticework of intricate tribal-style designs. It's only when her gaze drifts to me that the pretty flush returns to her cheeks.

"Kyla, am I glad to see you!" Carl says.

"Well, that's a warmer welcome than I ever received at the Daily Grind." Kyla grips her purse, smiling with a look of relief. She's trying to come across as confident, but her body language is saying something else entirely.

"You might not be so happy once you've been dealing with this mess all day." Carl's hands drift across the chaos that is our reception area.

"It'll all be fine," she says brightly. "Leave it to me. I'll shout if I need anything."

"Can you deal with the booking system first?" Carl asks, running his big hand over the top of his hair. "It's a miracle we have any customers left. It's such a mess."

"Sure. That'll be no problem."

Wasting no time, Kyla drops her purse under the desk and takes a look at the disheveled diary that is currently controlling all our workload. Flicking through, she can see that we're booked out months in advance. I wonder if she realizes that we squeezed Luna into the schedule because she asked us to. If she notices, she'll probably believe it's because Luna's a celebrity, but it wasn't. It was just to put a smile on Kyla's face.

The rest of the guys arrive as Kyla's getting settled; Lex and Dex, and lastly, Kase and Kole. They're all smiles when they see her, and her blushes are cute as hell.

When the phone starts to ring, Kyla immediately takes the initiative and answers, responding to the customer in a natural and friendly way. In response, Carl's tense shoulders relax almost immediately.

Customers begin to arrive, and Kyla glances around, realizing that she's not yet familiar with the shop layout.

"I'll show you the place," I say, and she nods gratefully.

It doesn't take long to point out where each of us works. The customers all settle into conversations with their artists. There are some intrigued looks directed toward Kyla. I guess she's not what they're expecting to find at Ink Factor, but I'm happy she's here.

"I'll leave you to it," I say when she's settled back in at reception.

"Sure. And thanks." The smile she gives me is accompanied by another little flush of color across her cheeks. For the first time in my life, I get the urge to pinch her there like some adoring auntie fussing over her cute niece! It's an urge that's way more affectionate than I'm used to. My eyes drift to her wrists, and I imagine what they would look like bound in rope, shackled above her head. Would she plead with me to stop? Would she beg for more?

You never can tell.

I finish my first client, filling in some of a large back tattoo that I started a month ago. It's going to take a few more sessions to finish. He's a big guy with a low pain threshold, so dividing it into manageable sessions is the one way we're going to get it done. As I drift to the back of the shop, intending to make a cup of coffee, I find Kyla leaning against the office door jamb, talking to Carl.

"There's this system that I think we should implement. It has a reasonable monthly fee and will really revolutionize how customers move through your organization."

"Sounds awesome," Carl says, already foraging in his pocket and pulling out his wallet. I'm stunned when he hands over the company credit card, but when I see the flicker of a smile passing over his lips, I get it. He's desperate for help here and is more than happy for someone else to take on some of the work he struggles with. "Pay for whatever you need," he adds.

"How about a decent coffee machine?" I say.

Kyla swivels quickly, finding me close behind her, my height no doubt causing me to loom large. The way her pupils swell at the sight of me is intoxicating, and I know I could get between her legs if I wanted to. It might take some work. I'm sure she'd try to put up some resistance, but she wouldn't hold out for long. I might sound like an arrogant asshole, but it's not that. Some people just have chemistry. It's there, crackling in the air like a change in energy or a calling of chakras. Who the fuck knows?

What I'm certain of it that Carl would be against it.

"Forget about it," Carl snaps. "But anything you need, Kyla."

"Well, I was looking at the hardware we'll need to support it."

"Sounds good," Carl says.

"Alrighty then." Kyla retreats with a raised eyebrow.

Maybe she was expecting to need to justify herself more, or maybe she just feels bad that I'm not going to get my coffee machine.

I hope it's the latter.

When she's back at reception, I step into the office. "That girl is going to get us get our shit together," Carl says. "I have a good feeling."

"I do too," I say, but I'm not talking about work. There is something about Kyla that's already under my skin. Her need to please is obvious need to please and there's a spark I've seen in her eyes when I challenge and tease her. She's that perfect mix of submissive with a bite of rebellion—exactly the kind of girl I love to tame.

"I know what you're thinking," Carl says, shaking his head.

"What am I thinking?"

"How good she'd look strapped to your bed."

There's no point in denying it. We've known each other too long. "She'd look pretty special with your handprint on her ass too."

"Fuck," Carl mutters, but I know his mind's gone there. He's looked at her nicely rounded butt and fantasized over what it would feel like to spank it. Men might be outwardly restrained, but inside our minds, it's full-on fucking depravation. "We can't go there," he huffs, not concealing his disappointment. "We need her to want to work here. Fucking, heartbreak, and work are not compatible."

"Sex and heartbreak don't have to go hand in hand," I remind him.

"For men, maybe. But for women, they're close bedfellows."

Maybe he's right. Having Kyla working here makes things complicated, but I like messy. I like a challenge. I like pushing the boundaries and finding new limits. I like punching through resistance.

I was the firstborn. My mom always said that's what made me the pioneer and the challenger.

"So Kyla's off-limits," I say, wanting to be clear.

"Let's see how she fits in. Maybe she'll like it here. Maybe she won't."

"And if she doesn't?"

"Then she's fair game." Carl nods, not realizing that he's just set up a big reason for me to make Kyla's life here difficult. If she quits, there will be nothing stopping me from bending her to my will: nothing stopping Carl either, or any of the men in this place.

She's one woman, and we're eight horny men circling her like vultures.

What would she say if she knew what we were thinking?

She'd probably run as fast as she could from us all.

Or maybe she'd like it.

6

KYLA

My first day at Ink Factor is a breeze. All my previous work experience tells me it shouldn't be this easy to fit into a new place of work. I think back to my teacher training placement and how sad I felt when I realized that I'd trained in a role that didn't suit me at all. Too much chaos. Not enough order. Being out of control just sent my nerves into a horrible buzzing state that made me want to claw off my own skin.

But here, everything is about order. Or at least, everything about my job.

The tattoo artists deal in the chaos of blacks and colors, riotous artwork, and more restrained designs. They're animated and funny, filled with male boisterousness and sex appeal that has me flustering over everything when they're around. But when they're working, I can really focus.

Toward the end of the day, Kole disappears through the front door, appearing ten minutes later, pushing the door open with his back and holding a giant white cardboard box.

I jump to my feet, wanting to help but by the time I get there, he's already inside. "What have you got there?" I ask as he glances around for somewhere to put it.

"A cake," he says. "I work at a youth boxing scheme in the evening and on weekends, and one of the kids I teach is turning sixteen today."

"So you got him a birthday cake?"

Kole shrugs like it means nothing. "The kid's in a group home. He doesn't have anyone else to show him that they care or that his birthday means anything."

He rests the box on the low table in the customer waiting area and straightens, flexing his hands. I've noticed little white scars across his knuckles and wondered what caused them. "That's real nice of you," I say. "I'm sure he'll really appreciate it."

"We're throwing a party after the class. It's a surprise, but the rest of the kids know. The guys here are helping to organize it."

"Do you need more help?" I ask without thinking. Putting the fact that it's my first day aside, I'd love to help Kole do something so awesome.

"You don't need to do that," he says, nodding with appreciation, even as he turns me down.

"I'd like to, though. What do you need? What can I do?"

"I wanted to get him a gift of some sort, but I haven't had time to think about what to get him," Kole says. "Do you have any ideas?"

"How about a watch?" I say, remembering my dad and how proud he was of the watch his dad gave him on his eighteenth birthday. It wasn't a particularly expensive brand, but he loved it all the same.

"That's actually a great idea." Kole sticks his hand in the pocket of his black jeans, his eyes lowering to the floor as he roots around, pulling out a bundle of notes. I whistle, and he laughs, shaking his head.

"That's quite a stack you have there," I say, wiggling my eyebrows, wondering at how odd it is to see someone carry so much cash these days. My dad always used to carry cash, too, unfurling it whenever we needed anything. As Kole unwraps a stack of bills and hands it to me, a flutter of something warm and new spreads through my chest.

"A man should always carry cash," he says, "At least, that's what my dad always says. Do you have time to step out and get one? Choose whatever you think."

"Of course," I say.

Later that evening, with the watch wrapped in shiny silver paper and tied with a bright blue ribbon, I help Kole load the cake into the trunk of his car. Kase is with us, stuffing helium balloons into the back seat. "I think Ryan is going to be embarrassed as hell," he says to Kole. "You know how he hates anyone making a fuss over him."

"He pretends to hate it because he thinks it's a weakness to want it," Kole says, revealing a perceptiveness that doesn't fit with his gruff exterior. Maybe he sees that in Ryan because it's how he feels himself.

"I'm coming," I say softly. "I'll help with the drinks and cleaning up. That way, you can focus on making sure Ryan has the best time."

Kole's eyes find mine, their stormy grayness assessing me, searching for motive maybe. We haven't known each other for more than a few days, so I don't blame him for being wary.

"That's awesome," Kase says, shutting the door with a thud. "We can always use help."

Kole gives me a simple nod and begins to round the back of his car, stopping to open the rear door and holding it open for me.

He doesn't say anything as I slide inside, clutching my brown leather purse on my lap. When he shuts the door, it feels like his way of saying "okay then," without ever verbalizing his agreement.

The rest of the men from Ink Factor are waiting outside the boxing club when we arrive. They're holding bags and boxes of supplies, and as I scramble out of the car, I can see crates of soft drinks and bags of chips poking out the top.

There are already five scruffy-looking teens waiting for Kole to unlock the door, and they eye me with interest as I make my way behind Kole, carrying the balloons. The birthday boy isn't here because there's no discussion about the cake and balloons. Everyone troops into the dark boxing gym, and I breathe in air that smells stale and slightly damp. The whole building has a rundown feeling to it, but the actual equipment seems well maintained. A huge boxing ring stands in the center, flanked by training mats and heavy bags hanging from the high ceiling. Kole heads through a small side door into what I'm assuming is a kitchen area. I trail with the balloons, searching for somewhere to keep them out of sight.

"What's the plan?" I ask as Carl drops a huge heavy box of drinks onto the white laminated countertop.

"The plan is to let these kids work out all the anger they've built up over the past week and then surprise Ryan with the cake," Kole says. He's looking around as though he's lost something, then begins to open drawers, some of which aren't level on their runners.

"What are you looking for?" I ask.

"A knife that we can cut the cake with," he says, retrieving what looks like a meat cleaver. I'm not sure how safe it is for a kids' boxing gym to have such a potentially deadly weapon stored so insecurely, but what do I know about training kids to fight? This is all outside of my experience.

Dex drops two bags of food next to the drinks, followed by Lex, who has a shallow open box with plates, napkins, and plastic cups, all featuring the number 16 in bold blue lettering.

I stick my head around the open door to the gym and find that it's now filled with a rag-tag group of teens in t-shirts, shorts, and sweatpants, all crowded around Kole and leaning in to hear what he's saying. They spread out to begin a warm-up routine, following Kole's instruction in a way that's almost military in its discipline. The man is a machine, his body toned and honed for this role.

"He's good with them, isn't he," Noah says from behind me.

"He is," I agree.

Kole chooses that moment to strip off his shirt and wipe his face with it, and my heart practically stops in my chest. God, his body, is stunning. There is no other word for it. Sweat-slicked skin hugs perfectly sculpted muscle, and everything is enhanced by the black ink that covers his body. I've never seen such a sexy man in person, only on the cover of men's health magazines that rest above the newspapers in my local store.

I clear my throat, embarrassed to be feeling a flush rising up my cheeks, and Noah chuckles softly. "You don't need to be embarrassed about looking at a man appreciatively," he says. "That's just natural."

"I wasn't looking appreciatively," I blurt. "I was just thinking he must work out a lot."

"He does," Noah says, folding his lips as though he's trying to stifle laughter. Ugh. He's so annoying.

"Are you guys gonna stand there gawping at Kole, or are you going to help?" Carl says, shaking his head as he unpacks the drinks.

"Not gawping," I say. "And if you tell me what to do, I'll do it."

"That'll be music to Carl's ears," Noah says with a wink.

"Can you just be a grown-up for five minutes?" Niall says, punching his brother on the shoulder.

"Why the hell would I want to do that?" he says. "Adulting is boring."

"There are kids in there who take life more seriously than you," Carl snorts. "And it's our job to make them feel like kids for a change."

That comment seems to chasten Noah, and he grabs a bowl from Carl and begins to empty chips into it.

We work for the next half an hour, making sandwiches and cutting up fruit, placing cakes and cookies onto platters, and heating pizzas in the old oven. We talk and laugh, finding fun in everything, and I get a chance to see the goodness in all these men who've willingly given up their time to help a friend and a kid in need.

When the boxing class is finished, Kole appears in the doorway, still shirtless but now with a towel draped around his shoulders. He rests a hand on the top of the doorframe, the stance stretching his gorgeous chest. He catches my eye as I look him over in all his glory, getting hot between my legs at the sight of his armpit, for fuck's sake, and smiles.

"This all looks awesome," he says softly. "Can I borrow the men to put some tables out?"

"Give me something manly to do," Noah says, striding toward the door. Poor baby didn't enjoy slicing the tops off strawberries.

Niall rolls his eyes, and Nash mumbles, "Sorry about my brother," as they all disappear from the kitchen, and I'm left shaking my head at how much I already love spending time with my new colleagues.

They're nothing like I expected, and I feel unkind for expecting them to be arrogant tattooed assholes.

The party doesn't last long. It's a school night, and most of the boys have to get home before curfew, but they tuck into the food and drink and rowdily help their friend celebrate. Kole sticks close to Ryan, always there to support him and make sure he's having a good time. He's like an extra-cool big brother, and the boys very obviously all love him.

"He's good at this," Kase says, his eyes trained in the same direction as mine.

"He really is," I admit.

"I'm really proud of him," he says softly before he walks away to join his brother.

We all sing the happy birthday song, and Ryan grins widely as he gets to blow out sixteen candles. I offer to take photos of everyone, and they pose around the cake, with the boxing gym providing a strange backdrop, but nobody cares about anything other than throwing their arms over each other's shoulders and joking as I try to get a good shot.

Ryan is lucky to have such an awesome place to come, with friends and mentors who really care.

And I'm lucky to have found a place to work with genuinely nice people with genuinely good hearts.

It doesn't hurt that they're all sexy as hell.

For the first time in a long time, I find myself looking forward to tomorrow and another day of work.

7

KYLA

It's the end of the last day of my second week, and Carl insists I leave before the rest of them. My plan was to meet Dawn for some after-work drinks, but I'm a little early, so I perch on a bench seat and pull out my phone.

"Hey," I say when she picks up. "I'm already done. Can you meet earlier?"

"No can do, sweet cheeks," she says, exhaling a long theatrical sigh. "But I'm worth waiting for, I promise."

"I know you are, you idiot," I say.

"But stay on the phone. My boss might own the time I physically clock my ass out, but my attention and where I direct it is my own. Tell me…how was your day?"

"Awesome," I say, breathing my own long sigh of relief. "I'm so happy that I never have to go back to that coffee shop. I could kiss you."

"Forget kissing me. What about those sexy inked gods you work for?"

"It's all above board," I say, shaking my head even though she can't see me. "It's a workplace. Strictly professional and all that jazz."

"Professional shmefessional," Dawn huffs. "Over a fifth of married couples meet at work, and those odds definitely go up if you're the only woman in a team of nine."

"Can we stop having this same conversation over and over? Luna keeps trying to convince me that I need a poly relationship like hers, and you keep telling me I should be more focused on dick than I am on my work. In the end, I'm just too vanilla for any of them."

"Vanilla can be a great flavor when you slather it with chocolate sauce and sprinkles," Dawn says. "And anyway, you need to get out there if you're ever going to experience anything new."

"Experiencing new things in the bedroom isn't something I'd even know how to ask for," I say. "At least at the ice cream shop, you can ask for a taste before you buy. With sex, you just have to take whatever flavor is on offer. I just don't know what flavor I want or how to find out."

Dawn snorts. "You have to try a lot of flavors before you die," she says. "Fuck the patriarchy's idea that a woman has to stay chaste before marriage. We don't get used up or stretched out, or whatever other fucking misogynistic fiction men have touted around to control us. We get more experienced and more comfortable with our bodies. We gain confidence to ask for what we need. How is that not better than suppressing all our desires and wants?"

"It isn't better," I say, but inside, I'm still tied up with the idea that too many lovers are a bad idea. More lovers equal more heartache.

"You don't sound convinced," Dawn says. "And maybe I won't be able to convince you. Maybe having some experience will show you."

"You think I need to try out having sex with lots of men to see if having sex with lots of men is a good idea. Isn't that like eating a whole burger to decide if you like the taste of meat?"

"Not at all. Each bite of that burger will taste the same. Fucking eight different men will be like tasting eight different burgers. Some will have relish, and others will have bacon or pickle or extra cheese…"

"I hope we're still talking about the burgers here because cheese and men are two things that definitely shouldn't go together in the same sentence."

There's a fumbling sound on the end of the line, as though Dawn dropped something, and all I can hear is muted laughter. "Shit. I dropped my phone. You can't be saying things like that without warning, Kyla. There's only so much suppressed laughter a girl can manage while she's supposed to be working."

"Sorry that my pathetic sex life is causing you so much amusement." I bite my lip, my mind drifting back to Carl's inked forearms and Noah's unbelievably sexy lip ring. Before I have a chance to think about the six other sexy Ink Factor men, Dawn interrupts with a muffled chuckle.

"Your sex life isn't pathetic. It's just subdued. We need to bring it to life. Inject it with some color."

"Is that a tattoo shop reference?"

"I bet those men would love to inject you with some cream."

Now it's my turn to snort. Oh God, the thought of any one of them pumping me full of cum has me crossing my legs. And what about eight of them, one after another. I'd become a vessel of their pleasure, so messy and sticky.

I fully place the blame for my filthy thoughts on Luna and her crazy ideas.

"No one is injecting me with anything," I say as heat

spreads over my cheeks. "Especially between my legs. My body is a temple of isolation, and it's going to stay that way."

"You make it sound totally awesome," Dawn says, dragging out the last word sarcastically. "I can completely understand why you'd want to remain in your nun-like state when you have eight potentially awesome fuck-buddy candidates under your nose on a daily basis."

"They're not fuck buddy candidates. They're workmates. You can't look at all men as just dicks on legs, Dawn. They have brains, you know. They have wants and needs and aspirations, just like us."

It's at that moment that a big warm hand rests gently on my shoulder, and I almost jump out of my skin. My phone tumbles out of my hand as I swivel, clattering onto the bench, but it's forgotten when I find myself staring straight into the warm honey eyes of Noah.

Oh shit.

How long was he behind me listening?

I can hear Dawn's muffled voice coming from the phone, but I'm completely mesmerized. The drumbeat of my heart is the volume of club music in my ears. "We're going to the Red Devil. You want to join us?"

I shake my head, but that's where I'm supposed to be meeting Dawn. I guess we'll need to change our plans. "I'm meeting a friend," I manage to say, but my voice is a ridiculous breathy whisper that sounds like I'm asking for sex.

Oh damn, I wish I was asking for sex.

I wish I were begging for it, and Noah was looking down at me, biting his lip before agreeing to fuck me senseless.

When Noah draws his hand back, I feel the loss of his connection more keenly than I ever have. "Your friend can come too, especially if it's Dawn. She's got some crazy energy."

I snort because that's a perfect description of my friend. "Maybe," I say. "She's still working."

Noah nods, sliding his hand into the pocket of his snug black jeans. He's so tall that I'm craning my neck to look up at him, and with the sun behind his body, he's illuminated like an angel in an ancient icon. A dark angel, maybe.

"Well, the offer's there." He glances over his shoulder to where the rest of my workmates are standing. Oh hell. I really need to pick a place to talk about sex that isn't so close to my place of employment. Or maybe just stop talking about sex altogether. I've stopped actually doing it, so maybe ceasing the verbalizing won't be so hard.

Ugh.

"Okay, thanks. I better get this." Fumbling around behind me, I finally grasp the warmth of my phone and put it to my ear. Noah nods, already turning to return to his friends, and my breath leaves my mouth in an overwhelmed whoosh.

"Was that one of the guys from Ink Factor?" Dawn giggles. "Did he seriously just come up behind you while you were talking about sex with them?"

I cover my face with my free hand, curling my body forward. "Yes. Oh my God. I'm so embarrassed. After they overheard me calling them deities, they're going to think I have a weird sexual fixation."

"Don't be embarrassed," Dawn says. "They know how hot they are. They won't be surprised to hear that you agree. And we are totally still going to the Red Devil."

"WE ARE NOT! There is no way I can face them all now. Noah's going to tell them what I was saying."

"*If* he heard something. The chances are that his mind was somewhere else. Men aren't renowned for their concentration or their ability to pick up subtle cues."

"I don't think my cues were subtle." Squinting my eyes, I shudder with a surge of embarrassment that runs through every cell of my body. "Can you leave work soon? I was going to go to have a drink, but now I'm stuck on a bench until you're done."

"Hang on a minute." I can hear Dawn's steps as she investigates the whereabouts of her boss. "I think he's gone," she gushes happily.

"You mean he doesn't say bye when he leaves?"

"The man has zero social skills. I'll be with you in ten minutes."

I don't know if Dawn is just a fast walker or if she's so excited to get to the Red Devil that she runs from her office, but she's charging toward me in a flash.

"You're having some sex tonight," she says, grabbing me by the arm and frog-marching me toward the bar.

"I am not," I say. "I haven't shaved my legs in two weeks and forget the forest. I'd need a lumberjack to tackle the growth between my legs."

"Haven't you heard that the bush is back, babe?"

"No, I haven't."

"Real men aren't put off by some natural hair. I heard it on TikTok, so it must be true."

"Are you sure it's not just a load of thirst traps trying to appeal to older women who can't be bothered with the maintenance anymore?"

"Maybe," Dawn laughs. "But I think we should run with it. Make it a thing. Who wants to approach their most sensitive area with a blade? If there were no male pressure, we'd all be walking around like seventies porn stars."

"True." I snort with laughter as my heart starts to flutter with nerves. The scarlet flashing sign for the Red Devil beckons ahead. "I need to act professionally tonight," I say. "Please. No matchmaking with my colleagues. No sex talk. No mention of overgrown bushes. I want them to take me seriously as a work colleague."

"That ship sailed," Dawn says. "They're probably in there right now discussing which of them is going to rub their ink all over you." I give Dawn a fierce look, and she puts her hands up in mock defense. "You know I have your best interests at heart, babe. No one said that you can't have awesome sex and still maintain a great working relationship."

"Errr…I'm pretty sure that most companies have a no-fraternizing policy because work relationships are such a disaster."

"Only if they go wrong," Dawn says, winking as her hand meets the door handle to the bar.

I guess I have to face them all sometime, but the idea that they're inside discussing my desert-dry sex life has me cringing all over again.

8

DEX

"She was talking about having sex with us?" I rub the scruff on my chin, staring at Noah, who's grinning like the Cheshire cat. I'm trying to decide if he's telling the truth or just pulling another one of his stupid pranks. I swear the guy wouldn't take a funeral seriously.

"I swear," he says, holding his hands up like he's surrendering to an enemy. Even with all his gestures, I'm still not sure I'm buying it. "She was talking about how inexperienced she is, and whoever was on the other end of the line must have been suggesting that she uses us for sex."

Carl makes a grumbling sound in his throat, but he doesn't jump on Noah for talking foolish like he usually would.

"What, all of us?"

"She mentioned fuck buddies in the plural, and polyamory, and eating lots of burger."

"Burger?" Lex furrows his brow in confusion.

"Something about eating lots of meat." Noah nods as though his rambling has just explained everything.

I down a few big gulps of ice-cold beer, watching everyone around me and trying to put all the pieces together. "How long were you eavesdropping over her shoulder?" I say in the end.

"Long enough."

Nash punches his brother on the shoulder. "Didn't Mom teach you any fucking manners? No good ever comes from listening to conversations that don't include you."

"I think a lot of good could come from this one."

"You're quiet." I nod in Carl's direction, but for some reason, he avoids my gaze. What am I missing here?

"The poor girl needs us bunch of assholes like she needs a hole in the head," Lex says.

Kase clears his throat and nods toward the door, and we all turn to see Kyla and her friend Dawn entering the Red Devil. Dawn is looking around, but Kyla's eyes are lowered. The poor thing must be embarrassed as hell. Right on cue, her cheeks turn a pretty shade of pink, and she heads straight to the bar and waits for the barman.

When Dawn spots us, she waves, beaming with a grin that matches Noah's almost exactly.

This is awkward.

It shouldn't be. I've never understood why sex is such a big deal to so many people. It's a bodily function, like eating and breathing. We're creatures made to bond through touch and designed to experience pleasure together.

Kyla's not a teenager. She should be free to embrace her sexuality if she wants to. But the way she's acting, it's like Dawn's egging her on, and she's flustered at the thought. It's cute but a little sad. Maybe she's been hurt in the past, or maybe she's just a whole lot more innocent than she should be at this stage in her life.

"You don't say a thing," Carl says firmly. "Leave the conversation you heard out of whatever comes next. The poor girl doesn't need eight dudes leering at her, and she certainly doesn't need to feel uncomfortable in her workplace."

"Yes, boss." Noah gives a sharp salute, which Carl greets with a scowl. Out of the corner of my eye, I watch Kyla and Dawn buy their drinks. I can't predict whether they'll come and sit with us or sit somewhere else. If I could place a bet, I'd put money on Dawn pushing Kyla in our direction and her resisting, which is exactly what happens.

Dawn grabs Kyla's hand, and there is definite pullback that is unsuccessful. By the time they reach our booth, Kyla's face is a pretty shade of strawberry that matches her sickly drink.

The volume of the music rises as Dawn leans in to ask if they can join us. Kyla swivels to where the DJ is bending over the sound system, her face illuminating in the colors of the flashing lights that are pulsing fast to encourage dancing. She sips her drink, avoiding the gazes of all of us, and I can't sit for any longer and leave her so uncomfortable. When I slide out of the booth, Lex's hand grabs mine. "You heard Carl," he says.

"I heard him."

When Kyla senses me close, she jumps, making her drink slosh around in her glass. There's a skittishness about her that needs to be tamed and a tenseness that needs to be relieved. This girl is an unexplored island, a place of natural beauty that just needs to be revealed. "Do you dance?" I ask to break the ice.

She shakes her head, her chocolate eyes widening with fear. Of course she doesn't. A smattering of freckles dusts her pretty nose like the universe sprinkled her with glitter. My fingers itch to trace between them like the dot-to-dot puzzles I used to play on long car journeys when I was a kid.

In my mouth, I push my tongue, piercing back and forth, as my mind slides into the gutter. I'd love to watch my brother undo all the little buttons of her shirt and part the fabric. I'd love to hear her moan when the hardness of his piercing flicks against her nipples. Watching her let go of all her constraints and come undone would be something else.

I know what Carl said, but I don't agree.

This girl needs us. She needs us to show her all the different ways a woman can experience pleasure. Between us we could cover a whole load of kinks that would open Kyla's eyes and give her some sexual confidence. It would be a gift.

But how do I make that happen?

My favorite saying is *The truth will set you free*. I guess I have nothing to lose by testing it out. But first, I need to talk to Dawn and ignore Carl entirely.

"So, how's that tattoo?" I ask. It was me she convinced to mark her with YOLO, and I did it because I could see how much it fits with her attitude to life. While I grazed her skin with my machine, she told me all about the plans she has to travel with her boyfriend and the long bucket list of crazy experiences she wants to make happen, like bungee jumping and white-water rafting. How is this girl friends with somebody like Kyla, who loves making files for piles of paper?

"It's awesome," Dawn says. "Brent loves it so much and he's the one who gets to see it the most." She does a mini twerk to demonstrate what she's hinting at, and Kyla looks away, embarrassed.

"I wanted to ask you something about that trip you were talking about. I'm gonna get another drink. Can we walk and talk?"

When Dawn glances at Kyla, I can see she's worried about leaving her friend, but she does it anyway. She's like a mom leaving her reluctant daughter at a playdate she didn't want to go to.

I don't wait until we're at the bar to get right to the point. "Noah told us what he overheard," I say, watching her green eyes widen. "But I want to make sure that he's not embellishing."

"It's no secret that I think Kyla needs to have more fun," Dawn says without hesitation. "She's been uptight since her last boyfriend cheated on her. It's like she's anticipating that every guy is going to be a douchebag. She won't let herself go enough to experience life. She needs to have some fun with some guys who know their way around a woman's body. Men who can show her all the different flavors there are out there without breaking her heart."

"Like a man buffet!"

"Exactly." Dawn slaps me hard on the shoulder to emphasize her agreement. "She's just so reserved, but underneath, I know she's just waiting for someone to help her break out of her shell."

"Like a butterfly," I say, waving the barman over to order another beer. "Can I get you another?"

"You can!" Dawn grins happily. "I'll take another Red Devil, and so will Kyla. If I ply her with booze, maybe we'll get her on the dancefloor."

A quick glance back at Kyla reveals that she's in deep conversation with Carl. I know it's going to be shop talk. Carl's stepping in to get things back on the professional track. But I don't want it straying back into Boredomsville.

My brother always says that I have a crazy imagination. My brain doesn't switch off. It likes twisty situations, and it likes challenging puzzles.

Kyla is like a Rubik's cube that's just out of the box. All the colors are ordered because no one's had any fun. Kyla needs us to twist her colors into a kaleidoscope. She needs to be played with until her stickers are peeling, and her joints are squeaking.

"What if I had an idea?" I say, still puzzling through all the crazy iterations in my brain.

Dawn takes a long sip of the red cocktail through her straw and then clutches the side of her head. "Brain freeze!" she gasps. "Tell me your idea."

"Maybe we could be Kyla's man-buffet. We could make it a game. Something that she could feel in control of. We can each write our kink on a piece of paper and put it in a bowl. Kyla could pick one whenever she was in the mood, and we'd deliver on an evening that is all about her experiencing new things."

I'm expecting Dawn to ask more questions. Maybe try to find out what kinks I'm talking about, or at least whether we're all single and good guys. Instead, she rests her cocktail on the bar and throws her arms around me. "I knew Kyla was meant to come and work with y'all. I just knew it. All of this is her destiny."

"Well, I'm not sure about destiny, but she'll have a great time if nothing else."

"So will you." The look in Dawn's emerald eyes can only be described as filthy. If I didn't already know what kind of person she is, I'd wonder about her willingness to pimp out her friend, but this just fits with Dawn's motto for her own life.

YOLO. It's such a ridiculous phrase, but I get why Dawn feels so passionately about living her life that way. None of us know when we might be checking out. We only have so many years while we're still young and able to do crazy things. With age comes responsibility and expectations, and our ability to step outside of all that is curtailed.

It's been a while since I let my hair down; a while since any of us did. The shop has taken over all our lives, and like Kyla, we've had bad experiences with relationships in the past. There's been a hiatus from women in Ink Factor for the last three months that needs to be broken.

If I can convince Kyla, I know the rest of my buddies will be on board. How could they not be?

Kyla picks that moment to turn from Carl, and our eyes meet across the crowded bar. It's like she knows I'm thinking about her, and a thread of awareness has hooked us to one another. I bite my bottom lip as my idea spreads like warm chocolate through my mind.

Can I convince her?

The rising blush on her cheeks tells me I can.

There isn't much that can't be accomplished with positive thinking and a little planning.

By the end of the night, I'll have her fully converted to the idea. And I'll deal with Carl tomorrow.

9

KYLA

Ever since Dawn and I arrived at the bar, the guys have been looking at me funny. Even though Carl has been talking to me about the new booking system, my heart hasn't stopped thumping against my ribs.

Could I be any more mortified?

Definitely not.

Seriously, I should have just stood up on my first day and told them all I'm a sexually frustrated hermit who thinks they're all sexy enough to lick chocolate off.

At least it would have been upfront.

This time, I have no idea what Noah heard or how he's relayed it to the rest. I have no idea how they reacted either.

My cheeks tingle with mortification, and I down the rest of the cocktail that Dawn returned from the bar clutching. She had an odd grin on her face that definitely spells trouble. Probably not trouble for her either. Most likely trouble for me.

I make my way to the restroom, using the time alone in the cubicle to relive my utterly devastating levels of embarrassment. At the mirror, I press my cool hands against my cheeks and smooth the frizz out of my hair while I try to reverse my seemingly never-ending blush with a pep talk.

Get a grip, Kyla. It's only sex. It's natural for women to think about sex. It's natural for them to think about sex with eight tattooed gods. They're probably not even surprised. This is probably par for the course for such gorgeous specimens of manhood. In fact, they'd probably have been more shocked to hear that I *wasn't* thinking about jumping their bones.

It doesn't have to change a thing, I tell myself. Just get on with the night like nothing happened. If I don't bring it up, maybe none of them will.

The alcohol in my bloodstream chooses that minute to soften my mind and my knees. The delicious buzz makes me even more convinced that my pep talk has hit the mark.

By the time I stroll out of the restroom, I'm feeling confident. Until I bump right into Dex.

My shoulder thuds against his concrete rock of a chest, and breath whooshes from my mouth with the shock, but Dex seems unphased.

"There you are," he says, as though he's been searching for me all along.

"Here I am." I smile brightly as Dex gazes down at me with eyes so warm I all but melt on the spot. What must he look like with his long hair out of the messy bun? Does it hang around his shoulders, all sexy and tousled? Would he let me run my fingers through it?

Oh Lord.

"So, tell me, Kyla. Is Noah right that the blush on your cheeks is because you've been having impure thoughts about us?

"Impure?" I stutter. I mean, I know what the word means, but I wasn't expecting it to come out of Dex's mouth, accompanied by a small but wicked smile.

"Yeah, you know. Thoughts that put a blush on your cheeks, like the one there right now."

His tattooed hand rises so his fingers can brush softly over my heated skin, eyes never leaving mine.

"Dawn thinks you guys are sexy," I babble, cringing as his smile broadens. "She keeps telling me that I should make the most of it. She's crazy that way, unlike me."

I look down, somewhere between Dex's broad chest and narrow waist, but he doesn't let me stay that way for long. When his hand tips my chin up, I know I'm in trouble. And when he ducks his head so he can talk closer to my ear, my knees feel as though they might give way.

"I think you can be crazy too, Kyla. You just button yourself up so tight. But maybe Dawn's right. Maybe you should make the most of us. Maybe we can all play a little game. No strings."

"A game?"

"Yeah," he says. "Eight dates. Eight different kinks. You can decide which you like the best."

"Eight kinks?" What is he talking about?

"Think of us as a big box of chocolates. Carl is the bitter dark chocolate that's infused with chili. Lex is the fruity orange cream center. Kole is the chocolate that you think is going to be caramel but turns out to have the nut inside. We each have something different for you to taste, and when you're done, you'll know what kind of chocolate you like the best, and you'll have a whole lot more confidence to pick the right kind of chocolate for you in the future."

Oh my God. Is he seriously propositioning me with a sex buffet?

Seriously?

Am I living in reality, or have I slipped into some kind of alternate universe where gorgeous men like him are interested in slightly disheveled-looking organization freaks who struggle to have fun like me?

This can't be happening. I don't know what to reply. My head is swimming with images of my Ink Factor colleagues naked, sitting in a large plastic chocolate tray, just waiting for me to pick them.

How would I pick? I bet they'd all taste amazing.

Blinking fast, I try to clear my head.

I shouldn't be thinking about how my work colleagues would taste. There is so much about it that is just straight-up wrong.

But Dex smells so good, and the warmth and sheer masculinity rolling off him have me dizzy and dazed.

"You want to help me work out what kind of man-flavor I like?" Even as the question leaves my drink-addled brain, I'm already shrinking with shame. What the hell do I even sound like?

"I want to help you have some fun, Kyla. I want you to feel gorgeous and special and desired. I want you to know all the different kinds of pleasure you can feel and be confident enough to ask for it with whoever you fall in love with."

"Love," I scoff. "I'm not interested in love."

Dex touches my cheek again, this time allowing his fingers to play with a strand of my hair. "That means you need us even more than I thought."

"But we're workmates," I say.

The way Dex shrugs makes it clear that it isn't something that he sees as a barrier to his plan. "We can have drinks together, can't we? We could watch a movie. We could eat dinner together. You wouldn't think anything about that."

"But none of those things involve sex."

"But they could involve feelings, and feelings can be way more disruptive than sex."

"Maybe we shouldn't do any of it," I say. "Just to be on the safe side."

Wobbling a little on my feet, I grab Dex's shoulder for stability. His shoulder that's like a huge hunk of granite. "Maybe," he says. "Maybe means you're thinking about it."

"I'm not."

When his hand rests on my waist, every fiber of my being seems to still. I don't blink. I don't breathe. I'm a marionette, waiting for the movement of his fingers. He dips low again. His lips are so close to the shell of my ear that I can feel their warmth. "I'd love to watch you come," he whispers, and my grip on his shoulder intensifies involuntarily. "I'd love to see the look of ecstasy on your face. Are you warm between your legs? Is your body telling you what your mind is denying?"

Oh my God, it is. It so is.

If we weren't surrounded by people, I'd slump against Dex's body and tell him to take me, here and now. I don't even care about how wrong it is to risk screwing up this job. I'm loose-limbed and loose-brained from too many cocktails, but for the first time in a long time, my mind feels clear.

I've been slowly dying in the wake of my last relationship. My poor lady garden is overgrown with tumbleweed, and it's so long since anyone explored it. I'm desperate to know what it would feel like to truly enjoy sex, not be waiting for the person I'm with to finally care enough to ask if all the rubbing and thrusting is doing anything for me.

This is my chance to find out.

Luna Evans told me to go for it. She told me that I

should work on manifesting my ideal life. She's a superstar with the perfect life, isn't she? Maybe I should listen to someone who seems to have it all.

"A game?" I ask Dex, moving my hand to touch the ribbed collar of his tight, black shirt.

"A game where we're all the winners, every time." Dex smiles, his fingers trailing over the tips of mine, sending a visible shiver up my spine and over my scalp. Winners. Every time.

I want to be a winner. I want these men to help me win so much that I forget my name and how many summers I've existed on this earth without sunlight. I want them to burn me with their passion and consume me with their desires. I want to truly know all the feelings that are described in every romance novel I've ever read.

"I'll leave you to figure out the rules," I blurt before the tentative side of my consciousness has a chance to come to the fore. "But I'm willing to play."

From the sparkle that forms in Dex's eyes, I can tell he's pleased, but I can also sense surprise. It's cute that he wasn't sure that I'd be a done deal. It means he isn't arrogant about himself or his friends.

"I can't wait to play with you," he says. Then his lips brush my ear, and a shiver of anticipation passes through me that is so strong, Dex sees it again. "We'll take good care of you, Kyla. Really good care."

And for a second, I feel tears burn in my throat. No one has ever said that to me before. No one has ever promised to look after me. I've been fending for myself for a long time. Taking care of other people too. I always give too much to every relationship I've ever had, and it's left me feeling hollow.

It's why I've stayed away from men.

Dawn is the only person in my life who really looks out for me.

I swallow down the emotion that doesn't fit with the moment at all. I don't want Dex to know that behind all this fun and flirty talk, I'm a little broken. I want to be the shiny dime that he's polished me to be. I want to relax into the game and play to have fun. Stupid it may be, but for once, I'm going to live by Dawn's tattoo. You only live once.

If eight inked gods want to show me a good time, who the hell am I to say no?

10

LEX

"You told her what?"

I press my finger to my ear and wiggle it back and forth, wanting to make sure I don't have a blockage that's making my brother sound nonsensical.

Dex reaches behind his head and tugs out the band in his hair, letting it fall around his shoulders. "I told her we're going to play a game with her. Each of us will put the details of a date and a kink onto a piece of paper and put it into a bowl. She gets to pick one out whenever she wants, and whoever's paper it is gets to take Kyla out and show her a good time."

"A date I'm fine with, but a kink?"

"I don't know why you're acting like some kind of monk. We've all known each other for long enough to have had plenty of drunken discussions about what gets us off. There's enough variety in our predilections to blow Kyla's mind."

"Oh yeah, so what the hell are you going to put on the

paper?"

"Voyeurism," my twin says, with a swift shrug of his shoulder.

"You want to watch her fuck someone else?"

"Maybe," he says. "Or maybe I'll just watch her pleasure herself."

"Shit." Shaking my head, I reach for the glass of water I intend to drink before I hit the sack. There's no way I want to have a hangover tomorrow when I've got so many appointments to work through. "What about me? What do you think I'm going to put on the paper?"

"You can put whatever you like, but I know it's going to involve eating stuff off her naked body."

He's got me there. I just love spreading delicious things over a woman's skin and using my tongue to clean her up.

"What about the rest?"

"That'll be up to them. I reckon Nash will go for the gang bang. He's always the one who finds the girls who want to fuck triplets."

"You're probably right."

"And Kase loves almost getting caught, so he'll probably go with something risky."

I shake my head, remembering when Kase was arrested for picking up a cheerleader in college and giving it to her in the car.

"What about Kole?"

Dex runs his fingers through his hair, glancing up at the smooth white ceiling. "I don't know…he's less predictable."

"And Carl?"

"That fucker's going to boss poor Kyla around."

"I'm scared to ask about Niall and Noah," I admit, screwing up my face as I recall some of the conversations that we've had with too much alcohol coursing through our veins.

"Outdoor sex and bondage," Dex says without hesitation.

"The poor girl." I frown, trying to imagine how Dex managed to get Kyla to agree to this crazy scheme. "Did you tell her all this?"

"Of course not," Dex says. "It's a game, and the whole point is the element of surprise and anticipation. She won't know until she picks, and then she'll have a little while for the details to settle in that pretty head of hers. We'll have some time for the anticipation to build. We need to take this seriously because it's not about us getting to fuck Kyla. It's about us showing her that she's a goddess who gets to seize life by the balls."

I wince at the imagery, but I get what Dex is saying. Kyla isn't exactly a seize-life-by-the-balls kind of girl. She's an organize-a-mess-of-papers-into-pretty-pastel-files kind of girl. She needs to know that a life that isn't organized can be amazing. She needs to feel exactly how awesome life can be when you shake out your hair.

"You know Carl is going to rip your balls off for this," I tell my brother. Dex is a clever guy, but he has a blind spot for other people. What seems to make perfect sense to him often gets lost in translation when he tries to convey it to others.

"Carl has been looking at little miss Kyla like she's food, and he's a starving man. I'm pretty sure he's already spanked and fucked her in his mind a thousand times. He might pretend to be the pillar of restraint on the outside, but inside, he's as deviant as the rest of us."

"Speak for yourself," I say. "Kyla's a really nice girl to talk to. It's not all about fucking."

"I know that, bro." Dex pushes his chair back, metal feet making an aggravating sound against the tiled floor.

"But for her, it is. Don't you see? She's had a shitty time with previous relationships. She needs to have a good time so she can leave all that shit behind."

"And you know all this how?"

"You can find out a lot from a friend," he says, grinning. "Dawn's a good friend. She's looking out for Kyla's wellbeing."

"By suggesting she gets back on the horse but with eight horses?"

"Dawn's a YOLO kind of girl. She wants Kyla to be willing to live a little. To Dawn, this is like giving Kyla the best birthday gift in the world."

"I don't understand girls. I never will."

"Why do dudes always think that women are so different from men?" he huffs, loosening his hair so it spills around his shoulders. "We all want to feel good. We all want to feel close to other people. We all want to have fun. I'm sick of women buying into the misogynistic idea that their body count diminishes their value. As far as I'm concerned, if a woman has experiences that make her feel good, whether it's in or out of the bedroom, I'm a happy man."

"My brother the feminist," I say, making a joke when I actually feel quite proud of him.

"I'll deal with Carl, and there's not going to be any pushback from the others. As long as Kyla's happy, they're all going to be ecstatic."

"You're probably right. I've gotta say that it sounds like fun. Take a girl out for a good date and show her the time of her life, all while competing with your best friends."

"It's definitely going to bring out the competition between us all."

Dex picks up his jacket from the back of the couch and strolls to his room, whistling in the way he always has when he's happy. It's the first time I've heard that telltale whistle in a while. I don't think my twin's been unhappy as such. More that there hasn't been anything going on in our lives that's been inspiring. But if Kyla's what it takes to put the pep back into his step, then I'm happy.

Despite drinking practically a gallon of water before I sleep, I still wake up with an ache behind one eye. Dex makes us both a power smoothie that's the color of a stagnant lake, and I sip it slowly on our walk to Ink Factor. By the time we get there, whatever Dex put in my drink has worked its magic.

Something's worked its magic on Kyla too. Gone is the neat shirt and pants combination. Today she's arrived in a slouchy black jumper that hangs off one shoulder, revealing the perfect skin of her shoulder, and a pair of ass- and thigh-hugging black jeans that leave nothing to the imagination. Noah is hanging around the front desk like a fly on shit, and Carl is currently chilling on the customer couch, pretending to look at his phone but watching Noah like a hawk.

If Dex thinks he's going to convince Carl of his idea easily, he has another thing coming.

"It's the X twins," Noah says.

When Kyla turns and sees Dex and me, her cheeks turn the color of a raspberry. "Morning, everyone," Dex says, walking with his shoulders noticeably straighter than usual. "Are y'all feeling good or nursing monster hangovers?"

"Hangover," Kyla admits, rubbing her left temple.

"I had one too, but Dex made me a magic potion, and now I'm fine."

"Can you make me one too?" Kyla asks, biting her lips. "I really did drink way too much. I can't remember half of what I said last night."

At the last part, she stares pointedly at Dex, and there is no mistaking what she's saying. Anything she agreed with him last night is off the table. Whether she remembers or not, I suppose it doesn't really matter. Is Dex going to remind her?

I glance at my brother, noticing that his posture isn't as upright as it was. He turns to me, and it's like looking in a mirror. Ever since we were kids, we've been able to communicate with each other without saying a word. He asks me with his eyes what to do. I nod to tell him he should make the smoothie and tell Kyla what they discussed. I get the feeling she's testing to see if Dex was drunk and didn't mean anything he said.

"I'll go get the produce," Dex tells Kyla. "Anyone else want a power smoothie hangover cure?"

"Me!" Niall shouts from the back.

"And me," Kole says, ducking his head around the wall to give Dex the thumbs-up.

I head to my station, dumping my phone onto the counter and glancing around to make sure everything's where it's supposed to be. There's something new—a small tablet on a stand. Kyla appears behind me. "Did you see the tablet?" she asks.

"Yeah, what's that?"

"I'll show you." She moves closer, reaching around me to pick it up, leaving her pretty floral scent in the air for me to inhale. Damn, she smells good and looks good. An image of her on my bed with her skin spread with chocolate flashes through my mind. Dex has planted ideas that I can't forget. He needs to get this game off the ground for sure. "It's all part of the new system," she says. "Each of you will have a tablet. You'll be able to use it to check out your bookings. You give it to your clients to fill out their records, and you can take images of their tattoos before they leave. It'll help us keep track of everything."

"Wow, okay," I say, moving closer so I can see the screen as she flicks through each of the different sections.

It'll be good to be able to keep on top of bookings and check out the customer's previous work before they come in.

"There's also this section," Kyla says. "It's going to be a reference tool for customers to use when they're looking for inspiration. You'll be able to add to it using your designs."

"That's pretty cool," I say. Carl might have resisted taking on an administrator for the place, but when he finally gave in, he picked a good one.

"It is, isn't it?" She blinks her long lashes, gazing up at me in a way that makes me want to lean down and kiss her lips. I totally get where Dex is coming from. There's something so innocent about Kyla, but an essence that tells me she just needs to be brought out of her shell. The question is, will she do it? Maybe I shouldn't leave this to Dex to figure out. Maybe I should step in.

We're so similar on the outside that even our own mother sometimes gets us mixed up, but where my brother is tough and assertive, I have an easier temperament. Dex might push too hard, but I know I won't.

"You do remember what you talked about with Dex last night, don't you?"

On cue, her pupils swell, making her eyes darken with arousal. Her tongue flicks out to moisten her lips as though she's thinking about kissing me. "He didn't mean it. It was all just the alcohol talking."

"Oh, he meant it," I say. "And I think you did too."

"Carl won't like it," Kyla says, and I have to bite my lip to stop myself from smiling. She's relying on Carl to put a stop to it because she can't do it herself.

"I'm sure Dex told you that Carl is our problem, not yours. All you have to do is pick a date and leave us to the rest."

"You guys are crazy," she says, taking a step back and pressing her hand over her heart. I bet if I did the same, I'd feel it skittering as fast as a mouse's.

"Maybe," I say. "But I don't think so. I think we know exactly what we're doing, and you're going to love every minute of it."

I reach out with my hand and entwine my fingers with Kyla's. She's so warm, and uncertain, but when I take a step closer, she doesn't push me away. "Do you want to know what we'd do on my date night?"

A little whoosh of breath leaves her sweet lips, and she nods, sending a rush of heat to my cock.

"I'd cook you your favorite meal and serve your favorite drink, and after, I'd lay you naked on my kitchen table and eat dessert off all the delicious parts of you." On cue, Kyla shivers, and I lean closer to whisper in her ear. "But that's just one date, and you're going to experience eight."

"What about my job?" she says.

"Nothing about this will affect your job here. What happens outside of Ink Factor stays outside of Ink Factor. Tell me you want to, and everything will be set. You can choose your first date later on. If you want, we can keep the discussion about it outside of work. What do you think?"

Kyla blinks again, lowering her eyes as she inhales a quick deep breath. There's still a flicker of doubt, but when her hand squeezes mine, that flicker is snuffed out. "Okay," she says breathlessly.

"Okay."

I'm shocked by the rush of relief that passes through my body. It's not the sex that's driving it either. It's something else entirely.

How long has it been since I really spent time thinking about giving someone the perfect date? Too long. How long has it been since I went on a date with someone that I actually enjoy spending time with? Just as long.

Kyla's sweet and interesting, pretty, and funny. I can't wait for her to pick my date out of the bowl.

How long will I have to wait? I hope it won't be too long.

Now I just have to tell Dex that his plan is on.

And leave him to deal with Carl.

11

KOLE

I catch the tail end of the hissed discussion between Dex and Carl. Noah and Lex are involved too, and by the time I enter the back office, it all seems to be calming down.

"This is the bowl," Dex says, holding out a white plastic bowl we usually fill with chips. "Everyone needs to write down three things. Their name, the details of the date, and the kink."

"Now, this sounds interesting," I say. "Is this Kyla thing going ahead? Because my plans for her are already well and truly drafted."

"It is," Dex says firmly.

"I've been overruled," Carl says, running his fingers over his intricately braided blond hair. It's the first time I've heard Carl agree to be overruled in a long time, so I guess his cock is driving his surrender this time. Even the strongest men get driven by their cock rather than their minds sometimes. It's the reason that the human race has propagated for so long. Those base urges are powerful. "But that doesn't mean I'm getting involved."

"What?" I ask.

"I'm not putting a date into the bowl. At least one of us needs to remain professional and on the outside of this. As the person who hired Kyla in the first place, I think that person should be me."

"I don't know how you're going to resist," Noah says. "I know I couldn't pass up the chance."

Carl shrugs, his blue eyes flicking to the ceiling as though he's trying to draw on reserves that are just out of reach. "I'm a man. I'm used to dealing with the fact that life doesn't always go as we want it to."

Is that a hint that we should all be stepping back and resisting like men? Because I call bullshit. Sometimes, men need to know when to step forward, and this is one of those times.

"Give me the paper," I say.

Dex hands me a small piece of white paper and a black pen, and I quickly scratch out the details of my date and desires in my curly cursive. Folding it, I hand it back, to be met by Dex's dark eyebrow arched with interest. "That was quick."

"That'll be the only thing that will be."

My quip is met by some low chuckles from the rest. "And this is a competition?"

"Yep," Dex says. "That part of it is to ensure that Kyla has the best time through this whole process. At the end, she's gonna vote on her favorite experience. So make it good."

"I always do," I laugh. "So, have you guys put your dates down onto paper?"

"I have," Dex says. "And Lex. Can you give these to the rest?"

"Sure," I say. Taking the paper from Dex, I duck out of the office and back into the shop. The music is pounding loudly, and the sound of the machinery rumbles in the background. Kase is working on a man's shoulder when I pop into his booth. "It's on," I say. "Here's your paper. Name, date, and kink."

"Sounds interesting," the customer says.

Kase rolls his eyes. "You have no idea!"

In the next booth, Noah and Niall are talking. "Here. Write down your name, date idea, and kink, then give it to Dex."

"It's on?" Noah's slow smile has a wolfish or sharklike quality to it. Out of all of us, he's had the biggest boner for Kyla. Or biggest visible boner, in a metaphorical sense.

"It's on. Where's your brother?"

"He's piercing nipples, so maybe leave his paper here, and I'll give it to him."

"Nice," I say.

And that's it.

My cock stirs in my jeans; the prospect of being let loose on Kyla's curves already sending heat through me.

She's sitting at reception, staring at the screen of her computer but she loses concentration when I lumber toward her. "I'm going out to get lunch," I say. "Would you like something from the deli on the corner?"

"Sure, that would be great. They do an awesome soft cheese and smoked salmon bagel. And an iced tea?"

"Sounds good."

Kyla reaches beneath the desk for her purse, by I wave my hand. "Don't worry about it," I say.

As I push the door to Ink Factor open, I have to squint against the brightness of the sun's warm rays. The walk to Mike's Deli is short, taking me past the florist and the coffee shop where Kyla used to work.

"Hang on, Kole," I hear, and when I turn, Kyla's there, clutching her purse.

I watch her rushing toward me, taking in the pretty swish of her chestnut hair as it swings around her neck, already wondering what it'll feel like to slide my fingers into the warmth of her nape and tip her face to mine.

"I need to get some fresh air," she says. "To clear my mind. So many spreadsheets, I'm starting to see squares floating in front of my eyes."

"Spreadsheets definitely aren't my thing," I say. "Give me a patch of blank skin and a tattoo gun any day."

"I wouldn't have a clue where to start," she says.

We carry on to the deli, walking side by side, the sound of the wind rustling through the trees settling my soul. I haven't had time to get to the gym this week, and my fists itch for the thud of the punchbag. My palms, on the other hand, are itching to slide over Kyla's curves. The rest of me is hungry to take her to places she's never been before.

"I think we all have it in us to be creative. All kids love to draw, and they do it without fear of judgment. They relish getting their hands dirty and are happy to represent the world in ways that don't match what they're seeing. It's when we become conscious of others that we lose that ability. We judge our creative skills against other people's. We want to be perfect. So many people stop being creative before they've ever had a chance to find out what they're capable of. Creativity should never be about what others think. It's something that comes directly from inside you. Enjoying the process is the main thing. If you forget about the end result, you'll try, and then learn, and over time you'll become more satisfied with your abilities."

"You know, I never thought of it that way," Kyla says. "I just always felt that my drawings were amateur compared to my friends'. I used to get embarrassed to present my art in class. As soon as I could give up drawing and painting, I did."

"If you don't like drawing and painting, you could try sculpture or collage."

"What's collage? Like, cutting up bits of magazines?"

"It's about using paper, fabric, photographs, images, textures to create something."

"That actually sounds like fun."

At the door to the deli, I grab hold of the handle and yank it open, allowing Kyla to enter first. At the counter, we both place our orders. Mike knows my usual anyway, and Kyla sticks to her smoked salmon bagel.

"Takeaway?" Mike asks, looking between us with interest. The guy is always asking me about my relationship status. He's Italian and has been married since his late teens. He can't understand how a man can get to his late twenties and not have a wife.

"Shall we eat here?" Kyla asks, her eyes widening with uncertainty. She's nervous about something, but I don't want her to be. I want her to feel comfortable in my presence, but I know women don't always. Maybe it's my height. At six-foot-two, I'm towering over Kyla, and she's not particularly short for a woman. Or maybe it's my tattoos. My arms are a latticework of hell symbols—demons and skulls, hellfire and death. It all fit with the anger I felt after my dad died, at the same time that I accumulated the faint scars that run up my cheek and the crookedness to my nose. My brother would say I have a short fuse, but it wasn't really that. My fuse is long. It's just my nerves were frayed too close to the edge.

"Sure. I don't have another client for thirty minutes."

There's a small table by the window, which Kyla grabs while I settle the check and find our drinks from the open-fronted fridge.

When I sit, Kyla's twisting her hands together on the table. "What kind of art do you like? What kind of pictures do you have up in your place?" I ask her.

"I don't have much art. Just photographs of family and friends."

"Well, if you could choose something, what would you pick?"

"I like black and white photos from the past. You know, the kind of thing that shows an era."

"Hollywood movie stars?"

She shakes her head, reaching out for the saltshaker even though we don't have anything to season. "Not well-known people. Just ordinary people."

"Yeah, I like those too. And the old black and white film reels from the past."

"Yeah. The days when everyone wore a hat and their Sunday best. People didn't have a lot, but they always looked well put together."

"They did. I guess they didn't have the option to buy fast fashion made in a sweatshop halfway across the world. It was all quality stuff made locally. Tailor-made from natural fabrics."

"Exactly." Kyla smiles as she takes a sip of her iced tea, turning to glance out of the window at a passing mom pushing her twins in a double stroller. Her eyes linger on the cute girls, who must be around nine months old. Their hair is secured into topknots, complete with purple bows, and they're both clutching a white unicorn toy.

Mike crosses the deli to set our food in front of us on white square plates. He's made an extra effort with the presentation today, as though he wants to contribute to making this thing that he thinks is a date more special. He gives me a wink too. "Let me know if you need anything else," he says before winking again. Damn, the man has no tact.

"Does he always do that?" Kyla says, taking a bite of her bagel.

"The winking thing?"

She nods, chewing and then rolling her eyes with pleasure.

"He thinks you're my girlfriend, or at least, he thinks I'm trying to make you my girlfriend."

"If only he knew what's really going on at Ink Factor." Kyla raises a brow and fixes me with a look that is far from shy. It's a real surprise to see her being so upfront.

"Dex has some interesting ideas."

"He does," she says.

"I wrote down my ideas on a piece of paper before we left for lunch, but now I'm thinking to change something."

"Really? Why?"

"Just something we talked about. It's steering me in a different direction."

"Well, now I'm intrigued."

"You weren't intrigued before?"

Kyla lowers her bagel, resting it in the white paper it was wrapped in and uses a napkin to dab her lips. "I'm intrigued and a little scared."

"Well, you definitely don't need to be scared. There's not a man at Ink Factor who'd ever do anything to hurt even a hair on your head."

"I get that," she says. "But it's more than that?"

"Oh yeah. What?"

"What happens if I like it too much?"

Now there's something that none of us had even considered. Or at least, it's not something that passed through my mind. My focus has been on making everything as good as possible for Kyla, but she's right. What happens if we all want more than one night? What happens after the game is done? I don't want to freak her out by adding to her concerns. I guess we'll all need to live with that risk and deal with it if it happens.

"I think that'd be a good problem to have," I say.

"So, am I gonna pick when I get back?"

"Yep, and then if you want, you can choose the night for the first date."

"Tonight," Kyla blurts. "If I leave it, I'll change my mind. I know it. My mind has an almost unfathomable capacity to freak me out. It'll invent a million and one reasons why all of this is foolish, and I'll end up regretting not going ahead. I know I will."

"I'm glad to hear you have so much faith in us."

"Something like that," she smiles.

We spend a few more minutes eating and talking. Kyla tells me some stories about her gruesome ex-boss that make Carl seem like a patient angel. On the way back, she asks me about my brother, and I fill her in on our dynamic. She smiles to hear that I'm always introduced as the one with the temper when Kase is hardly a saint.

Back at Ink Factor, everyone is working but the white plastic chip bowl is resting on the reception desk, just waiting for Kyla's slender fingers to investigate its depths.

"Remember, if you pick out mine, the date is going to be a surprise."

Kyla nods, her hand swirling the eight pieces of paper around.

Pick mine, I think. *Pick mine.* It's a one-in-eight chance, and I've beat worse odds.

What would it be like to be her first? Maybe my kink isn't the kind that would be best to start her off with, but my date could be. I guess it's all in the hands of the gods, or universe, or whatever power is out there choosing our paths.

Finally, she settles on a slip of paper, bringing it close to herself and looking around before she opens it.

Her eyes flick up to mine. "It's Lex," she says softly.

I don't know what Lex has written on his paper, but I'm sure it's going to be something that Kyla can handle. He'll build her confidence up for the next man and the one after that.

Wherever I am in the running, I don't care. When I finally get my date with Kyla, it's going to be awesome.

12

KYLA

"I can't believe I'm actually doing this," I say to Dawn, clutching the phone to the side of my head as I make my way to the address that was written on the piece of paper. It said: *LEX, A HOMECOOKED MEAL, DESSERT.*

I've never heard that dessert can be thought of like a kink, but I guess that's how ignorant I am of sex things.

"You're going to have the time of your life. What could be better? A man with gorgeous brown hair, tattoos on a physique that should be immortalized in marble, who can cook and likes sweet things?"

"Yeah, it all sounds good when you say it like that, so why is my mind throwing up red flags over and over?"

"Because your mind will make red flags out of going to the store. You're always so risk averse."

"I'm trying not to be," I say. "Somehow, between you and the men of Ink Factor, I've become a project."

"Pretty much every single woman in the world, and most married ones, would wish to switch places with you right now, Kyla. Don't you forget that. The universe isn't just smiling at you. It's sending you a colossal Cheshire-cat-style floating grin right now, complete with tooth glints."

"I'm here," I say, looking up at the building that Lex's note has brought me to. "He's lives in a nice building."

"You see. As if he didn't have enough going for him, he has great digs too."

I blow out a big tense breath, bouncing on my toes like an athlete getting ready for a run. "Tell me I can do this?"

"You can do this," Dawn says. "You're going to blow him away and have the best time ever."

"I hope so."

When I reluctantly hang up the phone, I stare up at the building again, approaching the central door with trepidation. There's a large pad of buttons, and I find number eleven, my lucky number, pressing it hard before I change my mind.

When the door buzzes, I rush to yank it open, heading for the elevator. It looks like number eleven is on the third floor, and walking up the stairs won't do anything for my complexion. My antiperspirant doesn't need any more testing than it's getting right now.

I only get time to straighten some wayward strands of hair in the elevator mirror before the doors spring open, and there's Lex, standing in the doorway of his apartment, dressed in gray joggers and a fitted white tee with bare feet.

And oh my God, the sight of his feet sends a volcano of heat rushing over my skin. What the hell is wrong with me?

"Come in," he smiles. "It's good you're on time because everything is ready."

I want to say something, but my tongue has fastened itself to the roof of my mouth and my brain cells seem to have slithered out of my ears. He looks so good. Too good, really.

Too good for me.

"I've made you a cocktail. I can't promise it's as good as the Red Devil, but it's along the same lines."

Phew. Maybe with some liquid courage inside of me, I might be able to function like a normal human being. "A cocktail would be awesome," I say, as I finally get my legs to function so that I can walk through the door.

Lex's apartment is amazing. White-tiled floors extend through the entire open-plan space, reflecting the tall windows and state-of-the-art kitchen. The scent of delicious food fills the air, and I glance around, searching out the personal touches that make a home. Along the wall, there are shelves covered in photographs. I drift toward them, smiling at a much younger Dex and Lex with their arms around each other's shoulders and one with a mom and dad too. The twins look like a carbon copy of their father. There are also plenty of photos of them with the other Ink Factor men, at all stages of childhood into adulthood.

"You like photos," Lex asks, handing me a red cocktail in a wide glass with a thin stem.

"Photos are always of special moments. They always feel happy."

"Our best moments," Lex says. "The happiest memories."

"Do your parents live nearby?"

"They do. About thirty minutes away. Far enough that we get to live our own lives, but close enough to have lunch over there at the weekend."

"That sounds perfect."

"Do you want to take a seat while I serve up?"

"Sure."

I follow Lex to the small square dark wood table that is already laid out with silverware and placemats. On the counter, two white square plates sit on what looks like a hot plate. Seriously, this guy isn't just rustling up a home-cooked meal. He has all the gear to make this like a gourmet restaurant experience.

"For starters, we have prawns and scallops with a light lemon drizzle and a fresh herb salad."

"Oh my God, I love scallops, but I'd never be brave enough to cook them at home."

"The trick is to not cook them much at all."

Lex sets the plate in front of me, and I marvel at the gorgeous presentation.

"Dig in."

"There's no *digging* about it. This is a savor-every-bite kind of experience." I guess this isn't the first time that Lex has cooked up something delicious for someone else, but his expression is still bright when I make a moaning sound of appreciation. "This is so good."

"My dad is a chef. He had his own restaurant while we were growing up, but it got too much for him, so he closed it. Now he works part-time for someone else. He gets to switch off from work when he's not there. Having your own business is a twenty-four-seven commitment."

"Is that how you feel about Ink Factor?"

"At first, but I think personalities lead to different roles being taken on in a group. Carl has shouldered most of the burden of the business side of things. I like going to shows to pick up on the new technology and techniques."

"That sounds fun."

"It can be. Mostly I just like keeping my head down and doing great art for people. I love the customers' response when I've made their idea come to life."

"It's a big responsibility," I say. "It's something they'll

most likely have on their skin forever."

"Exactly."

"And what about you? Where are your parents?"

"My family was originally from Austin, but they moved to a small town when I was a teen. I moved here after college and never wanted to go back."

"So you get to see them on the holidays?"

"Yeah. I try. It's not always easy to get time off, especially when I was working at the coffee shop."

"It should be easier now. Just let Carl know when you want to make the trip home."

"Okay, thanks.

Lex carries on talking about the recipes he's learned from his father, using his hands in an animated way that makes him larger than life. He seems really close with his family, which is always a good sign—a good sign when it comes to boyfriend requirements. Not so important for a one-time hook-up, I tell myself.

When we're done eating, he takes my plate and, after five minutes' more preparation, presents me with a plate of pasta—thin flat linguini curls in a light buttery garlic, herb, and lemon sauce with wilted spinach. The scent of lemon is fresh, and the parmesan adds something wonderful and nutty.

The first twirl of it around my fork is silky and perfect, and the first bite is out of this world. "You know, this is a relatively simple dish, but I'd be capable of messing this up without any assistance."

"What could you possibly do wrong?"

"Overcook or undercook the pasta, so it's hard or glued together. Put too much lemon, so it's sour. There's no end of ways that I could make this taste awful."

"If you had my dad as a teacher, you'd be fine too," Lex says. "He's really patient, and he lets me experiment."

Nodding, I take another sip of the cocktail, suddenly conscious that dessert is the next course. "I think you took his temperament," I say. "Dex definitely doesn't have the same patience."

"No, Dex came out of the womb screaming. He's passionate, and he lets things bother him a lot."

"You're good for each other," I say, and Lex nods, his soft brown eyes searching my face, for what I'm not sure.

"Do you feel comfortable with me?" he asks softly.

"I do," I say, and it's true. Even though we're new friends, there is something so peaceful about Lex, and he's made me so welcome in his home.

"You know that dessert could just be dessert. If you decide that you aren't comfortable with Dex's game, I'd be fine with that. I have no expectations at this point. This is all about you."

Maybe he sensed my nerves when I arrived, but I don't have any nerves now outside of the usual butterflies in my belly that are normal on a first date. This is a first date with a difference, though—a first date with expectations of sex.

"I want the dessert you planned," I say, resting my hand against my stomach to try and still some of the bubbling anticipations.

Lex grins, his tongue piercing glinting in the low light. I've never kissed a man with metal in his mouth. Will it feel different? Will he use it to make me feel good? Isn't that what piercings are all about? Will he have any other piercings? A shiver runs up my spine that is part uncertainty and part arousal. I know so little about this man, but I'm so eager to find out more. My hands tremble as I lower my silverware, knowing that there isn't much time left before he's doing so much more than smile at me across a table covered with empty plates.

His hand reaches across and takes hold of mine, cradling it gently. "Wanna come and see my bedroom?"

Now that is a nice way to phrase it: no sex references or anything sleazy or cringy. When I push back my chair, my heart begins to speed in my chest. The light pink camisole I'm wearing feels suddenly flimsy, and the jeans too snug. I'm aware of my body in a way that feels alien to me, every curve and bone filled with a buzzing vibration.

I'm over-sensitized.

Hyper alert.

When Lex leads me through a door into a small hallway with two doors, my throat tightens. "This is my room," he says, resting his hand on the door. "Ready?"

I don't even know what I'm supposed to be ready for.

Dessert?

Is that's what on the other side of this door, or am I dessert? Or could it be a combination of the two?

A quick nod, and Lex pushes the door open. Inside, the room is softly lit by one shaded lamp on the nightstand. His bed is big, with a soft-looking comforter and more pillows than I'd expect on a man's bed. At the end of the bed is a pile of towels and on a low table, a spread of delicious things that would definitely constitute dessert. A tub of chocolate spread stands next to a tube of squirty cream and a cheesecake. There are strawberries and raspberries and what looks like a small tub of ice cream sitting in a bowl of ice.

There's ice.

I shiver again, imagining the feel of it trailing across my skin. Is that what this is? Lex is going to cover me in all his favorite desserts. Or maybe he's going to cover himself and let me lick them off. Either option sounds unbelievably awesome and sweet as hell, literally and metaphorically.

It's the perfect way to begin this crazy game, and my heart begins to settle into a more normal rhythm.

This is it. The moment that I force myself to break

down the barriers I've put around myself since James cheated and I realized I couldn't cope with the teaching job I'd been building up to for years. The moment I lost my footing and started not to recognize myself in the mirror.

Who was I without the man I thought I loved and the career I thought I wanted?

Who will I be after I let myself go and do things with this sexy man that will probably set my cheeks on fire for the rest of my life?

Lex pushes the door closed, allowing the latch to click into place. He turns the lock too, which I know is for privacy rather than to trap me in his lair. His hand slides under my hair until it rests, hot at my nape. His mouth rests against the skin of my shoulder in a long, soft kiss. "You smell of vanilla and blueberries," he says softly, kissing the base of my neck and resting his other hand possessively at my waist.

"Like dessert," I whisper, feeling his lips curve against my sensitive skin.

"Can I undress you, Kyla?"

Oh God, the feeling of his warm breath against my ear and his hands on my body makes me tremble. I'm putty in his hands, or maybe something foodier, like bread dough.

Words won't form in my mouth, so I nod, and he doesn't waste any time in sliding the straps over my shoulders and unfastening my bra at the back. I keep my eyes closed, safe in the darkness, while this man who hasn't even kissed my lips yet, strips off my layers of clothes as though he's peeling a ripe fruit. Every new part bared is kissed softly until my knees are weak and my whole body feels languid. By the time I step out of my jeans and lacy panties, my face is as hot as a furnace.

"Just look at your pretty skin," Lex says, using the back of his hand to caress my belly and up to the underside of my breast. When I open my eyes, he's close, staring down at the tight peaks of my nipples and maybe lower.

While I was getting ready for tonight, I debated over whether he'd expect me to clear the forest, but I decided that I don't care. I left everything the way I feel comfortable because that is what this whole thing is supposed to be about. Dawn made me laugh once when we were talking about landscaping the lady parts. "If they don't like bushes, they've gotta stay out of the garden," she said. I confess that I trimmed everything neatly, though.

Looking at Lex now, I don't think he gives a shit about anything except the fact he has a naked and willing woman standing in front of him, waiting to be directed.

I turn in my lips to moisten them, and Lex takes my invitation, bending to press a gentle kiss to my mouth.

It's the kind of kiss that I know I'll think about tomorrow and have to press my fingers to my face with the memory. It's the kind of kiss that I'll remember in years to come with a flutter of my heart. Damn.

Standing on tiptoes, I reach my hands around Lex's neck, drawing us closer, forcing the kiss deeper, feeling the strangely unfamiliar piercing against my tongue.

And just like that, his hands are under my ass, and I'm being lifted against him.

13

LEX

I feel like a neanderthal to admit that I'm pleased to be the first that Kyla picked. The slight tremble in her hands and the uncertainty in her posture make this a whole different kind of experience. I'm used to girls throwing themselves at me, stripping off their clothes in a hurry to fuck. I got to unwrap Kyla like the world's best birthday present, and I maintain my control until her tongue touches mine, then all bets are off.

She's naked and perfect, and I'm hungry for my dessert.

A little whoosh of air leaves her mouth when her back hits the comforter. I kiss my way down her body, tasting her neck, the space between her breasts, and the dip of her navel before I stand, drawing back to enjoy the view.

Damn.

Kyla is all woman.

Curvy and soft, with freckles across the tops of her breasts and the prettiest little nipples I've ever seen. She's set soft waves into her hair tonight that show me she was anticipating that this was going to be a special night.

I can't wait to reveal it all. But first, I need to undress.

It's not a secret that there's a certain way to tug off a shirt that sets girls' hearts fluttering, and maybe other parts of their body too. With one hand, I grip the back of my shirt and tug, revealing my body to Kyla with a flourish.

Her reaction is what I expected. The main tattoo that decorates my chest, abs, and lower torso tends to elicit that response. It's a huge snake that curves its way down, disappearing beneath the waistband of my gray pants. My brother has a matching one, and both of them were done by Noah. He has a special skill for reptiles, marking their scaly skin with perfection.

I drop my pants, too, revealing that I'm not wearing any underwear. My cock is hard, and I fist it as the surge of heat builds in my groin. Kyla's eyes widen, and her lips part. But they're not the only parts of her that open for me. Her legs fall open in an involuntary invitation.

Or maybe it's voluntary. At this point, all her nerves might have vanished.

What to use on her first?

I have a smorgasbord of sweet treats at my disposal, but I can guarantee that there's not a dessert on the table that will taste as sweet as Kyla.

As I crawl on top of her, everything I need is within easy reach. But first, I need to tell her my plans for her. Bracing myself on my hands, I smile down into her wide-eyed gaze that is filled with anticipation. "Are you okay with getting messy, baby? I promise I'll clean you up after."

A little nod is all I need, and I grab the chocolate spread, knowing that it's a great first food to use. The way it melts against the skin is just delicious, and the pressure needed to lick it away will have Kyla's back rising off the bed.

What could be better than a writhing, squirming,

beautiful woman covered in chocolate?

"Don't you need to put down the towels?" she asks.

"Are you planning on making a mess?" I joke.

"Definitely put them down. I won't relax if I'm worried about the sheets getting dirty."

It takes a few seconds to spread the towels around Kyla. Anything to make her feel relaxed, and then I begin painting her with the chocolate I scoop onto the tip of my finger. The first stroke of it across her nipple has her skin breaking out in goose flesh. I guess it's a little cold, which only adds to the sensations. Licking it away is my favorite part. The sweetness spreads over my tongue, and her tight little nipple draws into a harder point. My piercing grazes her sensitive skin, and her eyes widen at the new sensation. The moan that leaves her lips makes my cock kick, but I'm not ready yet.

I'm here to show Kyla that she deserves time and effort. I want to show her that any man worth his salt will consider her pleasure first. And in the process, I get to do it the way I like.

Her body's unmarked with ink, but I can mark it with chocolate. I can paint pictures of the things that I think would fit with Kyla's personality. A rabbit, slightly timid but with a strong kick. A butterfly, fleeting but stunning. A set of scales for fairness and the weighing of decisions. I mark each one out messily across her stomach, licking in between until I'm closer and closer to the apex of her thighs.

Kyla's arm is tossed across her face as though she needs to shut out anything visual to fully focus on the physical touch. Her body moves with every stroke of my finger and tongue, but when I spread the chocolate on the inside of her thigh, she goes completely still.

Now it's time to change things up. I put the jar back on the table and reach for the ice cream. Hot and cold work so well in driving a woman crazy. The drip of melting ice cream over Kyla's clit will make her flinch, but the warmth of my tongue will be the ultimate antidote.

It's cold on my finger, so I don't press it directly to her skin. I leave it to melt and drip down, watching Kyla gasp and squirm, bending to lick away the sweet, creamy vanilla.

She groans as I use the metal in my tongue to create more friction.

Oh God, the taste of her is intoxicating. The scent of her sends a buzz that travels over the back of my head and down my spine. The hunger I feel for this woman is a desperate coiling thing, like the snake that twists down the front of my body and wraps around my cock. She's barely touched me, but we're already entwined.

I let the ice cream drip again, and Kyla moans as her hand reaches out to grip my hair. I don't think she knows whether she wants to steer me toward her pussy or drag me back, but whatever. I'm licking this woman until she comes. Food aside, this is my mission, and the bite of pain as she drives me forward only makes my cock harder.

I know when she's close. Her hips are antsy, and her moans higher in pitch. Her grip tightens until my hair is loosened from its fastening, and then she says it.

"Please."

How could I possibly deny her when she asks so nicely. I slide two fingers inside her heat and press up, and then Kyla's coming and coming like a vice against my hand.

I give her a minute to relax again, and when she does, she peeks at me from behind her arm. "Holy fuck."

"Are you hungry for dessert now?" I wriggle my eyebrows, eliciting the sweetest giggle from Kyla.

"I'm hungry for all the dessert." She looks pointedly from the table to my cock, and it's that moment that I become sure of something. This girl isn't a one-night thing. She's not going to be someone that I can walk away from.

She's a keeper. The kind of girl that mommas the world over want to point their sons toward.

But this whole thing is just about sex, and after tonight, she's going to spend time with my brother and each of my buddies. It doesn't matter how good I make this or how much I want her to stay over tomorrow and the next night and the one after that.

This game wasn't designed for me. It was designed to show Kyla a whole world of fantasies.

And when we're done, she gets to go out into the world knowing a whole lot more about herself than she did at the start—ready for whichever lucky man happens to stumble into her path.

The thought makes me want to punch something.

14

KYLA

I didn't know it was possible for ice cream and chocolate spread to break a person's brain and body. I feel wrung out and heavy in a new and delicious way. And we haven't even had proper sex yet. I haven't got to explore Lex's gorgeous body or touch the most epic cock I've ever seen.

There are more dessert items on the table that I want to slather all over Lex and feast from.

He's made me a monster.

A hungry, dessert-eating, cock-swallowing monster.

I don't even wait to find out if that part's in the plan. I grab a handful of soft cheesecake and smear it over the snake on his belly until it's curving, writhing body has disappeared beneath the creamy topping.

Lex gasps at the coolness, or maybe at my brazenness. Maybe he thought I'd be timid in this fantasy but I'm diving in headfirst.

You only live once.

No wonder Dawn had it tattooed on her ass. If this is the kind of life you get to live when you toss caution to the wind, then I'm all for it.

The first lick of cheesecake is like heaven. Lex's body's so hot, it's already starting to melt and trickle down his sides. I follow the trail with my tongue, and he hisses as I get lower and lower. With my index finger, I scoop up a bit of cheesecake and run it over the tip of his cock.

My eyes meet Lex's wide-open ones. He's propped up on his elbows, watching me with what looks like an expression of awe. I'm so bold that I don't drop my gaze when I bend to take his huge cock into my mouth. It's hotter than hell and as hard as an iron bar, and with one deep bob, it kicks in my mouth like an errant mule.

Lex's abs contract, the perfect ladder of muscle still smeared with delicious vanilla topping, and his mouth drops open as I lick him clean. Is it crazy that I just want to climb him like a tree and slide down onto his big heavy branch? I haven't ever been this into a man, especially after such a short time.

"Shit, Kyla, you're going to kill me."

"Sshh…I'm having dessert." I lick again, and smear more of the cheesecake over all the places I'm hungry to taste until Lex is doing exactly what I did, shaking and trembling, his hips thrusting upward, searching for more contact. I take him to the edge of an orgasm so many times, but he keeps pulling back, until he does what I was working up to all along. He grabs me and rolls until I'm on my back and we're smooshed together into a delicious cheesecake chocolate mess. The long bar of his cock presses hard against my swollen clit and his mouth crushes into mine, and it's a frenzy of hands and hips and legs until his hand starts searching in his nightstand for a condom.

"Hurry," I say, as he uses a towel to clean himself enough to roll the condom down and all the while, I'm imagining what it's going to feel like when he pushes inside me. I've never fucked a man with a cock this size. He's gonna make me feel it, whatever it is.

When he's poised over me, Lex pauses, dipping to rub his nose against mine in the sweetest way. "You ready, honey?"

"I'm ready."

When his cock notches at my entrance, I let out a little puff of air and urge my body to relax. The first inch feels like Lex is breaching a new barrier and then he's deep and deeper, sliding through my arousal like our bodies were meant to fit together. His brow is furrowed with concentration and his loose hair fans around his face. The snake across his body writhes as he cants his hips and undulates his waist, and I'm mesmerized like Eve must have been in the garden of Eden.

It feels so good to be with this man. When he dips his head to kiss me, he's greeted by my lips that are drawn into a smile. I can't hold the bubble of happiness that I'm feeling inside. I just want to let it out.

Lex has a new and special way of moving his hips that hits something deep inside me, building heavy heat between my thighs that almost makes me want to pee. I've never come through penetrative sex before, but I think it could happen. Lex could make it happen.

His hand reaches to the table, and he slips something between us. I jump at the sensation of the ice across my clit. He doesn't leave it there, just taps over and over and over until my whole body is drawn tight, back arched, face scrunched, hands grasping for something, anything to push me over the edge. And then it happens.

Oh, it happens.

I cry out, flopping back against the bed, eyes closed so that I can dwell in the dark cave of pleasure that Lex has encased me in, and through it all, he keeps moving, his cock swelling to impossible proportions. When he comes, he does it resting on just one arm, his inked bicep bulging, every muscle in his body drawn tight. "Fuck," he gasps, thrusting through wave upon wave of an orgasm that I can feel.

He flops on top of me, burying his face into my neck, his hot breath tickling my skin, and I wrap my arms and legs around him and laugh.

I laugh and laugh, and he laughs too.

It's an expression of happiness, and awe, and I guess of relief.

Dex was right.

This game is fun.

Dawn was right.

You only live once is the perfect motto.

I'm never going to be able to eat chocolate spread, ice cream, or cheesecake without thinking about sex, but that's okay.

As Lex reaches out to the table and begins to feed me strawberries, I conclude that this is the best memory I've ever made.

And I have seven more to go.

15

KASE

Why Lex arrives at Ink Factor in the morning, he's not alone. Kyla is there, wearing a pretty outfit that looks more like something she'd wear to a date than to work. He has his arm around her shoulders and presses a kiss to her forehead before he disappears to get his workstation ready.

Dex stayed at our place last night, and I see him making his way into Lex's booth and hear the two of them talking in muted voices about whatever happened last night.

I guess if Kyla stayed over, it must have gone well.

Carl is in the back, and I can't work out if he's bothered by this whole thing or not. If he is, he's doing his best to keep it under wraps. Maybe he doesn't want to be the only one of us that doesn't get a taste of Kyla. Maybe that's what's made him quiet and brooding. Or maybe he's bothered because it's a game and he's holding himself back from competitive. Carl is as competitive as the rest of us. Maybe even more so.

I watch Kyla place her bag beneath the reception desk, then start up the new computer. While it's loading the software, her eyes drift to the white bowl. She might have had a great night last night, but she's already thinking about what she has to come. Kyla knows she can pick out a new date whenever she's feeling like it. We're not running on a deadline. It's all about her and what she wants.

Will she pick out a date today or leave it until tomorrow? Maybe she'll leave it a week, and we'll all be walking around with raging hard-ons from the anticipation.

Her hand drifts over the bowl and pauses. She's definitely in two minds about what to do. Is she tired? Did Lex keep her up all night? Maybe she's sore and wondering if she can physically take another night of vigorous sex.

Her fingers lower, touching the paper. She stirs them around and lifts her hand out, but she's not holding anything. Her gaze drifts to the computer, and inside, my impatient internal voice is screaming at her to pick me, pick me.

I have something awesome planned for her, something that will awaken a darker side.

Her hand reaches out again, and I hold my breath. Is she going to pick?

Yes.

She whips her hand out, holding the small, folded secret. Glancing around before she opens it, I manage to duck out of sight before she spots me.

When she opens the paper, her cheeks flush. Kyla only leaves it a few seconds before she puts the paper in the pocket of her snug jeans. I watch as she takes a deep breath. When she stands, I duck back into my work area, pretending to sort out the ink. I have my back to the reception area, so I have no idea which direction Kyla's going in, or even if she's intending to tell whoever it is that is getting to take her out tonight. There's a soft tap on the partition wall behind me, and when I turn, she's there.

The flush is still evident across Kyla's cheeks, but she meets me, eye to eye. "So, you're taking me clubbing tonight?" she says softly.

Fuck. She did pick me.

There are two things Kyla needs to know for our date to work out well.

"Wear a skirt," I say. "And no underwear."

The little gasp Kyla makes is just about the sweetest thing I've ever heard, and her shock makes my cock twitch. I wait for her to protest, but she doesn't. "Meet me outside Club Crystal at nine pm."

With a quick nod, Kyla turns, and everything is back to business as usual.

For the whole day, all I can think about is what I wrote on Kyla's piece of paper. *KASE, CLUB CRYSTAL, EXHIBITIONISM.*

I hope she's ready to go on an adventure with me.

I'm outside Club Crystal at 8.45 pm. There's no way I want to risk being late and potentially missing Kyla. There's a chance that she won't wait, especially if she's nervous. The doorman, Gerard, is an old friend so I spend a few minutes catching up with him about family and work. When his eyes drift away to something in the distance, I turn to find Kyla walking toward me in a black minidress that finishes halfway up her thighs and has skinny straps that show off her gorgeous golden skin. She's walking slowly, her sweet tits bouncing with every step, and I can't take my eyes off her.

Whoever invented the bra was an imbecile. I'm not a man who enjoys prizing away constricting underwired bras from the chests of my girlfriends. My favorite time is when they're hanging out at home in loose shirts with the breasts in their natural state.

I swallow, the anticipation for the night building in my throat and between my legs.

Did she keep to the deal and come out without panties too? I guess I won't find out until I run my hand over her hip.

"Fuck," the doorman mutters under his breath.

"She's with me," I say proudly.

"Lucky fucker," he says, slapping me on the shoulder.

When Kyla's close enough, I reach out my hand to take hers, bending to press a kiss to her cheek. "You look amazing," I say, taking the time to breathe in her sweet floral scent.

"You look good too," she says, her eyes trailing over my smart attire.

I wanted Kyla to feel special, so I pulled out my most tailored suit and crisply pressed white shirt. It fits like a second skin, accentuating my broad shoulders. The flight of birds I have up my neck is also visible at the open collar, forever seeking freedom from the confines of my clothes.

"Let's go inside," I say, leading the way.

"Have a great night," Gerard calls.

I want to tell him we will, but I don't want to come off as arrogant or assumptive. As the door opens, the base of the music creates a wall of sound. It's dark in the club, broken up by the flashing colors of lights situated around the dancefloor. The long bar is down the left side of the club, and I figure we could both do with a drink. Kyla's hand grips tightly to mine, her eyes darting around at the unfamiliar surroundings.

What's going to happen between us tonight will only work if she trusts me and if she's willing to let herself go. It's going to take a level of connection between us that could be a step too far. I'm trying not to think too much about the possibility that she'll balk before the main event. I'm trying to remember that this is about Kyla and not about me fulfilling a sexual fantasy. This isn't my first time here or my first time playing with this kink, but it is Kyla's.

Maybe I'll be the one to take her too far.

"What would you like?" I ask as the barman dips closer for our order.

"A fruity cocktail," she says. "Surprise me."

"I'll have a whisky, neat," I tell the waiting man. "And a piña colada."

As the barman begins to prepare our order, I take my time to look Kyla over. Her lips are painted a dark red, a color I've never seen her wear before, and her shoes have a spiked heel that increases her height by around three inches. She's still a lot smaller than me, but the difference is less pronounced. I'm not the only one who's noticed how stunning she is. Across the dancefloor, I catch three other men tracing her curves languidly with their eyes. In this place, you're either a watcher or a person who likes to be watched. They must be wondering where Kyla stands on that scale and whether they'll get to witness her pleasure later. The thought settles hotly in my belly, anticipation building, but I have to be patient.

"So, how did it go with Lex last night?" I ask.

"Am I allowed to tell you? Did Dex make up rules about disclosure too?"

"There are no rules about disclosure, but I'll be transparent and tell you that Lex wouldn't tell us anything outside of that you had a good time."

"He doesn't want to give you any kind of insight that could improve your chances of winning the game," Kyla says, tucking her gently curled lock of hair behind her ear. Her fingers drift over the long earring she's wearing, a seductive move that I don't think is deliberate. Kyla doesn't seem to have any idea just how alluring she is.

"And what about you? Will you give me an insight?"

"Will I give you an advantage? No. You gotta do your best, Kase. Isn't that what your momma always told you, because my momma sure did?"

"My momma didn't tell me shit about doing my best at sex stuff, Kyla. What kind of momma have you got?"

She snorts with laughter, reaching out to take the pale cream cocktail that the barman rested on the marble countertop. "Not about sex stuff. About life in general."

"Well, I'm all about doing my best. I think you're going to like my best a lot."

"I guess we'll have to wait and see about that."

"Did you stay over at Lex's?"

She nods, taking a long sip of her cocktail. Around us, the music changes from something with a fast beat to something more soulful. People begin to make their way to the dancefloor, leaving the space around it feeling less congested.

There's something so opulent about Club Crystal. Maybe it's the muted purples shades or the huge chandeliers, or maybe the walnut bar. Or it could be the clientele. Everyone here dresses to impress. There's also the other part of the club that makes it more decadent than any of the others in the city.

The upper balcony, which extends over the dancefloor, is made mostly of glass. The balustrade and the floor are transparent. It's not a spoken or promoted thing, but couples who have an exhibition kink can often be seen up there, indulging in whatever brings them the most pleasure. Kyla doesn't know it yet, but that's why I bought her here. That's why I made the no underwear rule.

I lean in close, wanting to breathe in Kyla's scent and whisper into her ear. Some things have to be spoken that way to have maximum impact.

"Have you ever had sex in public?" I ask her.

"No," she says, but it's not delivered in a forceful way. Kyla's voice is breathy and aroused, exactly as I was hoping.

There's no fun in coercing someone to do something so far outside of their barriers that it makes them uncomfortable. Encouraging someone to do something that they'd previously been too shy to try but are eager to experience is something totally different.

"Will you come upstairs with me, Kyla?" I raise my head to glance up to the balcony. There's already one couple up there kissing. Kyla turns to follow my gaze, her eyes widening as she realizes the intention behind my question.

She blows a long, soft breath between pursed lips as though she's trying to physically push the nerves from her body. Her eyes search mine, seeking reassurance, I guess. This isn't simply about us taking a new kinky step in an established relationship. This is about her trusting me enough to have sex with me for the first time and do it in front of other people. It's a leap into the darkness, so I get why she might be uncertain. When she doesn't immediately respond, I bend to press a soft kiss on her lips, my heart thudding when we touch that way for the first time. "If you don't want to, we can go somewhere else, or I can take you home. You know there's no pressure for you to go ahead with any of the dates. This is all on your terms."

She blinks, glancing again at the couple on the balcony and then lower at the people whose heads are angled to the sky. Taking everything in, she straightens her shoulders, resolve forming and changing her posture. "I'm here to play the game," she says with a determination that comes as a surprise, and her hand slides into mine as though she still needs my encouragement to go ahead. Hell, that small gesture causes something in my chest to constrict. There's a vulnerability about Kyla but also an internal strength that I'm not sure she even recognizes in herself. As she blinks, her long lashes cast shadows over her high cheekbones, and I get an urge to press a soft kiss to the tender skin there.

She's like an unopened gift, wrapped up pretty, but what's underneath is even more tantalizing.

"Let's go," I say. We carry our drinks up the stairs. I allow Kyla to walk first, conscious that she's not wearing any underwear and might be grateful for my body as a barrier to prying eyes. Her dress is long enough that I don't get to see more than her sexy curvy thighs brushing together with each step. At the top, she looks around, finding three couples in various stages of passion. There's just one at the edge of the balcony, on the far side. The two other couples are sprawled over the plush purple velvet couches.

Kyla glances back at me, her mellow brown eyes alive with excitement and maybe a tinge of fear. It's funny how those two emotions can run hand in hand, taking us into dark places that we might never have dared to experience.

"Come," I say, leading her to the edge of the balcony. There's a low table that we place our drinks on, and then she stares out at the club, watching the dancers below. Her legs are pressed tightly together, but not for long.

Moving her hair over her shoulder, I duck to press soft kisses along the back of her elegant neck. My fingers trace the thin strap of her dress, moving it toward her shoulder in tiny increments. For the first few moments, Kyla seems resistant. Her shoulders are bunched, and her arms are clutched tightly against her chest. But the more I kiss and caress, the more she seems to relax. "Do you trust me?" I whisper as my thumb strokes lazy circles on her back.

"Yes," she says, turning to look me dead in the eye.

Do I deserve Kyla's trust?

Of course. I'd never do anything to hurt her. Tonight is about to bring excitement to her life and show her a different way of finding pleasure. Her trust is something that is important to me but knowing I have it makes this moment with her even more special.

She keeps her eyes locked with mine as I push the strap of her dress slowly down her arm. When the fabric moves over her breast, it gets caught for a second at the point of her nipple, but a little more pressure and it drops.

I can't see what Kyla looks like because I'm behind her, and her body is still twisted toward the club, but me seeing is not what this is about.

This is about knowing that other people are watching. This is about Kyla trusting me to expose her and knowing that she's excited about it too.

I allow my thumb to teasingly brush the side of her breast, watching her pupils dilate with arousal. Even in the low light, I can see her cheeks are stained red and her self-consciousness sends a wave of warmth through me. I stroke closer and closer to her nipple until I brush the pointed tip with the gentlest of pressures, and Kyla's knees almost give way.

"You know people are watching us," I say. "They're looking at your beautiful body, and they're jealous as fuck that I'm the one getting to touch you."

Kyla's lip's part, but she doesn't say anything. Her expression is glazed as though the sensory overload has shorted out her ability to communicate.

"Open your legs," I tell her, glancing down at the dancefloor beneath us. There are three faces upturned, waiting for a chance to see under Kyla's short skirt. "And look out there. Find someone who's watching and let them know you see them."

"Fuck," she mutters, her hands bracing against the balustrade, knuckles white with the effort to keep herself together. She's trembling, her arms breaking out in gooseflesh and her chest hitching with hastily drawn breaths. Balanced on her high heels, she slowly spreads her legs until her feet are about a foot and a half apart. Very gently, I move my feet until one is pressed to the inside of Kyla's ankle. I want her to feel it there and know that I'm the one responsible for baring her pussy to the strangers downstairs. I'm the one who's making this experience happen.

"Have you found someone?" I whisper, letting my lips brush the shell of her ear.

"Yes," she says.

"Man or woman?"

"It's a man."

"Good. Keep looking at him. Let him watch me touch you."

A shiver runs through Kyla's body, and in my pants, I'm as hard as granite, knowing that it's time.

I'm about to touch Kyla in between her legs and find out just how wet I've made her.

And then I'll show her just what it means to let go.

16

KYLA

I don't know who I am anymore.

This woman, who's standing on a glass balcony with her breast exposed and a man pressed to her back, is a stranger to me.

The man watching from the other side of the club has a smile on his face that can only be described as filthy. He's good looking which only adds to the experience. I'm pretty sure that he's banking these images for later when he's alone with his dick in his hand.

The idea is oddly arousing.

I don't think I've ever been someone's spank-bank fantasy before. At least, I don't think I have.

And I don't think I can deal with any more arousal. As I spread my legs at Kase's order, the wetness between them cools in the airconditioned atmosphere. There is no doubt about the mess I've made of myself, and in a second, Kase is going to discover my shame.

There's no rush in his touch. Everything about Kase is

slow and exploratory. He's an adventurer, and I'm unexplored territory. He's a pioneer, and I'm just along for the ride.

Beneath us, people dance to the pounding music, but maybe they're looking up, watching as his fingers stroke under the cheeks of my ass. Maybe they see when his finger slips through my arousal or when he plays by circling my little hole, teasing me to the point of gasping.

My hands are braced on the balcony edge, but that's not enough. My body slumps forward, one bare breast and one covered, resting over the top. Kase's foot prevents me from closing one leg, but there's no way I would tell him to stop. I'm too turned on, too crazy with lust.

I'm in a frenzy of longing and more desperate to come than I've ever been.

Am I brazen enough to tell him to do it? Slide two fingers inside me and pump until I'm a quivering mess?

I am, but before I can, he brings his hand around the front of my thigh, hitching up my dress, so my pussy is visible to everyone.

The heat I feel in my cheeks is a mix of excitement and shame. The man who's watching leans forward as though he wants to get closer, to see better, to imagine what it would be like to touch me.

Kase's thick finger slides down my belly, slowly, slowly, until it presses against my swollen clit, and I almost come from that one firm touch.

"He's watching my finger, but he's imagining it's his," Kase whispers. "He's imagining what you feel like, what you smell like, what you taste like. He wants to replace me so that he can play with you, knowing that everyone can see, that everyone is watching."

Even though I know what Kase is saying isn't strictly true—only a few people are watching at most—the thoughts are enough to trip a switch in my brain.

My pussy clenches, hungry for more. I don't think I've ever felt emptier or needier in my life. "Please," I whisper, my hips shifting for more swipes of his finger. Kase presses against my ass, the ridge of his cock a firm bar against the seam of my ass.

There's hardly anything between us. All Kase would have to do is undo a button and a zipper and yank down his pants and underwear. He could push inside me in a few seconds, and I wouldn't stop him. Knowing people will see his cock thrusting into me doesn't concern me at all. At this point, I'd get on my back and spread my legs to feel Kase spread me open.

"Please, what? Tell me what you want."

"Your cock," I whisper, knowing the man across the club might be able to lip-read. His smile grows wider. Can he tell how worked up I am? Does he know that I'm begging the big, sexy man behind me to fuck me without shame?

"Are you on the pill?" Kase asks. "I'm clean. I have to be to work at Ink Factor."

"I am," I say, my pussy drawing tight again. This will be the first time I've ever fucked a man without protection. The first time I'm going to feel what it's like to be filled with cum.

Kase doesn't waste any time in freeing his cock. Any finesse is lost when he yanks up the back of my dress and slides the hot bar of his dick through my arousal. When he notches at my entrance, he pauses, his hand gripping the hair at my nape. My mind flicks to an old fantasy, a forbidden thought of a man roughly taking me without my permission. The surrender to someone else's will. The desire to escape from him but also the building arousal at the idea that I'm a captive.

"Ready?" Kase asks, bringing me back to the present.

I nod, my body pushing back slightly with need. Oh

God, I want him so badly.

The first thrust doesn't take Kase deep. There's so much of him, but he works his way inside slowly but surely—his hand tugs at my hair, pulling my head up, forcing me to look forward.

"He's watching us," he says. "Look at him. Look at how much he wants you. He'd do anything for a chance to do this with you, but he'll never get that chance."

Rolling his hips, he uses his other hand to spread my labia open wide and tap against my clit. There's a roughness to his actions that makes my pussy clench. A desire to display me, too, in a way that seems animalistic and possessive. With every thrust, I feel my orgasm building, my whole body drawing tight but opening at the same time.

"He'll never get the chance to do this with you because you belong to me now."

"Yes," I say, even though I'm so crazed I barely know what I'm saying. Even though I know that Kase doesn't mean a word.

"Tell me again. Let him see."

"I belong to you," I say, forcing my hips back so my pussy can swallow him deeper. "Oh God."

The man below licks his lips as though he's imagining his tongue on my spread pussy, imagining the way I taste and the heat of my skin. Imagining making my clit swell even more than it is right now.

I'm lost between two men: the man behind me, responsible for all my pleasure, and the man he's allowing to be part of this, if only as a bystander.

How odd it is to feel like two men are part of my pleasure when only one man is touching me.

I wonder why Kase has this kink. What is it in his past that has made him want to display his sexual prowess for others? What is it that makes him want to share the woman he's with to a stranger's eyes?

Kase tugs on my hair as I come, keeping me upright through wave upon wave of the brightest pleasure. The moan that leaves my lips is something animal and desperate, but Kase doesn't seem to mind. He carries on fucking me through it all with the kind of precision that only a man with extreme control can deliver.

"That's it, baby," he says. "That's it. You feel so fucking good."

And I do. I feel awesome. Like a powerful and uninhibited goddess who's opened a box of treasures she never knew existed.

When Kase's cock swells inside me, it feels different from anything I've ever experienced. There's an intimacy to it, which is strange, seeing as we're not alone. All around us, there are people who know what we're doing. Downstairs, there are people who witnessed it all, the penetration and now the release. Kase lets go of my hair and bends to kiss my neck, his breath gusting over my skin fast and hot. His fingers find the strap of my dress and draw it up so that my breast is covered with the soft black fabric. Smoothing the skirt of my dress down at the front, he sighs. "You're perfect," he whispers. "Absolutely perfect."

And I feel it.

Like a dove, released from a cage to fly free into the perfect blue summer sky, I'm liberated.

Even though we're still joined, I turn at the waist so I can look into his ethereal gray eyes. The birds on his neck soar to escape the prison of his collar, and the affinity with my own feelings makes tears burn in my throat. I kiss him, slow and deep, our tongues sliding against each other lazily, unconcerned of any onlookers.

Eventually, I feel him slipping from inside me and sense him reaching into his jacket pocket. Kase presses a handkerchief to my entrance, catching the slip of cum that I can feel dripping from inside me. I wish I could touch it. There's a strange sense of loss that comes with him wiping it away.

When I'm clean, and he's tucked away, there's nothing to show what we just did. From the outside, we could be any couple, at a nightclub to enjoy the music, alcohol and even some dancing. I don't expect Kase to wrap his arms around me, holding me against him in a firm hug that squeezes the air from my chest. I don't expect the tenderness from him, but it's there.

"Are you okay?" he asks, but I can't find the words to reply. My throat is closed with emotion, so I nod and bury my face against his chest, relishing the moments of closeness.

Is this what they call aftercare?

It's more than I've ever had from a lover before, and my lovers have been relationships.

Kase isn't my boyfriend. There are no feelings between us outside of friendship, so then why does this feel like more?

We stand that way for as long as I need to pull myself together, and I do what I do best, stuffing down my emotions and firmly closing the lid on them. When I draw away, my smile is bright.

"That was awesome," I say.

"Our friend over there agrees." Kase nods toward the man, who's currently clapping his approval. I don't know whether to feel proud or mortified. "Shall we finish our drinks?"

"Sure."

Kase bends to pick up my cocktail and his whisky and finds us a free couch. We drink and talk, and it's so much fun that we stay for two more drinks after that, but then the night comes to an end. We both have work tomorrow after all.

At my door, Kase leans in to kiss me goodnight, and it's bittersweet. The urge to invite him inside is strong, but so is the feeling that it would be a mistake. This is just a game, and tonight we've played and won. Trying to make it into something more would only risk adding fuel to the already smoldering fire, the fire of realization that I like these men more than I should.

They're my colleagues, and this isn't about relationships or love.

This is about sex and exploration, and awakening.

If he steps over the threshold and we have sex again, it won't be part of the game. It'll be more intimate and searching. And if I fall asleep in his arms, what then?

It was hard enough to say goodbye to Lex. I can't make the same mistake with the rest of these men. My heart won't take it.

I wave Kase goodbye, holding on to the fact that tomorrow is another day and another date.

Maybe that'll help me forget just how much my heart already feels involved.

17

NIALL

On the day after Kase's date, Kyla doesn't pick another. She doesn't give any kind of explanation, so we're left wondering if the game will continue or if it's all over after just two. Kole and Dex are annoyed with Kase. They think he did something wrong, but Kase is adamant that their date was great, and that Kyla was happy at the end of it.

So we wait.

We're professionals at work, but we have fun together too. Kyla brings in an awesome tray of brownies, and we devour them with all the intensity that we're hoping to get to devour her with someday.

We have fun lunches at the deli, getting to know each other more, and it's all great. Kyla's cool with Lex and Kase so any theories about them putting her off the game seem wrong. Maybe she just needs time to recover. I've known these guys a long time. Fucking any of us would take it out of a woman's body.

Or maybe it's more than physical. Maybe it's the intensity of dates with men who Kyla is only just getting to know.

On day three, I'm uploading some photos of my latest creation—a Viking on the thigh of a fifty-year-old male—when someone clears their throat behind me. Turning, I find Kyla standing with a small piece of white paper in her hand. Is that what I think it is?

"I guess you're up," she says softly.

"Seriously?"

"Yep. Niall is lucky number three."

"Fucker," Noah says, appearing behind Kyla as though he followed her.

"I will be later," I snap and immediately feel bad because I shouldn't be flippant about any of this. "Sorry, Kyla. That came out badly. When it comes to my asshole brothers, my tongue is sharp."

"No one knows how to press Niall's buttons better than me," Noah says with a stupid grin on his face.

"What about me?" Nash says, sticking his head around Noah. Of course, he'd be there to interfere with my discussion with Kyla. My brothers are such nosy douchebags.

"Can you all fuck off so I can talk to Kyla? None of this is your business. You better apologize."

Noah and Nash turn their attention to Kyla and notice her flushed cheeks. Whether they've upset her or not, they are quick to say sorry and skulk away. I know they're bummed that I'll be the first of us to be with her. Noah was sure he would be. The guy has a thing about talking about the future as though what he wants is an absolute certainty.

"Are you good for tonight?" I ask her.

When she nods, my heart skips a beat. I place the tablet

on the counter and rub my hands on my jeans, inhaling a deep breath to quash what feels like nerves bubbling behind my ribs. I shouldn't be nervous about this. Sex isn't something I've experienced nerves about since I was fourteen and rutting with a seventeen-year-old in her bedroom while her parents slept on the other side of the wall.

I need to pull myself together.

I have a chance now to make tonight less awkward. All it will take is a soft approach. The rest will come later. When I cross the space between us, Kyla straightens herself. I run my hand over my closely cropped hair, a nervous habit that my brothers don't share. Kyla blinks up at me with wide, slightly worried eyes that I need to soothe. None of this will work if she has reservations.

The blue tank that she's wearing is the same color as the sky on a summer's day. I reach out to touch the fabric, moving slowly, so she doesn't flinch. My finger brushes her warm skin. "Are you excited about our date?" I ask.

"Niall, picnic outside," she whispers, nodding, the paper I wrote my date information on crackling between her fingers.

"Exactly."

"I'm excited," she says.

"Good. It'll be fun. I know the perfect spot, so I'll pick you up at seven pm."

"Okay." Her breath leaves her lips in a rush that I'm hoping is relief.

I touch her chin, tipping her sweet face to mine. "You know I'll look after you. We all will. There's nothing to be anxious about."

"Yes."

Bending to kiss her cheek gently, I breathe in the soft floral scent of her skin. "That's good. I'm looking forward to it." I've always loved a girl who blushes. There's something so cute about witnessing a person's physical reaction, especially when it's to my words and proximity. "Oh, and wear a dress."

Kyla smiles. "Easy access?"

"Exactly."

I arrive outside Kyla's apartment at 7 pm exactly and call up to let her know I'm there. She emerges from the building in less than five minutes, earning extra points for her punctuality.

Points?

I'm not supposed to be scoring her. She's supposed to be scoring me. But as I take in my gorgeous date, dressed in a floral floor-length cotton dress and pretty powder blue cardigan, with her hair swept up into a ponytail and her hands clutching her purse a little too tightly, I can't help but think that she's a ten out of ten.

"I hope you're hungry," I say, reaching out to take her hand for the short walk to my car.

"I resisted snacking on anything," she says. "I didn't want to spoil my appetite."

"That's good."

Her hand is small, soft, and warm in mine, and when I glance down at where we're connected, I'm struck by the paleness of her skin against the dark ink of mine.

For as long as I can remember, my brothers and I wanted to become tattoo artists. Our dad had a friend who was in the marines, and he had the most interesting ink covering his arms and torso. I used to sit in his lap and ask him about each one, and he'd tell me the most elaborate stories about the inspiration behind all the artworks.

The idea that tattoos can tell a story is what drew me to the profession. I also liked that it was a way that I could differentiate myself from my brothers. The ink I have on my arms is unique to me. My triplet brothers chose different places on their bodies and different stories too.

In many ways, we're very similar. Before the tattoos, even our own parents would struggle to identify us if we were still and silent. Now, there are no problems. We've created our own differences, and it made me feel just separate enough.

I wonder if Kyla will ask me about them. She doesn't have any herself and told us that she doesn't want any either.

I wonder how she'll react to my piercing. That's another difference between my brothers and me.

Opening the car door for Kyla is a way of me setting the tone for the evening. I'm here to take care of her in every way. I'm here to make her fantasies come true. At least, I hope my night fits with her fantasies.

In the trunk is a delicious picnic prepared by the deli near Ink Factor. I have candles and a small speaker for music. A few rugs and cushions so that Kyla will be comfortable. I've also downloaded this awesome app so we can look up at the stars. Thank goodness there's no chance of rain tonight, or I would have needed to find another venue for our outdoor escapades.

"Nice car," she says as she pulls the belt across her body.

"It's my dad's old truck," I smile, happy that she appreciates my passion.

"There's nothing old about this. It's vintage and in awesome condition." Kyla trails her hand over the dash. She's right. It is in awesome condition. This truck has been my passion for years, much to my brothers' amusement. There was a long period where I couldn't get her to start, but now they've had to eat their words. She's a beauty. All she needed was some tender loving care.

"It took a while," I say, "But I managed to restore it to

its former glory."

"You did this?"

I put the truck into drive and turn it, so that we're facing in the correct direction.

"I did. Every bit of it. I didn't have a clue what I was doing in the beginning, so it was a learning curve, but I loved every minute of it, even the frustrating times when nothing was going right."

Kyla nods. "I love learning too. It's why I wanted to become a teacher. I thought it would be a natural step to take my passion to others."

"So, what happened?" I ask, only to be met with a small shrug.

"I did all my training, and I got what I thought was going to be my dream job, and then I realized that I actually only like learning. I didn't enjoy teaching at all. It's just too much chaos, and I got bored telling people the same information over and over. I wanted to dig deeper. I wanted to explore and find out things that I didn't know. I wanted to lead the kids off the curriculum, but I couldn't. It was so narrow.

"Is that how you ended up at the coffee shop?"

"Yeah. I mean, it wasn't supposed to be a long-term thing. It was just until I found something else."

"And Ink Factor…does that fit with your something else?"

"It does right now."

I smile, feeling a bubble of relief that she's not planning to leave us any time soon. When Carl told us he was hiring a woman to help at the shop, I thought he was crazy. But Kyla's really become part of the Ink Factor family and made some awesome changes. I want her to stay.

It doesn't take us long to reach the lake. The parking

lot is a mess of gravel and dirt, but I get us close enough to the place I imagined would be perfect for our picnic. I'm familiar with this area, so I'm confident that I'll be able to navigate us back to the truck in the dark with the limited light of a flashlight.

There's a real feeling of serenity that lingers at the edge of a such a large body of water. It's peaceful, and the energy is as cool and still as the water. I come here sometimes when I need to think. The last time was when Mom told us she needed surgery on her heart. Thankfully, it all went okay, but she had me worried for a while.

I hope Kyla will enjoy the beauty of this place as much as I do.

The light is low, but as we walk, it's still possible to see the water rippling with the movement of fish, birds, and insects. When the wind picks up, it sends the dark surface shivering. I carry the heavy food basket and another bag, but Kyla is kind enough to take the bag of cushions.

"It's so beautiful," she says as we pause at the location for our evening together. It's not secluded. None of the land that borders the lake is. For privacy, I'd have to take us into the woods, but that wouldn't be half as romantic, or half as serene. I'm happy to take the risk that we might be discovered for the chance to share this awesome place with Kyla.

At this time of the evening, the only people likely to be here are those with a similar plan to ours, but as I scan the area, I can't see another soul.

Perfect.

Placing everything on the ground, I begin to spread out the picnic rug. Kyla drops the cushions, and I place them close together with the picnic basket in the middle. First food, then it'll be time for the main course.

"I'm not going to pretend that I'm in any way responsible for the delicious food. That's all down to the deli."

"Did you choose the menu?" Kyla asks.

"Yep. All my favorite things."

"Then I guess you are a little responsible for the food."

"What did you think of Lex's cooking?" I ask. Of all of us, he's the one who has the most impressive culinary skills.

"He knows his way around a kitchen," Kyla says, smiling at the memory.

I'm tempted to ask for more information about their evening together, but Kyla strikes me as the kind of girl who'd see disclosure as a betrayal of trust.

"Is this a favorite place of yours?" she asks.

As I begin to place all the yummy food on the blanket between us, Kyla starts to help herself. "It's a place I come to think, usually."

"So it's not where you bring all your women?"

She raises her eyebrows expectantly and tucks a lock of hair behind her ear.

"No," I say. "You're the first person I've brought here."

"So where do you usually take your dates? Is it always somewhere outdoors?"

"Are you asking me if I have to be outdoors to get off?"

Kyla snorts, popping an olive into her mouth. "The whole kink thing fascinates me," she says. "I mean, I never thought of sex that way before. I never imagined that men could have this many different things that appeal to them."

"Kinks are just part of sex. I guess, for some people, they become integral to their excitement and fulfillment, but it's not always like that. Think of it this way. I have a favorite chocolate bar, but I also like most chocolate bars. My favorite is special, but if I ate it every day, it would lose some of its appeal."

"So you like to ration your kink?"

"I wouldn't say ration. It's more that I'm conscious not to overindulge it. Do you ever hear a song that you absolutely love, but you know that if you listen to it too much, you'll get bored, and you don't want that to happen? This is like that for me."

"Well, I'm flattered that you're prepared to indulge it with me." When Kyla blushes, I just have to reach out and touch her face.

"You don't need to be flattered one bit. I'm the lucky one here. I get to have this special experience with a beautiful awesome girl. I've hit the jackpot."

She sighs softly, putting her plate down and shifting so that her legs are crossed beneath the fabric of her dress. "Can I ask you something?"

"Of course. Anything."

"How come you guys are all single? I just don't get it."

"What don't you get?"

She blinks her pretty brown eyes, outlined with soft liner and framed by long lashes. Beneath her freckles, her skin begins to pinken, and she clears her throat as though she's uncertain about saying whatever's on her mind. "It's just that you're all so…gorgeous…and I was expecting there to be a lot of arrogance there, but there isn't."

"So what you're saying is that you expected us to be douchebags."

Kyla shrugs one shoulder. "Guys that are blessed in the looks department tend not to be blessed in the personality department. It's like they never learn the skills of being a decent person because they've never had to try. Life comes too easy to the beautiful people."

I snort, shaking my head. "I've never been called beautiful before."

"Well, you should have been," she says. "All of you guys are like straight tens."

"If we're tens, then you're off the scale."

"I'm just an ordinary girl." Kyla pulls at the cuffs of her sweater as though the conversation is making her uncomfortable.

"There's no such thing as ordinary, baby. We're all unique. All exceptional. There's not another person on this earth who's like you. There's not another person who's like me. We're all just here trying to find our place and make our contribution."

In the distance, a bird calls and then sets into flight, its flapping wings disturbing the silence around us. Kyla chooses a mini sandwich and chews thoughtfully. "That's such a beautiful way of looking at the world," she says. "I don't know if I've found my place or my contribution. Do you?"

"I don't think we have one place or one contribution. Everyone we meet…every new situation gives us a chance to do more and be more. Like tonight for example. Being with you is giving me a chance to contribute a little to your life. After tonight, I'll always be a part of your story. Like a link in a chain, everything that happens after today will be layered on top of what we experience together."

"I'm happy you're going to be a link." When Kyla smiles, it's as though the sun has appeared from behind a cloud, casting a beam of warmth over and through me.

"I'm happy you're going to be a link in my life too," I say.

And I am. But it won't be enough. I already know that before we've done anything all.

18

KYLA

Looks can be so deceiving. The man sitting in front of me could be a cover model for one of the romance novels I love reading so much or even a model for a designer clothing brand. With his honey-colored eyes and strong nose and jaw, he's every woman's dream, but you'd never know from talking to him that he has any idea how sexy he is.

Niall is deep and emotionally intelligent. He's a man who's made me rethink my own preconceptions and tendency to jump to conclusions about people before I've given them a chance to show who they are.

He might be sexy, but that doesn't mean that his looks have any impact on his personality or the core of what makes him who he is.

He might look the same as his triplet brothers, but that doesn't mean they're all going to be alike. From what I can make out, they're all different, with varied interests and characters.

The picnic Niall ordered for us is diverse and interesting. The falafels melt in my mouth and the salad is crunchy with a hint of mint. Every bite is delicious and shows me that he's as adventurous about food as he is about locations for sex. The lake is spectacular, and not a place that I've ever even heard of before today. It's romantic in a way that isn't contrived or pretentious.

In just a little while, Niall has made me feel comfortable in his presence and more comfortable in my own skin.

Dex might have started this thing, but his friends are running with the baton. Dex saw how I needed more than what I was getting out of my life. He saw how much I was squashing myself into a neat little box, and now his friends are helping to prize the lid away.

As the sun goes down, the air cools a little. I'm glad for the sweater I'm wearing, and also happy to see that Niall brought an extra blanket for us.

As we finish our food, he packs it all carefully away and then moves the basket onto the grass. This should be the moment that I begin to experience butterflies in my stomach or a racing heart, but Niall doesn't leave any time for that. He takes a pillow and tosses it behind him before lying with his hands behind his head, staring up into the sky. "Do you like looking at the stars?" he asks.

"Living in the city, we don't get to see, many do we?"

"Exactly. Too much light pollution, but out here, when the sky is clear, you can see a lot. And look at this." Niall swipes his phone screen and selects a small blue icon on the screen. An app begins to open, playing some ethereal music before loading a skyscape that blows my mind. "See?"

Encouraging me to lie next to him, I glance at the sky and then the app, finding the real stars and then matching them to the constellations on the screen. Niall points them out one by one, saying their strange names in his deep, rumbling voice, and I shift closer so that I can see what he's talking about. At least, that's what I tell myself.

Really, I'm seeking out the warmth of his body, wanting him to get closer. The more time he takes over our date, the more impatient I get until I roll onto my side to watch him rather than the stars.

God, he's gorgeous. The ring he has through his eyebrow adds just a hint of danger, and his tattoos are just beautiful. I've never wanted to mark my skin, but the more time I spend with the men from Ink Factor, the more I can appreciate the permanent beauty of what they create.

Eventually, Niall must sense me looking because he turns and smiles. "What are you looking at, Miss K?"

"You," I say. "Do you ever get weirded out seeing yourself reflected back by your brothers?"

"No," Niall says. "They've been with me from the point of our creation. Although we have our differences, they're like an autonomous extension of me."

"I keep wondering if it's going to be weird, you know, being with Dex after Lex, or Kole after Kase. With you guys, I have to worry about two more versions of you."

"I think you'll forget the similarities because of the differences."

"I hope so."

"Anyway, each of the dates is going to be varied, so that should help too."

We smile at each other, and the silence between us joins the emptiness of the atmosphere all around us. Since darkness fell, the intermittent bird call has faded, as though they fell asleep with the disappearance of the sun.

Now it feels as though we're in this place all alone. The darkness, rather than feeling empty, is like a protective cloak all around us.

Niall reaches out to touch my hair, letting a strand pass

through his thumb and index finger in a way that feels surprisingly tender. Then he leans in to kiss me with the lightest of touches, sending the hairs rising across my scalp. Our kiss gets deeper as he rolls closer, his leg resting between mine, thigh pressing upward with light pressure that makes me want to moan.

The wind blows, rustling my hair and chilling my skin, and without missing a beat, Niall reaches for the spare blanket, drawing it over us.

There's something so sweet about the way he touches me, and combined with the setting. I feel as though I've taken a step into my past. This is the kind of date that high school kids set up to lose their virginity. I might not be a virgin, but being with Niall is new, and being outside is too.

His hand traces the line of my dress across my breasts, sending tingles through me like ripples across the lake water. My fingers trace the muscular strength of his back, drawing him closer, relishing his weight and warmth.

There's no shyness when he uncovers my breast, or nervousness when he bends to suck my nipples into tight, yearning points. I don't worry about what he will think of me tomorrow when he pushes up the hem of my dress and finds the delicate lace of my panties with the very tips of his fingers.

Tomorrow doesn't matter because this is all about today. It's about putting all the things that have wounded me firmly back in the past. It's all about living in the moment and letting myself feel. It's about shedding old skin and growing a new one that isn't scarred and fractured but new and shiny.

His first touch between my legs is tentative and gentle and even more arousing because of it. He's a man who knows what he's doing but doesn't want to rush. He's not using this experience to make things happen quickly. He's letting me adjust and enjoy.

Our bodies move with a synchronicity that should only be present between couples who've been together for years. When his fingers push inside me, and I cry out, my voice echoes in the emptiness around us.

My hands seek his skin, tracing the undulations of his abs and the roundness of his pectorals.

There's so much that is new to discover. When he opens his pants, I don't notice the piercing at the end of his cock until it grazes against my skin, and I tense.

"It'll feel good," he whispers as though he knows exactly what I'm thinking. "Don't worry. I know what I'm doing."

He doesn't ask me if it's okay to push inside me. He doesn't need to because, by that point, my legs are spread wide and my pussy is wet against his thigh.

Do I trust him not to hurt me? Absolutely. Niall is gentle and kind. A truly good man, through and through.

When he pushes into me with his big cock, I will myself to relax. The piercing feels unfamiliar but when he starts to move, I understand the hype. In seconds, I'm whimpering and begging for him to make me come, urging his hips forward with bossy hands, my mouth kissing him hungrily.

It's bliss when he thrusts into me with his big cock. The kind of bliss that arches my back and forces my lips into an ecstatic O shape. The bliss is almost unfathomable when he moves, hitching my leg around his waist and rising up over me so he can drive deeper. The flickering light of the candle casts his face in light and shadow. The warmth of his eyes is deeper, the cut of his cheekbones in sharper relief.

If I was a painter, Niall would be my muse for a masterpiece.

But I'm not a painter, just a person who lives to keep things neat and orderly. A person who finds security in control.

Tonight, my solace comes from the freedom I feel caged within Niall's arms as his body owns mine, over and over, and when I come, it's with his name dripping from my lips.

The stars gaze down at us, lovers for just a flicker of time in the age of the universe as he seeks his pleasure in my body.

And he finds it.

He finds it so well that his cry disturbs the birds who had disappeared into the forest around us. They take flight as his spirit soars.

Afterwards, Niall paints pictures onto my skin with his fingertips. He tells me myths and legends that the stars are named for, and we laugh at stories of his childhood with two annoying identical brothers.

I let him take me home and kiss me goodbye, like sweethearts who can relive their perfect night any time they want.

Except we can't because in a blink of an eye, we played a game and won.

And tomorrow there will be a new player at the controls.

19

KYLA

It turns out that the day after my night with Niall is actually my day off. I've been so caught up in the game and my new job that I only realize when I check my messages to find one from Carl saying, *Thanks for your contribution. I hope you enjoy some well-deserved time off.* It's so sweet of him, and it saves me from the embarrassment of turning up to the shop when I'm not supposed to be there!

In the morning, I take a quick shower and sort through my mail as I sip my super healthy berry smoothie. When it's a respectable time, I give Dawn a call.

"Want to meet me for lunch?"

"Hell yeah, sista! You just rescued me from the most boring task ever. I swear my boss is purposefully trying to destroy my last will to live today."

"Tacos?"

"You read my mind."

"Twelve o'clock."

"Be there or be square," she sings before hanging up.

My apartment is spotless by the time I leave, and I glance in the mirror by the front door, finding a new glow to my skin and brightness to my eyes that hasn't come from cleaning. Dawn's going to notice. I know she is.

She's also going to give me shit for making her wait days to find out what's been going on between the inked gods I work with and me.

But that's okay. I needed time to process what's been happening and time to work out how I feel about it all.

Outside our favorite taco restaurant, Dawn waits, wearing a perfectly fitted scarlet trouser suit and black spiked heels. Her hair is twisted into a knot, which mostly conceals the bright colors that tint the ends, and she's holding a small pink gift bag. She grins hard when she sees me, already filled with glee about the gossiping we're about to do.

"There you are, with a warm glow to your skin and pep in your step. Someone's been living their best life."

"Can we get inside before you start the interrogation?"

"I don't know. Can we?" Dawn threads her arm through mine and practically hustles me inside. A server shows us to a booth that's away from the other diners, which is a relief. I'm sure they won't want to hear the ins and outs of my recent sex life.

I don't even need to look at the menu. I'm so familiar with this place. We order sodas, and reel off our regular choices, and Lana, our waitress, leaves to relay everything to the kitchen.

"Tell me you've been having the best sex of your life. I just can't take the waiting anymore. It's not fair."

"I've been having the best sex of my life," I say with a sly smile.

Dawn's hands fly to her face, and her eyes bug out like a lizard. "Are you serious? I mean, I've been hoping that

Dex, who shall from this point on be called genius, had convinced you to go ahead, but I wasn't sure he had it in him. I mean, you're a hard nut to crack."

"Yeah. I'm not so hard with these guys," I say. My internal queen whispers, *three men in one week*, and my heart skitters. It could have been more but I always regret a binge. Better to space things out and really enjoy them.

"Tell me EVERYTHING." Dawn bounces in her seat like an excited toddler, and our server chooses that moment to return with our drinks. I've never seen Dawn shoot anyone such violent daggers from her eyes. When she's finally gone, I take a sip of my soda, knowing that I won't get much chance to once I get started.

"I'm three men down with four to go," I say.

"Four? I can't believe that's the part you focused on. Explain that part after you've talked about the three men. Are they good in bed? Are they hung? Was it worth all the hype? Are you happy?"

"Yes, yes, yes, and yes."

Dawn claps, drawing the attention of the table nearest us, and I shrink back in my seat with embarrassment. "Who, Kyla? Who?"

"Lex was first, then Kase, and then Niall."

"Wow…so you got a taste of one of each of the multiples. I guess you know what to expect from the rest of them physically."

"I hadn't thought of it like that," I say. They're all so different that the similarity in their looks has melted away.

"Go through each date, one by one, and tell me everything."

So I do. Our tacos come, and I add the spicy sauce with my tales of different dates and different kinks, and for once in my life, I seem to have rendered Dawn absolutely speechless.

If nothing else, all of this was worth it to see my friend with her mouth hanging open like she wants to catch flies.

"You are a sex goddess," she gasps at the end. "You've done things that I've only read about. I mean, I love sex but fucking on a glass balcony above a nightclub is pushing my YOLO boundaries."

"You'd do it if you got the chance," I say.

"Hell yeah, I would. Except it's not going to happen. Brent's a god in the sack, but he's a private man."

"You've got a good one there," I say. "No point in risking a good relationship to chase some temporary excitement."

"Yeah," Dawn says, but it's without her usual commitment. "So, what are the other kinks?"

"I have no idea. I'm not allowed to look until I pick another date. Even then, some of them have made it cryptic."

"I think I'm more excited than you are. Why aren't you bouncing in your seat?"

"It's not that I'm not excited." I play with the edge of my napkin, trying to find the words to explain to Dawn exactly how I feel. "I am with each experience that goes past. I get left with a little tinge of blue too."

"Why?"

"I guess it's because I have a really good time, and I enjoy their company, and we're awesome together, and it's fun, but then it's over, and there's no going back and no chance to experience it all over again."

"Over again?" dawn muses. "You think any of these guys would say no to another round with you?"

"It's not that. It's just that, while we're playing the game, everything's clear and straightforward. Our expectations are aligned, but once the game's done, I'm just supposed to go back to my life as though nothing happened. I just don't know if I can do that."

"Can I give you a piece of advice?"

I nod, and Dawn takes a deep breath, preparing to step into the shoes of a sage. "Live in the moment. That's what YOLO is all about. If you spend time worrying about what will happen in the future, you won't enjoy the present. None of us knows how our lives are going to pan out. We could drop dead tomorrow, and all our plans and dreams will be lost. That's why YOLO is so important. It gets us to focus on the things that are really important so that we can do them before it's too late."

"I'll try," I say with a smile that I know Dawn wants to see. "I'll do my best."

And I will. I really want to make the most of the next four experiences. I want to relish feeling like a goddess a few more times, and whatever happens when the game is done is something to worry about another day. But I know what I'm like. In a way, by living this experience, I've freed a part of myself, only to have to put another part in a box.

Maybe all freedom comes at a price.

"Anyway, I got you something." Dawn grabs the pink bag from the seat next to her and passes it to me across the table.

"What is it?" I say, peering warily inside. It wouldn't surprise me if it was a sex toy of some sort. Dawn has no sense of propriety. Whatever it is, it's wrapped in pretty tissue.

"I had a feeling that your underwear might not be as exciting as it should be after so much time, so I thought I'd buy you something that'll put hairs on the chest of anyone lucky enough to get a look at you."

"Are you serious?"

I tear the tissue, and inside is something made of gorgeous black lace. I want to pull it out so that I can see it in all of its glory, but a restaurant isn't an appropriate place.

"I'm always totally serious about lingerie! And even more serious about sex."

"Well, I don't know who's going to get to appreciate this, but whoever it is will be told that they owe it all to you."

"You still have to pick your next candidate?"

"I do, and I have no idea what I'm going to get with any of them. I thought they'd have revealed their dates and kinks by now, but they're holding all their cards close to their chests."

"You know what we should do?" Dawn says, reaching into her purse and pulling out a small notepad with a pen attached. "We should write down what we think for each of the men left. Whoever gets closest has to buy the other dinner."

"I feel bad doing that."

"It's a game, Kyla. This just adds some fun."

Shaking my head, I raise my eyebrows, and Dawn flicks open the pad. "One of them has to be into group sex," she says. "Seriously. It seems like all dudes are into running a train with their buddies."

"A train? Ewwww…that sounds so gross."

"I'd lay back and get run over by the Ink Factor train and say thank you after." She laughs so hard that the servers glance over at us from where they're congregating at the bar. The service in here isn't anything to write home about today, that's for sure.

"You seriously think one of them will want that?" The idea sets my lady parts squeezing but my mind scrambling. If that was on one of those itty-bitty pieces of paper, would I agree?

"If they don't, they're tamer than I ever would have imagined."

"Okay, who are you putting for that?"

"Noah. He's the most out there. I reckon he'd be all over that. And one of them must have put anal."

"Oh God. No. I don't think so."

"There isn't a man in this restaurant that hasn't jerked off to anal porn."

"I don't think I want that."

"Don't knock it until you try it," Dawn says, wiggling her perfect eyebrows.

"What else?" I ask, wishing we'd never started this game.

"How about spanking or bondage?"

"Maybe, but I'm not sure who?"

"Fisting?"

"For fuck's sake, Dawn. Are you trying to terrify the fuck out of me?"

This time when she laughs, she doubles over, clutching the pad to her belly. "For a woman involved in a filthy sex game with seven men, you sure are a prude."

"It isn't prudish to wince at the idea of a huge hand being stuffed where the sun doesn't shine."

"If a baby's head can come out, a man's fist can go up."

"Come on. Please. Don't do this to me. There are still four pieces of paper in that bowl, and I'm going to be shitting a brick every time I have to pick one out."

Holding her hand up, she dries her eyes with a napkin. "Maybe they'll all be into things like massage and whispering sweet nothings in your ear. Maybe it'll be softly-softly hearts and flowers."

The truth is, I wouldn't want that either. I don't think I could take too much romance from any of them. Romance will hook into the tender flesh of my heart and pull. It'll leave me feeling like I've been run over by a train, and not in a good way.

"I don't think I can guess," I say in the end.

Dawn slides the pad back into her bag. "Just enjoy it, sweetie," she says, reaching out to squeeze my arm. "Enjoy every minute of creating memories that will make you blush in your old age."

"They definitely will."

When lunch is done, I walk Dawn back to her office building, and we hug goodbye. On my journey home, I pass my favorite stationery store, and I can't resist heading in to see if they have anything new. On the center table, there's a display of new journals, and one jumps out at me. With a matt black cover and the words *DO EPIC SHIT* on the front, it seems made for me at this moment.

I haven't written a diary for years, but it feels like time. I'm doing epic shit that I don't want to forget. I'm finding things out about myself that I don't want to drift away when the experiences are done. Putting pen to paper can be hard, but this won't be a serious monologue. It'll be a genuinely funny recollection of a time in my life when I went outside the box.

Maybe it'll be the only time in my life that I get to be this version of me.

The trouble is, I like the person I am right now, and I'll do anything to keep her.

20

KOLE

When Kyla picks my date next, I'm on fucking cloud nine. I wasn't happy that my brother got chosen before me, but when Kyla went through with his date and enjoyed herself enough to continue the game, I felt more confident that she'd be okay with my kink.

Not everyone gets the idea of role-playing. Most people are happier being themselves, especially during sex. Taking the time to act out a different scenario needs a person willing to play. It takes someone comfortable with acting too.

Kyla seems intrigued by the idea. On the paper she picked out of the bowl, I wrote KOLE, CONNOR'S BAR, STRANGERS. I had to explain what I meant, and she seemed relieved that it was only role-play. After, it struck me that she might have worried that I wanted to watch her have sex with people she'd never met before. The poor girl was probably nervous as hell.

On the day of our date, Kyla leaves work at the end of her shift, but I hang around for another thirty minutes to help Carl deal with an issue at one of the franchises. After, as we're closing up, he turns to me with the expression of a Viking who just spotted an enemy on the horizon. "Do you think this game is going too far?" he asks.

"Kyla seems happy. The guys who've already gone haven't said anything negative. She's still happy to pick the next date. I think it's okay."

"I know I said that it was up to you guys, but I'm starting to wonder if I should have put my foot down at the start."

I pat his shoulder, hoping to offer some reassurance. "Carl, you can't control everything. There are seven other men in this business, and you weren't going to be able to say no against that much opposition."

Carl bends to lock the shutter. When he stands, it's with a posture that seems defeated.

"I think she's going to leave…when the game is done. While it's still going on, she's happy to come in, but when it's ended, things will get awkward."

"I don't know. We've all been upfront about everything."

"We have, but that doesn't mean that there aren't feelings bubbling under the surface."

I think Carl might be right, but I'm not sure if agreeing with him is wise or crazy at this point. I've noticed my twin staring at Kyla with a dopey smile plastered across his face. I've seen the homemade lunches that Lex has brought in for her and the way Niall always fetches her favorite soda from the store. My friends have already had a taste, and they all seem smitten.

Will I feel the same after tonight?

"My momma always tells me not to worry about things that haven't happened yet. I think that's a good approach in this situation. There are too many people involved, and that leads to too many variables."

"Your momma sounds like a wise woman." He shoves his hands into his jeans pockets, kicking the sidewalk with the toe of his black boot. "I kept myself out of this thing to try and preserve a professional space within Ink Factor. Kyla needs at least one of us to turn to if things go sour."

"And you want that person to be you?"

He nods, then shrugs his broad shoulders. "I did. But I'm conflicted because the more time goes on, the less confidence I have that it will make any difference."

"And you're regretting not having a chance to be with her?"

Carl shakes his head as though he's disappointed with himself. "When she walked in the door, I knew she was the kind of girl who would get under my skin. When I offered her the job, I was disappointed that I wouldn't get a chance to ask her out on a date. Now, I'm going to be the only one who doesn't know what it's like. Am I cutting off my nose to spite my face?"

"Maybe," I say. "But you're doing it for a good reason. You're doing it for Kyla."

"But she'll never know that. All she'll know is that I didn't put a piece of paper in the bowl. She must think I rejected her."

I glance at my watch, conscious that I have limited time to get ready. "I have no idea what she thinks," I admit, "But I can find out later if you like."

Carl turns, staring down the road as if he's searching for answers on the horizon. When he turns back, there's a brightness to his eyes that I haven't seen for a while. "Find out," he says. "Maybe it's not too late to change my mind."

I'm purposefully late to meet Kyla at the bar. From a vantage point across the street, I watch her arrive and disappear inside. I take my time, pulling at my cuffs and buttoning my charcoal jacket, giving her just long enough to find a seat at the bar and order a drink.

This goes against all my usual protocols for dating, but it's necessary to keep to the role-play I promised Kyla. All she knows is that we pretend to be strangers. We pretend to be the kind of people who meet and hook up, without any of the preliminaries of a normal date. It's like a movie; love or lust at first sight. There's a freedom that comes from letting go of all the normal parts of meeting someone and hooking up.

When I stroll across the road, I do so with a slightly different gait, leaning back more than usual, with my thumb hooked into the pocket of my gray pants. I'm Aaron Cole tonight. A banker who makes truckfuls of money and doesn't give a fuck about anyone. My aim is to pick up a woman and fuck her so hard she squirts. I'll leave her with a sore pussy and her mouth flapping open with awe and no way of contacting me the next day.

The door to the bar is heavy, and inside the music is loud with a thumping beat. There are more men than women, and for a second, I worry that some other dude is going to be chatting up my girl, but as I scan the bar, there Kyla is, looking like a rose amongst thorns, nursing a colorful drink.

I approach slowly and face the bar, waving down the barman so that I can order a drink. I don't usually drink bourbon, but Aaron Cole does. He likes it neat for the extra burn when he swallows it. Out of the corner of my eye, I take in Kyla.

There's something very different about her tonight. She's secured her hair into a tight, high style that pulls her eyes up at the corners, eyes that are outlined in thick black kohl. Her dress is a deep purple silk number with thin straps and a cut that clings to every curve. On her feet, she wears silver shoes that would look more at home on an actress at the Oscars than a woman sitting alone at Connor's bar. I think that Kyla has developed a character of her own.

"I don't know why you're looking at me like that," she says, sipping her drink through a straw and raising an eyebrow in my direction.

"Excuse me?"

"You're looking at me out of the corner of your eye. It's not polite."

I blink, taken aback for a second, but then I'm back in my role and Aaron's slow wolfish smile forms on my face. "Listen, lady. I'm allowed to look where the fuck I want and at whatever the fuck I want."

"Oh yeah," she says. "And I don't have a say?"

"No fucking way," I hiss, noticing the way her eyes sparkle as my voice gets low and rough. Taking a step forward, I rest my hand next to her on the bar. "You need to watch your mouth, lady. I'm a decent person, but I can guarantee that there are assholes in here who'd slap the lipstick from your lips if you talk to them that way."

"A decent person?" she sneers. "There aren't any decent people in this bar. Just lonely, broken souls, looking to cut themselves on other lonely broken people."

"Is that what you are?" I ask, raising my eyebrow. Kyla's good at this. Better than I thought she'd be.

"Why'd you want to know?"

"'Cause cutting myself on you seems like the best idea I've had all week."

When Kyla drops her lashes and shakes her head, my heart thumps in my chest. With role-play, you never know how it's going to turn out, but Kyla has it down. She's pushing a button that I never knew I had.

"You've got a smooth tongue, that's for sure." She rests her fingers on my arm and narrows her eyes. "Men with a smooth tongue are the most dangerous."

"Not if they know how to use it," I say. "Then they're the most fun."

She snorts, taking her hand away, and begins rooting around in her purse. A lipstick and a small gold mirror are retrieved, and she begins to paint her lips in a color that goes perfectly with the tone of her dress. As she holds her lips in an O shape, all I can think about is what my cock would look like covered with that shade of lipstick. I bet Kyla gives good head. I bet she'd get on her knees for the right man. The kind of man she's building Aaron Cole up to be.

"What's your name?" she asks, snapping the top back on the lipstick and pressing her lips together.

"Aaron," I say, "Aaron Cole. But we don't need to know each other's names to be friends."

"You want to be friends." Kyla downs the rest of her drink and slides off the barstool. In her heels, she's three inches taller than she is at work but still a whole lot shorter than me. She touches the collar of my shirt and then looks up at me, tipping her head to one side. "I don't need another friend, Aaron Cole. But I do need someone to show me a good time. Can you do that?"

Can I do that? Fuck yeah, I can do that.

I don't even reply to her question. I just take hold of her by the elbow and march us out the door. Connor's is a bar that is surrounded by office buildings and stores that are all deserted at this time of night. There's an alleyway down one side that leads to a small courtyard where the staff hang out and smoke. It's perfectly deserted and in the shadow of the building.

If Kyla wants me to show her a good time, it's going to be here and now with no pleasantries or romance. It's going to be raw and dirty like it would be between strangers who really were like Aaron Cole and whoever

Kyla is pretending to be.

I shove her against the wall, bracketing her with my arms on either side of her head. Kyla's eyes are bright and wild, her face still formed into an expression that is part of the role she's playing. My breathing is ragged with anticipation, my mouth hungry to taste every bit of the gorgeous woman standing in front of me.

She's going to let me, but not with any form of submission. Everything I get, I'm going to have to take.

"You look beautiful in that dress, but you'd look even more beautiful without it."

"You think I'm going to get naked in an alleyway because some stranger asks me to?"

"I think you'll show me your pretty tits. You'll let that dress drop to your waist and drive me crazy."

"You'd go crazy at the sight of my nipples?" Her tone is sneering, as though I'm pathetic for being as turned on by her as I am.

"I'd go crazy at the sight, and you'd go crazy when I suck on them. I'll have you so wet that you'll be dripping down your legs."

Kyla pauses for a moment, her eyes never leaving mine, then she drops her purse and the straps to her dress and smiles defiantly. "Let's see what you've got, Mr. Bigshot."

For a moment, I have to close my eyes because I'm hit with sensory overload. Then Kyla's hand finds mine and drags it to her breast. The sensation of her soft flesh against my rough palm brings me back into the present. She's perfect, not in an adult film star way but in a natural woman way. Her nipples are small and drawn into tight points as I use my thumb and finger to tease. My mouth waters to taste, so I do what I promised and dip my head, sliding my tongue over her skin, breathing in her warm floral scent.

Oh God, this is too much. This different Kyla really

knows how to flip my switch.

A soft moan emanates from her lips, and her chest rises and falls beneath my lips. In my pants, my cock is harder than granite, my hips feeling the primal drive to thrust into her. Then her fingers slide into my hair and grip, and I'm lost.

21

KYLA

We're strangers, I keep repeating to myself. Strangers who've just met and have enough electricity between them to want to rut in a dark alleyway where they could get caught at any second.

I don't know what's come over me. From the moment Kole arrived, strolling into the bar with a different way of walking, I slipped into a different me. A sassy, abrasive, and challenging version of myself who enjoys pushing the buttons of this man.

Gone is the Kole I have lunch with and who makes me laugh. Aaron Cole has taken over his body and mine.

Everything about him feels different; his demeanor and his voice, his actions and his tone. He should ditch tattooing and sign up for acting classes. With his pretty gray eyes, midnight curls, and rugged broken nose and scars, he'd make a perfect romance or action hero. But right now, his focus is on teasing me into desperation, and he's getting pretty damn close.

When I gasp, he loses focus and slams his mouth into mine. Our first kiss is deep and desperate, and I hook my leg around his hips, tugging him closer.

There's no consideration in my mind of his size down there. Kase was big, and Kole is identical. I know what it's going to feel like when he spreads me to open the way his brother did. I know my body can take the stretch, and when the bar of his cock presses against me, everything is confirmed.

Damn, he's so hard and big. Just the feel of him through layers of clothing has my knees weakening and my pussy fluttering. Even the cool, rough press of the wall against my back isn't worrying me. Whatever Kole is going to do to me will more than make up for any scuffs or scratches. Aaron Cole isn't a man who worries about women's comforts. He's a man who takes what he wants, and that is horny as fuck.

His hands grab at the fabric of my dress, yanking it up. His foot kicks mine to the side, opening my legs for his probing fingers. When he touches me, he finds me as wet as he promised, groaning at the physical manifestation of my arousal. Then he does something I'm not expecting at all. He drops to his knees and presses his face to my pussy, licking with a frenzy I've only ever imagined.

Aaron's hands grip my ass tightly, fixing me in position. From this angle, he looks like a man worshipping at an altar, and I sure as hell feel like his goddess. His talented tongue flicks my clit and then presses against it, driving me closer and closer to the orgasm that I'm almost weeping for. I grip his hair again, holding him exactly where I need him to be, and then it happens.

I beg. I plead. "Please."

I can tell he loves it because, in a flash, I'm stuffed with two thick fingers and coming like a woman possessed. There's no way to stand through such pleasure, but Aaron is there to hold me, his hands so strong that I feel like a rag doll in his arms.

When he stands, he's breathing fast. Drawing his hand over my breast, he cups my throat, using his thumb to stroke my jawline. "I knew you'd like what I got," he says, using his other hand to wipe my arousal from his chin. It's such a rough gesture that I'm shocked to find it turns me on. When he kisses me, I can taste myself in his mouth.

Drawing back, his storm-cloud eyes fix me with an intensity that I feel in my throat. "Now you're going to show me what you got."

Fuck.

Voices get closer as people walk across the street to the entrance of the bar. All it would take is one of them to stumble down the side of the building and discover us. But I can't think of that now. I have to stay in role and keep my mind on what's going to happen next. I'm going to let this stranger slide his cock inside me.

Kyla wouldn't do this. She could never let a man between her legs who didn't know her name. But in role, I can touch Aaron's face and kiss his lips, then turn to face the wall and spread my legs.

I wish I could see his expression as I tug up my dress and expose my ass. I wish I could know if this is what he wants from me, but this is all guesswork. But when his palm smooths over the rounded cheek of my ass, I'm pretty certain that he's happy.

"What are you waiting for?" I purr.

The sound of his zipper tells me the wait is about to be over for both of us.

Oh God, the press of his cock at my entrance is too much. The first inch feels impossible, then his hand presses against the small of my back, and he thrusts the rest in, deep and then deeper, until I'm struggling to keep my arms locked against the wall.

"That's it," he grunts when I push back against him.

"You love this cock, don't you? You want to feel how deep I can go with your hungry little pussy."

"Fuck me," I gasp. "Don't talk about it. Just do it."

And he does. Oh, he does so well. I'm up on my tiptoes, my whole body trembling as he spears me from behind. The flesh on my ass ripples with each thrust, his fingers gripping as though he loves my curves and wants to bury himself in them.

I want to come again, but I'm still too jacked up from the first time, but it doesn't matter. Everything about this night is perfect.

When Aaron comes, it's like an exorcism. His arms wrap around me, tugging my back against his chest, his big hand resting over my throat again. The warmth of his breath stirs my heart and dampens my neck while inside, his cock throbs and throbs its release into me.

I think back to the night at the club when Kase came inside me. It's only a few days later, and I've fucked his twin, letting him do the same thing. It's so wrong that the thought of their shared cum makes me close my eyes and sigh.

This is a game. I'm not supposed to be imagining what life would be like with all of these men as a part of it. I'm not supposed to be slipping into fantasies where they were all my boyfriends, or where I had a harem like Luna's.

It could never work. None of them have expressed any kind of interest in me outside of the game. Carl doesn't even want to take part. I mean, who turns down the option of free sex if they actually want it?

We both stand linked together, panting as though we ran a relay race until my sweat has cooled and Aaron has pulled out. He doesn't pull out a pocket square like his brother, but I forgive him. This isn't a swanky club, and Aaron doesn't strike me as a man who'd be bothered with aftercare.

But when he turns me in his arms, Aaron's smirk and swagger are gone, and Kole is back in his place. His hand cups my cheek and smooths my hair, his eyes searching my face. "Are you okay? Was that okay?"

"I'm okay," I say. "And it was more than okay."

"Really? You liked it?"

"It was perfect." The way his shoulders drop reveals how genuine his concern is. The way he kisses my lips gently stirs my heart. Between my legs, I feel wet and tender, and my knees are still trembly, but Kole is there to hold me up, helping me to adjust my dress.

"Perfect," he repeats, smiling so broadly that one dimple dents his cheek in a completely adorable way. It draws my hand to cup his face and smile broadly too. "What would you like to do now? We can go back into the bar. Are you hungry?"

"No," I say. "Not hungry at all, and that bar is a little noisier than I like. Maybe we could walk for a while?"

"You want to walk in those shoes?"

"I'm fine to walk in these shoes," I laugh.

As we emerge from the alleyway, Kole slides his hand into mine. He's so warm and strong, and it's a gesture that feels protective. He's showing anyone who might be looking that we're together and that it wasn't just a meaningless hook-up for a guy who just wants to tuck his dick back in his pants and walk away without a backward glance.

It's a gesture that stirs my heart.

We walk and talk about everything from our favorite meals—his is barbeque ribs, and mine is my momma's lasagna, to our favorite bands and even the books we've read and loved. I find out things about Kole that I wasn't expecting at all.

And at the end of the evening, I'm sad that it's coming to an end.

One more down. Three more to go.

But I don't want to think about that because then it'll be over, and I have no idea how I'm going to face that.

22

NASH

"Are you serious?" I growl as Carl finishes telling me about our most recent franchisee, who's been arrested for selling drugs out of the shop.

"I'm serious. I mean, the lawyers did all the background checks that are required, but nothing showed up. Either it's a first-time offense, or he's never been caught before."

"Or maybe he's used a fake identity."

"That's an option too."

"So, what's going to happen?"

"Fuck knows. It's just another heap of bullshit that I didn't need right now."

"It's not all on your shoulders, dude. You know that we're all here to deal with this stuff. That's what a partnership is all about."

Carl's shoulders slump as he fiddles with the label on his bottle of beer. "And my brother has been giving me shit too. He's asking for money again."

"I thought he had that new job...the one that was going to make him a truckload of commission."

"Yeah, it turns out it wasn't, or at least, he didn't put in the work to make the money he was hoping for. Now he's overstretched himself, and he wants me to bail him out."

I take a long drag of ice-cold beer and shake my head. Carl's brother has been dragging him down since we were kids. I know it's harsh, but sometimes people are born with the leech instinct. Their whole lives are about looking to see who else is doing well and finding a way to climb on the back of that success. Carl is a decent and hard-working man. It doesn't seem fair that he's constantly dealing with his brother's financial issues.

"You know you need to cut him off cold. This has gone on long enough. You don't owe anything to a man who doesn't think he owes anything to himself. If you keep enabling him, he's always going to be lurking over your shoulder."

"I know. I know. I told myself last time that I wouldn't do it again."

"As I remember it, you also told him that it was his last bailout."

Carl sighs and runs his hand over his braids. The tattoos across his forearm are all about family. There's a copy of a photograph from when Carl and Gavin were kids, standing in shorts with their arms around each other. Carl's always looked out for his younger brother, in the same way, he looks out for the rest of us. It's like he was born to be a father figure. He does it well, too, but that doesn't mean he doesn't feel the burden.

"You think I should tell him that I can't help him?"

"Absolutely. If I'd been a drain on my brothers like he is to you, they'd have told me to fuck off a long time ago."

"He's the kind of douchebag that will go and get a loan from someone shady. Then he'll be telling me that they're going to hurt him if I don't help him pay them off. It doesn't feel as though it will ever stop being my problem."

"Yeah, that would be harsh, but maybe getting a kicking from someone will knock some sense into him."

"You really believe that people like Gavin can change? I mean, I've been hoping that something will make a difference for so many years, but nothing ever has. Even when he had a decent woman in his life, she didn't manage to motivate him to stand on his own two feet."

"You mean Andrea?"

"Yeah. Poor girl got out of the relationship with a significantly lighter purse."

"I can't imagine ever expecting a woman to contribute to anything," I say. "When I finally find a woman worth sticking to who loves me, flaws and all, I'm looking after her like the queen she is!"

"I feel the same."

"Did you hear anything about Kole's date last night?"

Carl shakes his head, finishing the last of his drink before lowering it back to the table with a thump. "I heard that he had the time of his fucking life."

"Yeah. I heard that too. Kyla seemed happy today too."

"She did." Carl glances off to the side as though he doesn't want me to see the expression in his cool blue eyes. The thing is, I know him too well for him to hide anything from me. He's jealous. He's regretting staying out of the game.

"It's not too late, you know."

"Too late for what?"

"To put your paper in the bowl. I know what you said, but you can see that nothing that's happened so far has affected anything about our working relationships. If anything, the men in this place are walking on air and Kyla seems more relaxed than she ever has before. Maybe we should be writing a book about how to improve employee relations."

"Errr…somehow I don't think that many other organizations are going to buy into the 'fuck your colleague' school of management."

"I don't know…there's probably a whole bunch of sweaty business executives eyeing up their younger, sexier female colleagues right now, just waiting for an excuse to fuck them without getting fired."

"You're forgetting that the younger, sexier female colleagues need to actually want it. I mean, there was no pressure on Kyla to do anything."

"Ah…a flaw in my master plan for corporate domination," I laugh.

"Yeah, well, business studies never was your top subject."

"I'm all about the creative," I say. "So what can I do to wipe the misery off of your face? I mean, seriously, dude, it's like working with a black cloud."

Slumping back in his chair, Carl grips the arms of the bucket chair he's currently spilling out of. "There's nothing," he says.

"There's Kyla," I say.

"Yeah, there is."

For a few moments, we just stare at each other, me with a challenge in my eyes, and his gaze conflicted. Eventually, he leans forward and rests his hand flat on the table. "Aren't you worried that when Kyla eventually picks your paper out of the pot, you're going to enjoy it too much? I mean, she's pretty and funny. She's reliable and caring. There isn't anything I can say about her that would make her unappealing as a girlfriend."

"I think Niall and the rest of them are already hooked," I admit.

"And so maybe the problem isn't going to be that everyone feels awkward with each other after the game is done. Maybe it's going to be that we all have feelings for the same woman, and none of us are going to get to be with her."

"You know that celebrity that came into the shop with Kyla? Luna Evans?"

"Yeah, the singer."

"Exactly. I was reading about her online the other day. You know that she's in a poly relationship with seven men. They used to be her bodyguards, but now they're her lovers."

"Seven men?"

"Yeah. Apparently, it's not that rare these days. Poly relationships are on the rise. Did you ever watch that show, *McGreggors Uncovered*?"

"About the property developers?"

"Yeah. They're ten brothers in a poly relationship with one woman. They have kids together and everything."

"TEN MEN?"

Carl seems completely shocked at the idea, but I'm not. Maybe it's because I've always done everything with my brothers that I can see how easy it could be to live together and share one woman. At least we'd all be focused in the same direction. I can't imagine all eight of us at Ink Factor finding women who'd all get along and want to hang out together. It's hard enough to find a woman to love, let alone needing to find one who'd manage to love your seven buddies and their seven lovers.

"Ten, and they make it work."

"What are you getting at, Nash? You haven't even had your date with this girl. You have no idea what it's going to be like."

"But I've hung out with her at work. I've seen how well

she's dealt with this odd situation. Nothing seems to faze her. Nothing gets under her skin."

"You think you could love her and watch her be with the rest of us and not be bothered."

"I think that I love you guys, and if I loved her too, then nothing would be too difficult to make it work."

"Have you told your brothers you feel like this?"

Shaking my head, it's my turn to slump back against the soft padding of the booth seat behind me. I can talk to Carl. I can explain myself, and I know he'll listen to me without judgment. I know he won't ridicule me, no matter how crazy I sound. My brothers are a whole other ballgame.

"They'd give you shit," he says. "Especially Noah."

"He always thinks I'm too much of a planner. That I never focus on enjoying the moment. He's always telling me I need to stop thinking so much about the future and enjoy the present."

"In some ways, he's right. But we're not teenagers anymore. I'm all for finding hot girls to spend time with, but I also want a family at some point."

"Exactly. I don't know. When I look at the women we've dated recently, none of them have been ideal for building a future with."

"And you think Kyla is?"

I haven't even admitted this to myself yet, but I tell Carl without hesitation. "Yes. I think she is."

"How does the poly thing work, though? I mean, with eight of us, we'd only get to spend three nights a month with her."

"Or every night," I say.

"I know your kink is group sex, but what makes you think that Kyla would go for that?"

"Well, when she finally picks out my date, we're going

to find out."

"You put that on your slip of paper?"

I nod, and the grin that pulls up the corner of my mouth is wide and open. I hadn't thought about it at the time, but it really will be a great test to see if Kyla could be with us all. If she'd pulled out my date first, it wouldn't have worked so well, but if I go last, it might be the best way for us to move things on from just a game to something more committed.

"Yeah. I did. And I think I've got an idea."

"Why am I suddenly worried," Carl says.

"Because you know my ideas are always genius." I smile. As I tell him what I've got in mind, I see some of the tension leave his body.

You see, my idea takes away at least one decision that's been weighing Carl down.

And if he agrees, it could turn this game on its head.

23

KYLA

There are only three pieces of paper left in the bowl for me to pick out. Three more dates, and then this unbelievably awesome but confusing part of my life will be over.

I don't pick another date for a few days. After the intensity of my night with Kole, and the warm feeling that enveloped my heart after we parted, I thought it would be best if I allowed a little time for me to shake it off.

I've been telling myself that I'm not feeling anything. The strange sensation of attachment to the men at Ink Factor is just nature using hormones to link people who might have procreated. We might be living in different times, but our brains were forged hundreds of thousands of years ago, and we still carry around all the biology that helped our ancestors survive for long enough to create successive generations of humans.

I have to look at all of this in an unemotional way.

I'm on a journey of transformation, and letting my

heart get fish-hooked by sexy tattooed men who are only interested in rocking my world for one night is certainly not the sensible thing to do.

The sensible thing is to enjoy everything in the cool and calculated way that men manage every day. Set aside my heart and let my body take over. Rationalize so that my mind doesn't start trying to convince me of things like how perfect each of the men I've had a date with so far is, or how maybe Luna could be right. Maybe I want them all.

All morning, the bowl is whispering to me. It's telling me to pick a date and let someone cure the ache I have between my thighs. Just the thought of another night of unbelievable passion is enough to dampen my panties. The whisper of more pleasure is enough to dampen down the tendrils of worry around my heart.

As I reach and touch the three pieces of paper, the names of the remaining men spin like a Vegas slot machine; Nash, Noah, and Dex. Nash, Noah, and Dex. Who will it be?

My fingers are drawn to the most tightly folded piece. Whoever put it in the bowl wanted to make sure that the details wouldn't be visible to me before I selected it. That extra level of secrecy has my interest.

Nash, Noah, or Dex.

I inhale a deep breath and unfold, taking my time until the writing is visible.

What the hell?

Carl.

He wasn't supposed to have put his name in the bowl. He told me he was staying out of this to maintain a professional distance. He hasn't been himself since the start of the game, and I've been walking on eggshells in case he's mad at me.

I mean, he hired me to do a job, not become a sex toy for his staff.

And I'm doing the job. I'm doing it well, and I know he's pleased because he tells me every day how great everything is, but that hasn't stopped the corners of his mouth from sloping or the center of his brow from furrowing. It hasn't stopped the frustrated glances at the rest of the Ink Factor team, as though he's resentful of them partaking. As though he's jealous.

And now he's put his name in the bowl.

I have to sit down on my chair behind the reception desk and fold the paper back up into its neat, tightly closed original form. My hand goes to my mouth as I blow out a controlled breath through pursed lips.

I glance back at the bowl and then rummage to make sure I'm right. There are only two more dates left in the bowl, which means one of the others has pulled out, but who?

For the first time since the game started, I'm tempted to open all the remaining dates to find out what the hell is going on. Why would someone else not want an evening with me? Who could it be?

It wouldn't make sense for it to be just one of the triplets. If Niall didn't have a good time, then I'm sure both of his brothers would have made the decision not to go ahead. My mind drifts to our time under the stars, and I shake my head. Niall came so hard that night. And he's been the sweetest to me ever since. There's no way it's him.

So maybe Lex didn't have a good time. It was the first night, and I was more nervous than I've been since. Was our foodie sex a disappointment? Has his twin decided to pull out?

That wouldn't make sense either. This whole thing was Dex's idea. How could he be the one to decide not to go ahead?

My hand hovers over the bowl, but I can't do it. I can't

look without disappointing myself. The old Kyla would have had a pathological need to know and be in control. The new Kyla is working hard to leave all of that behind and let the universe sit in the driving seat. Fate is guiding my hand. Fate is steering this ship.

The game is all about living in the moment. It's about throwing caution to the wind. It's about taking control of my nerves and pushing through to become a more confident me.

Carl.

He's thrown his hat into the ring. Something's changed but I don't know what.

It's only then that I realize that I didn't register the other information on the paper. Opening the folds again, my eyes scan the details of what's to come.

CARL. MY HOUSE. CALL ME SIR.

Holy shit.

24

CARL

When Kyla appears in the doorway to my office, I know. It's there in the way she shifts on her feet and the way she grips the door frame tightly. It's obvious from the way her eyes meet mine just for a second, then drop to the floor.

My cock stirs in my jeans at the hint of her submission.

"You put your name in the bowl?" Her voice has a breathy quality that's new. If I could rewind time and watch her open my date, I would pay good money to see her shocked reaction.

Shit. Just putting the paper in the bowl was enough to give me full-on wood.

"You picked my name out?"

"Yes," she says. "I'll need your address."

"I'll write it down." Grabbing a pen, I find a sticky note and scribble my address out quickly. I write 8 pm because I want to have enough time to prepare.

I get up to hand it to Kyla and relish the way she watches me move. Her eyes gaze up into mine with just a little flicker of fear in their warm gaze. I guess she knows enough about domination and submission to have an inkling of what might be coming, but maybe not enough to be sure. Not all doms are the same, and I'm going to go easy on her tonight. My sweet little Kyla deserves training wheels for her first time.

If there was a second time, things could be different, but that's not part of this game. It could be part of the next stage if Nash's plans come to fruition, but nobody apart from Nash and I know anything about that discussion. I still think he's crazy. Kyla would never go for something like that. She's all about feeling in control, and living with eight men doesn't exactly lend itself to that kind of control. Between us, there are so many different personalities and needs. We're a mix of impetuous and thoughtful, lively, reserved, funny, and dry-humored.

All of the variables would be too much for her.

It's not exactly every woman's dream to live in an unconventional way, either. I've known the boys for more years than I care to count, but to Kyla, we're all new. How much work would it take for her to feel comfortable around us?

We have to let her make the decision. No pressure.

That's if the rest of them agree.

"I'll see you at eight," she says softly, narrowing her eyes slightly as if she's squinting to read what might be written on my face.

Can she tell that I'm already thinking about how I can make her want us for more than this arrangement? Does she know the deviant thoughts that are running through my mind?

I watch her as she retreats, the soft fabric of her sweater dress clinging to curves that I've been dreaming about since she walked through the door. Her knee-length boots make me think about the bare skin of her thighs, soft skin that would color pink with even the softest tap of my hand.

How much can she take? the dark voice whispers in my head. How far can I go?

A shiver passes down my spine, imagining how it will feel to order Kyla to her knees. I fantasize about forcing her mouth open with my fingers, so it's wide enough to receive my cock. Will she enjoy handing control over to me?

I think she will.

Kinks are a funny thing. Women who take control in everyday life often like to cede control in the bedroom. Men who are forced to be dominant in everyday life often like to find dominant women to have sex with.

The way we like to have sex can be very revealing about us.

I've always wondered why I get such a kick out of being in charge. I think maybe it stems back to never feeling like I had control of my life when I was a child. Or maybe I'm just a kinky fucker for absolutely no reason.

Without paying a small fortune in therapy bills, I guess I'll never know for sure.

The day drags past as I try to focus on my clients and their requests. I ink the face of a child onto his father's chest and an outline of a roaring lion onto the back of a huge man who arrived wearing a leather vest. That one will need to be completed in stages because, despite looking like he could crush a man's skull with his bare hands, he had a very low tolerance for pain. My favorite tattoo was inked onto the ankle and calf of a young woman. She'd released her first novel and wanted to remember the feeling. The design I created for her was an open book with swallows rising from the pages. She cried when she got to see it for the first time, and Kyla came to give her a hug. The way they sank into each other's embrace so naturally shows me how genuine Kyla's warmth and empathy is.

When Kyla leaves, she steps into my workstation to tell me she's going.

"I'll see you later," I say, fixing her with a look that I fill with dominance. Instinctively she takes a step back, and her gaze lowers to the floor, and it's like she's telling me that she's going to be a good girl for me.

Getting ready for the evening is easy. This isn't about wining, dining, and romance, although I'd love to make dinner for Kyla another time. It's about setting the scene for what's to come. It's pointless to wear more than just a pair of gray sweatpants because undressing isn't exciting to me. Watching Kyla undress is something else entirely. When she rings the bell, I inhale a long breath and force it out through my nostrils.

I feel like a bull: calm, huge, with a bubbling power underneath the surface. As I walk to the door, I roll my shoulders and click my neck on each side as my hands flex in anticipation.

When I yank open the door, I'm greeted by a Kyla, who seems smaller than she does at work. Her hands are clasped in front of her as though she feels a need to protect herself from me.

Maybe she does.

Some women like what I like. They find peace in submission and even relaxation in the pain and humiliation. Some women don't ever want to go back to sex without the power exchange. Will Kyla be that woman?

Her eyes scan my torso, taking in the huge skull I have inked there. There's menace in it, but also the representation of death, mortality, and the unachievable nature of immortality. Our lives are fleeting. For me, it's a reminder that life is too short not to be exactly who you are.

I don't say anything to greet her. I simply reach out and take her hand to lead her inside. When I close the door behind her, I see the tiny flinch she tries to suppress. I guide her into the living room, feeling a slight tremble in her hand.

I know she wouldn't be here if she didn't want to be. There's no pressure in the game. She's participating willingly, so the tremble must be about anticipation.

Kyla knows to expect something different but maybe not exactly what she's going to get. Uncertainty can be a powerful aphrodisiac.

"Can I get you some water?"

"Yes…please."

Oh, that little hesitation and the addition of "please" send blood rushing to my cock.

As I turn to seek out a glass, I know she'll see the tattooed image of Hades on my back. It's mostly black and gray, an image similar to the marble statues of ancient Greece. His eyes are empty of a pupil, but instead, inked with yellow and orange, as though his core is made from molten lava. He clutches the chain leashing the three-headed Cerberus. Despite him being the god of the underworld, for me, he isn't a representation of death. He's a reminder that a man needs to live a good life and that the end will come to us all.

Kyla gasps, and when I turn, her hand is pressed to her lips.

"Don't mind Hades," I say, used to the reaction. "He's mellow."

"He doesn't look mellow," she whispers.

"He's relaxed in his power." I fill the glass with cool

water, closing my eyes just for a second so I can recharge in the cloak of darkness.

"Like you?"

When I turn, Kyla has her head cocked to one side, observing. This girl is so perceptive. Some people are shallow streams, but Kyla is a deep lake. I read about these sinkholes in Mexico that you can dive in. The water is turquoise blue and so clear that you can see the bottom, despite them being ridiculously deep. Swimming there is difficult because it's freshwater, so there's no salt for buoyancy. Kyla is just like that.

A shiver runs up the back of my neck, setting tingles running like insects over my scalp, because underneath my dominance, there is weakness and fear too. I'm certain that it's something that all human beings feel when it comes to connecting with other people. This is supposed to be a game, but it doesn't feel like one. It feels like the start of something, but what, I don't know. I shouldn't be thinking this way because it takes me from the moment and propels me forward into a fathomless future.

For now, I have to push everything else aside and focus on giving Kyla what she needs.

Handing over the glass, I watch Kyla take a small sip at first and then gulp the whole thing down. I watch the way she keeps her eyes lowered to the counter where she's rested her purse. I watch her place the glass down and take a deep, steadying breath.

She's ready.

"If you want to stop at any time, you can tap me anywhere three times or say Hades, okay?"

When her eyes flick to mine, I think I see excitement. "Hades. Three times. Okay."

"Anytime," I reiterate. "I have to know that you're here because you want to be…that you're not feeling any obligation or pressure."

"I'm here because I want to be."

As her words settle inside me, I rub the round ball of my shoulder, contemplating how to begin.

Much like a writer feeling pressure to write the first words of their story, beginnings are always challenging for me. I want to throw Kyla deep, but my instinct is to protect her. This has to be about her experience, and I wouldn't be doing it justice if I gave her a half-hearted version.

"On your knees," I say.

Without a second of hesitation, she drops to the floor, her eyes cast onto the herringbone wood-block floor that spears its way across the room.

Oh God, the sight of her kneeling for me is just too much—such a willing sub. I reach out my hand to caress the side of her face, tracing her pretty lips with my thumb. "You have such a pretty mouth," I say. "I think it's time to fill it."

"Yes…" she hesitates, her lips parted "…sir."

Time stretches like the sweetest taffy as the word settles inside me. It shouldn't feel so good to have her address me with such respect, but it does. It feels better because I didn't need to instruct her. It feels better because her submission is all her.

"Good girl," I say, watching as some of the tightness in her shoulders releases. She likes the praise, and I like giving it. It's an awesome combination.

"Now, I'm going to get my cock out, and you're going to open these sweet lips and take it. You're going to swallow it so deep that it'll hit the back of your throat, and your eyes are going to water, but you'll breathe through it."

There's a tiny dip to her head that is all the permission I need. My cock has been aching ever since I wrote those words on a scrap of paper and placed it in a bowl. It's been aching at the thought of this moment, but I didn't do anything to relieve myself. I'm in control of my actions and my destiny. This is all for Kyla.

Reaching beneath the waistband of my sweats, I grab the thick bar of my cock, bringing it out like a weapon. Kyla's eyes fix on it, her bottom lips dropping down with what looks like shock. Or is it readiness to do as I've ordered?

I can imagine what it will feel like to have her mouth wrapped around me. Hot, wet, and tight. But there's another layer, an emotional one. That is what sends a skitter of sensation from the base of my spine upward. It's one of deep acceptance.

Women don't suck the cocks of men they don't respect. At least, not willingly.

They don't get on their knees for men they don't respect.

Everything about this situation tells me how Kyla feels about me.

The way I slowly push her hair behind her ears and caress her jaw should tell her how I feel about her. I might want to dominate her, I might even want to punish her, but that doesn't mean I don't have a deep and profound respect for her too.

When I run the tip of my cock across her bottom lip, she opens her mouth like the good girl she is. "That's it," I say, canting my hips to test the depth. She hollows her cheeks, and I want to grab for the counter to give me something to hold onto, but that wouldn't fit with my persona of control. I can stand here, my thighs and glutes tensed, my hand resting under Kyla's chin as I push further, touching the back of her throat.

A little moan reverberates around my cock, causing my hand to grip around her jaw. My knees are weak as the wet sounds of her mouth reverberate around the room. I slow my movement, exercising restraint. I would be so easy to come across her tongue. It would be so easy to let this burning need loose so my body can relax, but I'm not wasting it. Kyla's going to feel me come, and when she does, I'm going to fill her up and feel her sweet pussy milk me dry.

I draw my cock back, letting it snap up and slap against my belly.

Kyla's lips are wet with saliva, and her eyes are watery with tears but bright with excitement.

"Come with me," I order, tucking my cock back into my pants and striding toward the bedroom. Kyla gets up, and I hear the padding of her feet against the hardwood. The light in my room is muted, coming from a small lamp on my desk. I slump into the black leather armchair in the corner of the room and watch as Kyla looks around. I guess the décor is a mix of traditional bachelor style, with a sprinkling of tattoos and dusting of Viking. When I submitted a DNA test, I was hoping to find some Nordic DNA, and it turns out I'm twenty-three percent from Scandinavia. I guess that explains my bulky form, my crazy light eyes, and my blond hair that always looks better longer than it does short.

"Take off your clothes, Kyla," I say coldly. "Fold them neatly and place them on the desk."

She blinks, absorbing my words before her hands rise to her throat. She unbuttons the shirtdress slowly, taking her time to be precise and not to fumble. Her spine is straight, showing her strength even in submission. It's an intoxicating combination. The fabric parts slowly, revealing her soft skin illuminated by the warm, soft light of the room. My eyes follow as the delicate space between her breasts and her belly comes into view. She's wearing a gorgeous black lace bra and panty set that looks expensive and classy and fits with what this evening deserves.

I can spank her ass wearing luxury. If she'd been in white cotton panties, it wouldn't feel the same.

As Kyla slides the dress from her shoulders and her whole body is revealed, I slump back in my chair and sigh with pleasure. She's everything that I like in a woman. Natural and curvy, with dimples on her thighs and enough flesh on her hips for me to grab. She folds the dress, as I instructed, and places it on the desk. Then she stares at me questioningly.

"And the bra," I say. "Leave the panties."

She nods, reaching behind herself to deal with the hooks, as a blush like the pink of a sunset rises up her chest and over her cheeks.

Will her skin go the same color when my hand makes contact? Will she make the same sweet gasping sounds, moan, or whimper? I just can't predict what it will be like, but I can't wait to find out.

25

KYLA

Of all the men at Ink Factor, Carl is the most mysterious. He has a soft side, for sure. The way he treats me as an employee makes him the best boss I've ever had. But there's a cool side to him too. I wouldn't say cold. That's too harsh. But sometimes, when he tells me what to do, I feel a frisson of sensation, a strange dominance. From the start, I could tell he's happiest giving orders, and when it comes to Carl, I want to listen to every direction.

There's a high level of trust between us that has been built as we work together.

But that trust is going to be put to the test now.

Of all the experiences I've had as part of the game, this is the one I'm most nervous about. It's not so much that being ordered around makes me uncomfortable. Any of the other men could tell me what to do and I wouldn't even flinch. It's the fact that this experience is with Carl.

Carl, who I work most closely with.

Carl, who is cool and professional at work.

Carl, who could decide to fire me at any time.

Carl, my boss.

Just the thinking the word boss has a shiver skittering over my skin.

I've read a few CEO romances where the heroine starts a new job and discovers that her boss is a gorgeous but emotionally repressed billionaire. Carl might not be stupid rich, but he has everything else. He's reserved and calm, and now, he's looking at me practically naked with the same assessing gaze he uses at work. He's evaluating everything, deciding whether it's up to expectation. His face remains impassive, but when he folds in his lips, and they come up moist, I can tell he's hungry.

But what will hungry mean?

With every other man, it's meant sex, but I'm not so sure with Carl. He was so close to coming in my mouth that I could taste him, but then he stopped. Control is part of pleasure for him, and it seems to be as much about controlling himself as it is about controlling me.

Taking my dress off was easy compared to removing my bra. In my underwear, I have a layer of armor. I feel powerful in the black lace, like a woman who knows what she wants and doesn't care about the patriarchy's views about women enjoying sex.

But without the bra, I'm vulnerable.

As the straps slide down my shoulders, I can't look at Carl. His icy white-blue eyes are too intense. His fixed expression doesn't give me any hint of what he's thinking. As the bra comes away, my instinct is to cover myself. One arm goes across my chest as I fold the lace and place it on the desk.

I suck in my belly, not wanting the fullness of it to be so obvious to his gaze. I stand in front of him with my eyes lowered and my arm braced to cover my nakedness, waiting for more instructions.

What I get is Carl tutting. "Kyla, drop the arm."

I inhale a nervous breath as I allow my limb to fall and then feel the coolness of the air across my breasts. Maybe it's the air or maybe the knowledge that Carl's eyes are on me that tightens my nipples. Or maybe it's my own mind and the underlying feeling of danger that stirs between my legs. I'm not sure. Everything feels tangled and complicated.

"Come closer," he says, straightening in his chair.

The air around us is scented with his cologne, and it only gets stronger as I move to stand in front of his feet.

"Kneel," he says again.

Does he want me to suck his cock again? Maybe standing and coming was too difficult for him. I shift closer, raising my hand to reach for him, but his reflexes are fast, and he grips my wrist before I can make contact.

"Still," he says. "I want you to stay still."

With the back of his hand, he trails down the edge of my face, allowing his fingers to drift across my lips like the tender wings of a butterfly. I close my eyes while he caresses my neck and across the tops of my breasts. It doesn't feel overtly sexual. Rather, this touch seems reverential. He's worshiping my form with his eyes and his tender touch. When the back of his finger glances the point of my nipple, it feels like he's testing my responses.

I will my body to remain impassive, but who am I kidding. Gooseflesh breaks out all over me, and I worry that the tiny scrap of fabric between my legs won't be enough to stem the flow of my arousal. His hand moves lower, still with the same slow back and forth over my ribs. I hold my belly in tightly, but Carl tuts again. "You don't have to modify yourself for my gaze," he says. "I want to see you as you are."

Wow. Is he serious? I let my abs soften slowly, and he makes a low rumbling sound in his throat.

"You know how good you look? How soft and perfect?"

Do I?

I tell myself that I'm at peace with my body, but then I hold myself into what I think is going to be a more appealing shape. I judge myself against the women I see on social media. But Carl isn't interested in the aesthetic of someone else. He's touching me as though I'm the most precious thing he's ever seen.

"There are so many things I want to do to you, Kyla," he murmurs. "So many wicked things. Do you think you can take it?"

Even though I have no idea, I nod. If nothing else, I want to take what he has to give. I want to be Carl's good girl more than anything.

"Yes," I say.

"You remember what we talked about?"

I nod, remembering the instructions he gave me in his firm, low voice, remembering the way it felt to internalize his directions and demands.

"Get up and rest yourself over my knee. Brace your hands on the floor."

For a few seconds, I remain paralyzed as the realization of what might be coming hits me like a tornado. In that position, there will be no way for me to resist Carl's actions. No way to stop him from exploring or hurting my body.

I know if I told him I wanted to stop right now, he would. He'd listen and treat my wishes with respect. But I don't want to do that. I want to know the depths of this man's kink, and I want to understand my own reactions. This whole game is about trust and exploration. But it's also about facing up to uncertainty and forcing myself to go to places that fear might have prevented in the past.

What am I afraid of? The pain of his hand slapping

against my skin, or that I'll like it? The idea that he might be able to make me come in such a helpless and vulnerable position where I can do nothing but beg for his attention and hope that he'll give it to me? Or is it the idea of him seeing me so vulnerable and so trusting?

The last time I'd allowed myself to be vulnerable in front of a man, he'd smashed my heart to pieces. Being vulnerable isn't easy. Facing the chance of being hurt again makes me want to hide under a rock.

But I have to do this because I want to. I need to heal. I need to break through the horrible way my ex treated me so that I can stop living like a traumatized hermit and live my life.

I want to find love. I need to be loved. But love doesn't come without vulnerability and trust. It can't break through fear.

I stand on legs that feel weak and close my eyes for one, two, three seconds. Carl brushes my fingers with the tips of his, as though he feels my anxiousness and wants to help me. It's not easy to get into the position he wants me in. I have to bend forward and rest my body over his knees, bracing on my tiptoes and fingertips, holding myself as tight as a bowstring. Beneath me, his legs are thick and strong. A satisfied hum leaves his lips as his hand slides down over my back, lingering at the dip of my waist and then drifting lower. His warm, rough palm hesitates on the roundness of my ass, his thumb pressing into the flesh there as though he's testing the feel of it.

For a few seconds, I expect his fingers to drift lower, seeking out the wetness of my entrance. I expect him to play with me until I'm trembling and then stop, so I whimper and beg for him to finish me. But he doesn't.

The first slap of his hand against my ass is such a shock that I don't even feel pain. His hand immediately soothes with a tender caress so that my skin is confused. Am I feeling pain or pleasure, violence, or soft touch?

The second slap spreads red-hot over the skin, knocking the breath from my lungs and sending stars spinning into my vision. My whole body tenses until I'm a rigid arch of flesh across Carl's knee. My legs want to give way, but they can't.

Carl pauses as though he's waiting for me to relax again, but when I don't, his hand moves to touch the small of my back with feather-light touches.

"Good girl," he says softly, and I don't understand why his words make me feel so safe, but they do. They really do.

When his fingers leave my skin, I tense again, this time knowing what's coming, but the next slap doesn't feel like the first or second. The burn of pain is a low hum this time that spreads out like warm water being poured into a cooling bath. I still tense, but beneath my body's instinct to brace against the pain, my clit hums.

I don't know how Carl knows, but he chooses that moment to spread my legs and drag the tip of his finger over the thin fabric covering my pussy. Just that distant tickling touch is enough to almost make me come.

"You're wet," he says. "So damn wet. I didn't tell you to get wet, Kyla."

My pussy constricts against the brush of his fingers, and he hums his disapproval. "My good girl's being bad," he says.

As stupid as it sounds, I want to cry out and tell him I can't help it. He's so gorgeous and sexy, and this position he has me in just makes me want to fuck. The pain of his slap against my skin fills me with need. His growling, low voice licks over my skin like the roughest tongue.

Oh God, I want him to slap me again. I want my whole body to be filled with adrenaline so that when he fucks me, my head will explode. Already, my heart is racing in my chest. My mind swims with liquid pleasure. My pussy aches to be filled. Bracing my body again is the only way for me to tell Carl what I need without breaking the moment. Without taking some control away from him. This is his scene, and I'm just a puppet dangling from strings that he controls.

Slap.

The force of the blow makes my knees drop and this time I do cry out. "Any time you want me to stop, you know what you need to do," he says. As my skin burns, he traces a feather-like touch up my spine, making my body jerk out of control. I don't want to tell him to stop. I want to beg him to continue.

Slap.

I squint my eyes, bracing to feel the slither of pain.

Slap.

I'm so close to coming that all it would take is a tiny press of direct pressure against my clit. I squeeze my thighs together, contracting them in waves to try to push myself over the edge, but Carl's hand slaps the back of my thighs, causing me to jump forward. My ass is so high in the air now. He must be able to smell my arousal and know how much he's torturing me.

"Bad girl," he growls. "You think I'm going to let you make yourself come? We're just getting started."

"Please," I beg, squirming against him.

"What did you say?"

"Please...Sir." I don't even care that I promised myself I wouldn't beg. I don't care that I've admitted that I'm totally in his thrall. Carl holds me in the palm of his hand.

"Open your legs," he barks, and I jump to do what he asks with military speed.

Holding my breath, I wait as the cool air licks softly against my burning flesh. *Please touch me*, I whisper in my mind. *Please let me come.*

Carl applies the tiniest press just above my clit, and I gasp, wriggling for more.

"Still," he says. "Still."

Holding myself rigidly, fighting the urge to move, I brace for what he might give me. An orgasm so intense that I lose the capacity to hold my own weight. An orgasm so strong that I will wake the neighbors. It's there, bubbling beneath the surface, lingering on the tip of my clit like a dark promise.

Please, my mind begs again.

And then he does it. He runs his finger in a long stripe between my legs, and I'm coming and coming and coming.

"Oh, oh…" I pant as the darkness swallows me, and bright white fireworks explode against the obsidian. For seconds, I'm no longer in this strange room with a man who's half my boss and half my master. I'm alone and drifting in warmth and contentment.

I'm adrift in the kind of pleasure that starts in the mind and spreads through the body.

It's only when I come around that I realize the floor is wet under my feet.

26

NASH

I set my alarm early the morning after Kyla's date with Carl. I want to get into work before my brothers so that I can talk to him about what happened.

Will he share everything with me?

Carl is a private person about sex, but this situation is different. We're linked together through the game and our discussion about what could happen after.

Carl's night with Kyla feels like a pivotal moment, especially since he threw his paper into the bowl as a late addition. How did Kyla feel when she picked out his name? Was it a shock? Was she worried or excited?

The plan for him to go back on his word was a risky one, but he was willing to take it.

Now, as I get started on readying my booth and dealing with some of the outstanding admin from the day before, I wait to hear if the risk has paid off.

The distinctive thud of Carl's feet follows the ringing of the bell over the door. I duck my head out of my booth, and he notices my presence immediately.

"You're early," he says. "For a moment, I worried that we'd been broken into."

"How did it go?" I ask, not giving any more time over to pleasantries. There are six other men and Kyla due to arrive for work imminently and I need to get this conversation done.

Carl nods, but the seriousness of his expression doesn't match his eyes. Did something bad happen? I know Carl can be controlling and that he likes to spank his women. Could Kyla not take the pain?

"It was good," he says. "Really good."

"So why do you look like your dog just died?"

"It was intense, for both of us. I made sure she got home safe, but after the sex, she was really quiet?"

"Did she enjoy herself?"

Carl nods, his nostrils flaring at whatever memory he's thinking about.

"Are you sure?"

"She squirted all over the floor," he says. "It was the sexiest fucking thing that's ever happened to me."

"She squirted?"

"Yeah, you know. I don't think it's happened to her before. She was mortified until I threw her on the bed and fucked the living daylights out of her."

"Wow...that does sound intense."

"She needs some time to recover," Carl says in a tone that sounds like an order.

"That'll be up to her, boss," I say. "You know the rules of the game. Kyla controls the timeframe. Kyla controls it all."

"Except what happened last night," he says.

I watch him retreat to the back of the shop with a

shake of my head. Maybe it was wrong for him to put his name in at this stage. We could have waiting until the end. And me removing my date…was that fair to Kyla? Is keeping my date until the end fair? She only has Noah and Dex to pick now. Whichever one of them she picks last, she's going to realize that I'm the one who's pulled out. Is she going to be upset? And then when my date appears in the bowl the next day, will she be happy or just want this whole game to be over? It's impossible to predict.

I'm beginning to question if she'll even go through with my date. Maybe by then she'll be too overwhelmed to contemplate it.

The rest of the boys drift into the shop over the next hour. Dex and Lex look tired, and I initially imagine that they were out partying and maybe found some girls to take home. But when I ask what kept them up so late, they blame starting a new Netflix series. Hardly the rock-and-roll life we used to live.

Kole and Kase have more energy, arriving freshly showered from the gym. And my own two brothers? Well, they arrive with a huge box of donuts and tray of coffees for us all. I could kiss them, if I didn't find them so annoying.

Kyla is the last to arrive, blushing the moment she steps foot in the shop. The sex memories are really stacking up. Only me, Dex and Noah are uncharted territory for her.

Noah grabs a coffee and a donut and approaches her at reception.

"A sweet treat for sweet Kyla," he says.

"What's the bitter coffee for then?" she grimaces.

"Me!" he says, with a grin. "Sweet and bitter go together so well, and you only have two more dates to pick. Fifty-fifty it'll be me. Are you choosing today?"

"No pressure," I call across the shop firmly. "You

know that, Noah. It's up to Kyla when she picks. Kyla, don't mind my brother. He never could wait his turn."

She puts up her hand palm facing Noah and then me. "Seriously, dudes. No bickering today. My mind is scrambled as it is." Her attention focusses on Noah, who has now taken a step back to give her some space.

"I will be choosing today," she says.

"When?"

"How about now?"

Her hand hovers over the bowl, and she drops her head to one side, narrowing her eyes. "There are three of you left, and only two more dates. That means someone has dropped out."

Noah's head swivels and his brows draw downward in confusion. "I thought Carl didn't put his name in."

"Carl was last night," Kyla says. "I guess it's not you who pulled out?"

Noah shakes his head vigorously. "Hell no. Do I look like a man who doesn't know a fucking amazing thing when he sees it?"

Behind us, someone starts up their tattoo gun, getting ready to ink their first customer. What we're doing right now is hardly professional but fuck it.

Kyla snatches up the paper, and unwraps it. When her eyes flick up to Noah, I know immediately that he's next, and so does he.

"Yes!" He pumps his fist and ducks over reception to plant a firm kiss on Kyla's lips. "I'll write down the address," he says. "Come at eight pm. My brothers will not be home."

The nod he sends in my direction is all the instruction I need to find another place to sleep tonight. Carl has a pull-out and spare mattress for me and Niall. We won't mind freeing up the apartment so that Noah can have his night, and Kyla can feel comfortable to let go and not have to worry that two other sets of ears are listening.

Kyla seems startled by Noah's enthusiasm, bringing her hand to her chest as he practically skips to his booth to get ready for the day. Her eyes drift across the shop, finding me leaning up against the wall, watching.

"So it's you or Dex?" she says.

I play dumb, but I'm not sure why. It's not like denial is going to make Kyla forget what is obvious. "Me or Dex what?"

"It must be you," she says. "This whole thing was Dex's idea. Why the hell would he pull out?"

"I guess all will be revealed," I say, sounding like I should be a gentleman in a Jane Austen novel, not a tattooed brute.

Kyla's smile sends a clear message. She's relaxed about whatever happens next and I like that. It means that this crazy game that Dex set up is working for her as much as it's working for us. And if it's working for her, then maybe, just maybe, my idea isn't so far-fetched after all.

27

NOAH

Kyla arrives dead on time and dressed in a cute pink fluffy sweater and baggy torn jeans that look like something she might have borrowed from a previous boyfriend.

"Did you eat? I ask as I take the jacket that she's carrying over her arm.

"Yeah, I made some pasta."

"Mmmmm…I love pasta, but pasta doesn't love me." Patting my belly, Kyla rolls her eyes.

"There isn't an ounce of extra fat on that stomach, and you know it," she says.

"So, if you don't need anything to eat, can I get you a drink or three."

I begin to lead her to the kitchen, where we have a homemade bar that I fashioned with my brothers from an old drawer unit. It's well-stocked with spirits, mixers, and cool glasses. The ideal way to get a party started.

"Am I going to need three?" she asks, a hint of nervousness creeping into her voice.

"Well, that depends."

"On what?" She cocks her head to one side and rests against the door jamb, watching me with appraising eyes.

"How willing you are to give overall control to me?" I ask.

"Maybe I'll need more than three," she says, drifting into the room so she can take a closer look at the bar. "This is very cool. Can you make cocktails?"

"I can. Name your drink."

"What about sex on the beach? Do you have orange juice?"

"I have everything I need to make your dreams come true."

Kyla snorts as I take two tall glasses and rest them on top of the bar. I head to the fridge to fill the ice bucket and find the freshly squeezed juice. I need vodka and peach schnaps and some sickly-sweet grenadine for the drippy sunset effect around the edge of the glass. When I'm done assembling our drinks, I realize the Kyla's drifted off to look at the shelves on either side of our monster-sized TV. "Who's the reader?" she asks. "It's definitely not you."

"What are you trying to say?" I snort, slightly taken aback. I might not be much of a reader of fiction, but I keep up to date with world politics and economics. Despite choosing not to go to college, I had the grades that would have got me in. It always amuses me when I come out with something current and intelligent-sounding and find astounded expressions as a result. Shocking people can be fun.

"You don't strike me as a person who would want to spend time in another person's shoes. You seem more than comfortable in your own."

"Is that why you read?" I ask, remembering the black

and red cover of the book I caught Kyla buried in at the deli one lunchtime.

"For sure," Kyla says. "My life isn't the worst, but it certainly isn't the most interesting."

"Are you sure of that?" I hand her the drink and take a sip of my own. It's the perfect mix of sweet and sour with the warmth of alcohol as it hits the back of my throat.

"Right now, I'm reading a dark mafia romance. I guess I'm kind of glad that my life hasn't taken that kind of turn."

"Exactly," I say. "But I'm sure there are some romance novels out there where the heroine has lots of kinky fun with a tattooed hero."

"There are lots where the heroine has kinky fun with lots of tattooed men at the same time."

"Really!" I say, leaning a little closer. "And have you read any books like that?"

"I might have done," Kyla admits, sucking cocktail up her straw with bright eyes.

"Well, my night might not live up to that kind of excitement," I say.

"Noah, cocktails and ribbons," she murmurs, as though she's still trying to work out what it means.

"So, you have me, and you have the cocktail. Now all I have to provide are the ribbons."

"Ribbons don't seem very kinky." Kyla hands me her empty glass and raises an eyebrow.

"Anything can be kinky with the right person in control," I say. "For example, that banana over there. In one person's hand, it's just an innocent little fruit, but in my hands…"

Kyla holds up her palm, the imagery of the banana seemingly too much for her. "You said nothing about bananas on that little slip of paper. I think I'll stick with the ribbons."

"It's not an either-or situation," I smirk, sliding my hand around hers so that I can lead her to the bedroom. I've tried to set the scene without making it like something from a tacky third-rate 1970s porn movie. I've covered my bed in my plain white cotton comforter, with matching pillows and a soft gray woven throw. The light comes from a muted bulb in my black lamp, resting on my nightstand. Candles seemed too cliched, but this feels just right.

I've left a mellow playlist on in the background too. Somehow, music has the power to turn a cold empty room into an inviting space. I hope everything I've done will relax Kyla enough for her to let go and hand all control over to me.

"Are you planning to tie me up?" she asks softly, making her way around the bed and fingering the thick red ribbon that is already fixed to each corner of my bed.

"Will you let me?"

She takes the ribbon and wraps it around her left wrist, testing the feeling of it by pulling away from the bed the way she might if she was struggling. It pulls tight around her skin, the bite obvious from the way it indents her flesh. Her lips part at the sensation, pink and soft-looking, totally mesmerizing. There's another roll of thick ribbon on the nightstand that she notices.

"What's this for?" she asks.

"Your eyes. Have you ever been blindfolded before?"

Her brown eyes find mine as she shakes her head. "I would never have guessed that this would be your kink," she says softly.

"What would you have guessed?"

"Dirty talk," she says. "You have a way with words."

"Oh, I like dirty talk too." I take a step closer, then another, moving slowly, so that I don't startle her. Kyla seems skittish and nervous tonight, a contrast from the controlled and confident woman she is at work.

"Do I get a safe word?" she asks.

"Of course. That's yours to pick."

"Banana," she says, tucking her hair behind her ear as I get close enough to reach out and touch her.

"Not banana," I say. "Because if that's your safe word, you'll never be able to actually ask for the banana."

Swatting her hand at my arm, she shakes her head. "Seriously, are you not content with pushing my boundaries with these ribbons? You want to go even further?"

"I want you to go as far as you want," I say. "Whatever you want, I will deliver."

"I'm sure there would be things you wouldn't want to do," she says with an arch to her eyebrow.

"Maybe." I smile, "But I don't think you'd be stepping that far out of my comfort zone."

"Tell me what you want me to do," she says, with a curt nod.

Tipping her chin, I dip my head, running my lips across hers with a featherlight touch, waiting until I feel her first tremble. She'll learn that what I like can't be rushed. It's about slow, torturously good pleasure. Layer upon layer of sensation that curls toes and elicits begging. She won't understand it now, but she will when we're done.

"I want you to give up all control to me," I whisper against the pretty pink shell of her ear. "Take off all of your clothes and lie on the bed. I'll do the rest." I half expect her to resist or tell me she wants me to do it, but she doesn't. With quick efficiency, she strips off until she's completely naked, her beautiful body illuminated and shadowed by the dim light. She's close enough for me to touch her, but I don't. I wait, my eyes trailing what she's revealed, taking in the tightening of her nipples and the gooseflesh that creeps over her skin.

It's not cold in the room.

I made sure of that.

But maybe my gaze is making her shiver.

The thought sends a tickle of sensation down my spine.

"On the bed, Kyla," I whisper, not needing to ask twice.

She takes orders like a pro, sitting quickly on the side of the bed and swinging her legs until she's lying in the center. When she opens her arms and legs, so they're close to each corner of the bed, my cock surges in my pants. Oh God, she looks so perfect like this, and she'll look even more perfect when my ribbons are fastened around her slender wrists and ankles. She'll look sensational when I tease her, and she strains, pulling at the ribbons, seeking freedom to resist that won't be there.

Cupping my cock, I give it a squeeze, then begin the work to tie Kyla to my bed, making her my slave.

It doesn't take long because there's no resistance. With each knot, her fingers curl, and her ankles flex, testing the binds enough to know they're there. She keeps her eyes closed, which I expected. There's a shyness about Kyla that is tantalizing, as well as buried confidence, which rears up every so often, catching me by surprise. I undress, dropping my clothes onto the hardwood floor, my eyes never leaving Kyla's curves.

I know her anticipation will be building and building. Behind the blackness of her eyelids, her other senses will be heightened. She'll hear the rustle of my clothing and my footsteps at the bedside. She'll hear my breathing increasing in speed, but I'm not close enough for her to hear my pounding heartbeat.

My hands are itching to touch her, my lips tingling to kiss her. My mouth waters, imagining how she'll taste against my tongue. Closing my eyes, I inhale a deep breath, but she's still there behind the darkness of my eyelids, the image of her smiling from behind the reception desk at Ink Factor, tossing her head back and laughing at one of my jokes, standing outside on the day of her interview, nervous but excited.

She's been lingering in my mind since the first time I saw her. At first, it was just physical; a desire to touch her, to claim her, to own her. But now, it's something deeper that fills my chest with a nervous ache. It's about being something special to her.

I have a lot to live up to. My friends have already taken turns to please her. They've taken her on dates and given her new experiences. Her mind is already full of excitement and pleasure. I need to be something different and special. Glancing down at the tattoos I've marked my body with, I get the unwelcome feeling that I'm not going to be able to do it. I'll blend in like the rest of them. She won't remember what I did with her. It'll just blend in with the memories of the others. Maybe she'll confuse me and Niall and Nash in her mind, the way everyone has since the day we were born. Maybe I won't be enough.

"Noah," her voice whispers in the darkness, bringing me around from my thoughts.

"Yes, baby," I say, taking a step closer.

"Tell me something funny," she says. "My heart is beating so fast; I need to hear your voice."

And just like that, the anxious ache around my heart melts away.

Kyla's here with me, and I can make her see what that means. I'll show her how it can be between us. I'll make her laugh, and then I'll make her come.

If I try, I know I can be enough.

28

KYLA

I wish that I was brave enough to keep my eyes open and watch Noah's every move, but I'm not. My eyelids are a welcome shield against my emotions.

Somewhere in the room, Noah sighs, and it sounds happy. His footsteps bring him closer, and the bed shifts next to me. "You want me to make you laugh?" he asks softly. My whole body braces for his touch, my limbs stiffening in their binds. The tips of my nipples feel so sensitized that all it would take is for his mouth to suck hard, and I think I'd come.

Is that why he likes this? The sense of anticipation, of control.

It's so different from what I thought he'd be like in the bedroom.

Funny by day, I imagined him taking me to a comedy club and maybe engaging in some dress-up. Something that would make me giggle. But this also kind of makes sense.

People generally take on the role of the joker to cover up deeper feelings. They find attention and validation through being lighthearted, but there's always something darker beneath—feelings of inadequacy or somber thoughts they want to hide.

Noah seems that way.

I wonder what he's hiding beneath the humor. I wonder if he knows that people don't just like him for being a comedian. They like him because he's kind. He sees the humanity in everyone, and he uses his talent to make them feel at ease. It's what he did for me that first day, and he's never stopped.

It's what he does now with a stupid dad-joke while his fingers gently trail up the side of my ribs, soothing in the way you would a skittish horse.

When I laugh, I can almost feel his smile, and my fingers itch to reach out and touch his face, wanting to confirm that it's there.

"Now, the time for jokes is over, Kyla," he says, fingers trailing up the side of my breast and ghosting over the point of one nipple. My body reacts immediately, back arching, legs tugging at the binds.

There are many things Noah could do to me while I'm restrained this way. Things that I've never done before. Things that I'd never dare to ask for. I wonder how far he'll go, but I find that I don't really care. This is his night. This is his chance to take what he needs from me, and I'm happy to give him everything.

Well, everything is within reason.

"Do you like feeling powerless?" he whispers closer to my ear than I was expecting. Already my sense of where he is in the room is diminishing.

Do I? It's hard to be sure. I like the anticipation of his touch. I like not knowing what's coming next. Although I'm strung as tight as elastic, it's a relief that nothing is expected of me. All the control is with Noah, and with the control comes responsibility. It's his job to please me and to please himself. There are zero expectations from a person who cannot move more than a few inches in either direction. "Yes," I breathe because it's true and because I know he wants to hear it. This is his kink, after all.

And before I have a chance to prepare, the weight of him kneeling between my legs shifts the mattress. The cool ribbon is wrapped over my eyes and around the back of my head, fastening at the side in a secure knot. I test my sight, finding that the blindfold conceals absolutely everything. Now it's no longer my choice to see or not, I feel the loss of my sight.

I'm reduced to four senses: hearing, tasting, smelling, and touch.

I can hear Noah's breathing, feel the press of his knees between my thighs and smell the delicious scent of his cologne. It's something deep and spicy, sexy and dark. When he runs something across my lips, my tongue darts out to taste, it's his thumb. I can tell by the thickness of it and the ridges of his skin, hardened from holding the tattoo gun.

"You have such a pretty mouth," he says softly. "Such soft pink lips and a voice that's warm and smooth."

I shiver as his thumb moves to caress the line of my jaw and down the length of my neck, drifting across my clavicle. As he gets closer to my breasts, my arms strain at the restraints, instinct urging me to protect myself and cover up against his hungry gaze.

But I can't.

There's nothing to stop him from touching me where he wants. There's nothing to stop the press of his mouth between my breasts, or the trailing of his tongue over my nipple. There's no stopping him from licking and nipping and no way of preventing my own body from reacting.

Every touch is sharper. Every feel of his breath against my skin is more tingly; every anticipation builds and builds.

I want to press my thighs together and enjoy the friction. I want to beg him to stop and to ask for more all at the same time. My head is a confused muddle of sensation, desire, and fear.

Fear that I won't like what he does. Fear that I'll like it too much.

Fear that I'll never have this again.

My fingers flex in their binds again, wanting to know what it feels like to touch Noah. My eyes want to see his beautiful eyes, sculpted face, and ever-quirked lips. I want to kiss him and hold him and feel him move inside me. I want a connection with this man, who always seeks to bring people together with laughter.

But I won't get that tonight. I'll get this restrained version where Noah's in charge of how we are together. I won't feel his skin beneath my fingertips. I won't see all the ways he lights me on fire.

His breath licks over my spread pussy before his tongue, and the heat is enough to make me buck. A large hand rests on my belly, and his voice is a soothing hush. "Still," he whispers, pressing a soft kiss to my thigh. "Still, and I'll give you what you need."

The first press of his tongue on my clit has me writhing again, but he draws back as I move. It's not enough that I'm tethered to his bed. He wants me to stay as still as a statue while he touches me. I know for sure it won't be possible. Even if I control my breathing and try to relax, my whole body is on high alert.

Licking out again, I can feel the smile on his lips as I moan, and the unfamiliar graze of his lip ring against my flesh. A finger strokes my entrance, finding me wet, and a satisfied hum leaves his lips. With every lick, he slides a finger inside me, hooking up against the bundle of nerves that makes me want to grunt. I try my hardest to stay still, but the closer I get, the more I need to move. I want to tear the restraints away from my limbs and push Noah to his back, sliding down on the big cock I know he has and riding him until I reach the pinnacle of pleasure. I want to feel him buck against me, chasing his own pleasure. I want to flip the dynamic, so I'm the one in charge.

I wonder if he'd like that as much as he likes this. I guess I'll never find out.

"You taste like honey," he says. "So sweet on my tongue. You feel like silk inside. I can't wait to fuck you."

I groan, his words licking places inside my mind that his tongue could never reach. His fingers twist inside me and the word please spills from my lips like a drink overturned. *Please.*

Noah sucks on my clit, once, twice, three times, and I'm lost. There's no holding my hips still through the orgasm that tightens the ribbons at my wrists and ankles. There's no stopping myself from straining to close my legs while wave upon wave of contractions clenches my pussy around his fingers.

"That's it," he murmurs against my thigh. "That's it, baby. Let it all go, so I can start all over again."

I'm still fluttering in the recesses of my mind as he makes good on his promise, his tongue skating around my clit in gentle circles that don't feel like anything to start with but become maddeningly sensual over time. His fingers, which never left my pussy, move slowly too, as though he's stroking inside me rather than fucking into me. The emptiness of my vision makes the sensation brighter and sharper. My body is a piano, and Noah is a maestro, tapping at my keys, playing the perfect concerto of my pleasure.

Please escapes my lips again, this time higher pitched. He's taking longer to push me toward the pinnacle this time, the delay more maddening than I would ever have thought possible.

"Patience," he whispers, drawing back enough to let the orgasm slip away.

Fuck. Do I need to keep quiet to get what I want? He really does want to keep me bound and gagged, even if the latter is not literal.

So I wait. I hold my body perfectly still, and I allow my mind to swim in the darkness, absorbing every lick, every touch, until I'm vibrating inside with all of the pent-up pleasure.

When I come, I can tell that Noah's surprised. The pulsating waves of my pussy contracting are the only outward sign. This time, his smile against my skin is even wider.

"You're perfect," he whispers, kissing his way up my stomach, licking my nipples, nuzzling my neck. I'm not so sure about that, but maybe I've learned to be perfect for him.

His thumb trails my bottom lip, encouraging me to open my mouth. Climbing higher, he rests his knees under my arms. I can sense him leaning over me, bringing his cock to my lips. It's thick and rock-hard as he traces where his thumb had been, giving me a chance to object.

I don't.

In the darkness behind the scarf, I imagine what he must look like, looming above me like an avenging angel. His gorgeous muscular inked body braced and taut, anticipation narrowing his eyes and drawing his brows. My tongue licks out like it's seeking the sweetness of ice cream, finding the smooth head of his cock instead. The hiss Noah makes is sharp, almost pained, but he doesn't pull away. Instead, he shifts, bracing his weight on the headboard so the bed creaks, allowing his cock to pass over my lip and into my mouth.

It's big.

So big that my jaw aches just from allowing it space to pass between my teeth. One of his hands cups my face like I need encouragement.

I don't.

There's no room for me to move, to facilitate this act, but that's not what Noah wants anyway. His hips cant gently, easing his cock in and out of my mouth, and all I can do is take it.

Do I feel violated?

Maybe a little.

Does it feel good?

Oh yes. Yes it does.

Noah's using my mouth to steal pleasure that I'd willingly give. He wants to take it, though. My powerlessness is a flick of an illicit switch, magnifying every little sensation.

"Mmmmm," I hum around him, not able to control my pleasure, and Noah mutters a curse under his breath, his hips shifting with a little less finesse.

"You like that, huh?" he says, stroking my cheek. "You like your mouth stuffed full of my cock. You want me to fill that pretty throat of yours so you can taste me and swallow it down?"

I twitch my head up and down, and I hear Noah's breathless chuckle as though he was right next to my ear, not high above me. Without my sight, every sound is heightened, every touch a million times more vibrant.

"Tut-tut," he whispers, drawing back. "You think I'd give away what I have to give that easily? I'm a patient man, Kyla. Can you be patient?"

I want to yell, NO, and have done with it. No is the truth. I'm not patient at all. I'm hungry and eager, wanting to find out everything about this man, to taste his pleasure and feel his surrender.

What would he want me to say?

No is defiant. It goes against his wishes. But yes is submissive. I can't work out if that's what he wants from me or if the fight is part of his kink.

So I say nothing. I'm immobile and impassive, and I wait.

And wait.

And Noah draws back, his mouth beginning to explore the rest of my body. And God, it's so hard to stay still and silent. It's so hard not to show him that I love the way he kisses the skin at my wrists and the underside of my breasts. I love the trail of his fingers like whisper-soft feathers. I love the fleeting press of his warm body that hints at what it might be like if he'd just rest himself over me and push inside.

I'll beg for that if he doesn't give it to me soon. I'll plead for his cock to stretch me open. I'll strain at the bindings to be able to touch him because I'm getting to the point that I can't take anymore. I just can't.

"You ready for the banana?" he asks, so close to my ear that his breath feels wet.

For a second, I think he's serious. Then we both erupt into a messy splutter of laughter, and all the tension is dispersed just like that.

"I'm ready for your banana," I say softly. "And I wouldn't mind having my hands back for that."

"Just your hands?"

I think about it, weighing up the pros and cons, but he doesn't wait for me to answer. The ribbon binding my right wrist is loosened by eager fingers, and then Noah's legs settle against the inside of my thighs. "You get one hand back," he says. "The rest of you is still my prisoner."

The blood begins to prickle at my fingertips, so when I

touch him, there's a weird disconnected feeling, as though he's a ghost and I'm seeking to touch something that isn't real. Noah seems that way sometimes. All the men of Ink Factor do.

Too good to be true.

Intangibly perfect.

Too special for me.

When he pushes inside me, it feels so good that I can't hold in the moan that surges from deep within my chest. Tears prick my eyes, knowing how close I'm getting to the end of the night and the end of the game.

"You're so fucking tight," he whispers against my lips, his voice strained as though he's gritting his teeth. The angle he's fucking into me gives so much friction to my clit that it's almost painful. There's no shifting to change it either. I'm still tethered to the bed, totally in Noah's power. "You feel so fucking perfect," he grunts, this time kissing me in a deep and frenzied way that sends me tumbling down, down, down into the very depths of pleasure. The orgasm sneaks up on me, sending me spinning with a whip-crack of pleasure, and Noah fucks me through it all, his hand pinning my still-tethered arm to the bed. I use my free hand to clutch at his perfect ass, pulling him deeper, urging him harder, wanting to know what it feels like when he comes inside me.

I don't know if he's wearing a condom, and I don't care.

"Kyla," he moans, his hand gripping my hair. "Baby."

Then his cock is swelling, and his body is seizing and I'm lost in the power of his orgasm and the powerlessness of the darkness surrounding me.

I expect Noah to get up quickly, untie me, and send me on my way, but he doesn't. He stays settled between my legs, playing with my breast lazily, pushing my blindfold away from my eyes so he can smile down at me. I blink a few times, even the low light of the lamp too much. "There she is," he breathes in a way that sounds relieved.

Did he worry that I wouldn't enjoy his kink? Was he scared that I'd be upset?

The way he grazes my cheek with his smiling lips makes me smile too. "Did you like my banana?" he asks, and we laugh again, wracking our bodies so much that he slides from inside me.

"I LOVED your banana." Stroking my hand over the side of his face makes his eyelids droop with pleasure. Exhaling long and low, he reaches out to untie my arm and then attends to my ankles. When I'm free, I flex my joints, grateful to have movement.

Noah, kneels up, watching me, uncertainty clouding his eyes.

What should I do now? Go? Stay? This feels awkward.

My eyes drift to the door, but before I can say anything, Noah grabs the remote from the nightstand next to my head. "Wanna watch some TV?" he asks. "I can make us another cocktail?"

"Make me a hot chocolate, and you've got yourself a deal," I say.

So that's what he does.

For the next two hours, we watch stand-up comedy specials, laughing at jokes that are so close to the bone they almost hurt. My hot chocolate is served with whipped cream and sprinkles, and Noah tucks me beneath the covers like a burrito.

When it's close to midnight, I know I have to make my excuses to leave. Sleeping over isn't part of the game, and I want to exit on a high. "I'm going to turn into a pumpkin," I say. "Time to brave the night and head home." There's a definite drop to Noah's face that looks like disappointment, but I can't be sure. Sometimes I wonder if I'm crazy and constantly noticing things that aren't really there.

"I'll take you home," he says, but before he gets the chance to pull on his clothes, I've ordered a cab.

At the door, we gaze at each other like we're meeting for the first time. He has a sparkle in his eyes that I recognize from the first time we met. His fingers lace with mine, and he brings my hand to his lips. The cab rumbles its arrival outside as Noah releases my hand. "Your carriage awaits, Cinderella," he says.

"I'm not leaving a shoe," I smile. "These are my favorites."

Noah grimaces with disappointment, then his expression brightens. "You forget, Kyla, that I know exactly where to find you tomorrow."

I smile, hiding the sinking feeling in my stomach. As I make my way to the sidewalk, I try to shake the disappointment, knowing that the Kyla he'll find tomorrow is a work colleague and nothing else. Our fairytale night is over.

Tomorrow, I won't be Noah's princess anymore.

29

DEX

Part of me can't believe I've had to wait so long for my turn in a game that was my idea. The other part of me is happy that Kyla's gotten so far and is still happily participating. It's not so much that I doubted that my brother and friends would be able to keep her happy. It's more that I was expecting it to be too much for her. And now it hasn't been…now others, who have kinks as challenging as mine, have gone first, I'm not so worried that my date is going to be the one that will make Kyla balk.

Most importantly, now she's happily had sex with my brother, my date won't seem like such a big deal.

After she has picked my date out of the bowl, she finds me uploading pictures onto m tablet. "You're up, champ," she says, waving it with a smile.

"Seriously. I thought I was going to be last," I say.

Kyla frowns, lowering her hand. "You are the last. Nash didn't have a date in the bowl."

"He did," I say, cocking my head to one side. "I saw him put it in the bowl."

"Well, it's not there now. I thought you guys might have been comparing notes, and he decided he wasn't up for his part in the game."

"Are you crazy?" I say. "You think the guys in here are just in this to satisfy you? I can tell you one hundred percent that we are all happily and very selfishly taking part."

"Then why's he taken his date out of the bowl," she asks.

"I am not sure!" As far as I'm concerned, he'd have to be crazy to let a chance like this go. I'm sure there's more to this than meets the eye. "Anyway, you don't need to worry about that today. Today you let me take care of you."

"Is that what's going to happen later?" she asks. "*DEX, MUSIC, WATCHING.* It's very cryptic."

"No more cryptic than the rest," I say, although I don't know for sure. We didn't discuss what we were going to write, but I know they used the same format. Name, date, a hint at the kink.

"Don't worry about eating dinner. I'll pick you up at eight pm."

"Sure." Kyla's smile is bright, but there is something about her eyes that doesn't quite match the rest of her expression. A wariness or an attempt to hold something in. It settles inside me like the gray of fog, but then she's turning around and disappearing back to reception, and I shake my head, telling myself that it's all my imagination.

I arrive fifteen minutes early, eager to see Kyla and keen not to be late. She's ready early too, so I drive us out to my favorite place up a road that snakes up the curve of a steep hill until it reaches the top. There's a small layby there where a few cars can park to take in the view. There's a bench too, and at this time of night, it's nearly always deserted.

Thankfully, we're the only ones present. In the trunk of the car I have our takeaway, staying warm in a thermal picnic bag wrapped in a blanket. I know Kyla loves Middle Eastern food, so I bought us kebabs wrapped in soft bread and filled with fresh salad and a yogurt dressing.

Passing her the light bag, I reach for the other bag containing drinks and my guitar.

"You play?" she asks, cocking her head to one side.

"Did you think I was going to play you my record collection?"

"I guess I thought I would have known something like that by now."

"I used to play a lot, but I don't find the time so much these days."

Slamming the trunk closed, I lead Kyla to the bench. It's dark, but the town is spread out beneath our feet like a glittering carpet.

"Do you play an instrument?" I ask her.

"Air guitar while I'm singing in the shower count?" She takes a bite of her kebab and rolls her pretty chocolate eyes with deep satisfaction.

"No," I grin, "But I'd still like to see that."

"My shower antics are strictly a one-woman experience."

"Shame."

Kyla nods at the guitar case resting at my feet. "So, what do you play?"

"A little of everything. I've never found I wanted to listen to or play music from only one genre. It's the melody and the lyrics together that touch me. It has to be something that I can bring to life."

"So have you decided what you'll play for me?"

I shrug because I haven't truly decided. There are so many songs that I could play for Kyla. Some to tell her about the way she makes me feel, the way her softness touches me. Some because the melody gives me that aching feeling inside that only things of real beauty achieve. Some songs that got me through tough times, and some that made me think about love. "Do you have a song you'd like me to play?" Turning the tables is a cowardly move, but I don't fight it. Maybe it's right that Kyla should lead. It'll be less like I'm performing and more like I'm carrying out a service for her.

"I think I'll leave the decision to you," she says, raising her eyebrows. There's a little challenge in her expression. A challenge that tells me I need to get this right. What will Kyla like the best? She doesn't strike me as the kind of girl who wants to be romanced in a traditional way. If I sang her a love song, I think it would embarrass her. No, I think she understands emotion and pain. She understands weakness and uncertainty. Honesty and truth are what Kyla needs.

"Did you ever listen to The Civil Wars?" I ask. "They broke up a while back."

"Oh my God, I love them. I'm still holding out that they'll make up and get back together. The world needs more music like that."

"Remember when they did that cover of The Smashing Pumpkins' track?"

"Disarm?"

"How about that?"

She lowers her half-eaten kebab to the bench. "Forget about eating, Dex. You need to get that guitar out of its case and show me what you can do."

"Are you always this demanding?" I laugh, placing my food next to hers. Taking a napkin, I wipe my fingers clean before reaching to unsnap my well-worn guitar case. Pulling it into my lap, there's such a comfort in the way it feels against me. The wood warms to my body temperature, and my hand wraps around its long, elegant neck. A cool wind blows from behind us, ruffling Kyla's hair and making the sky feel closer around us.

The first pluck of the string sounds so loud in the echoing silence, but as I craft the melody, the sound created fills the atmosphere perfectly. The first words fit with the way I felt when I first saw Kyla. *Disarm me with your smile.* It's what she did that first day. There was an innocence in her that seems to be missing from people these days. It made me take a step back.

I sing without looking at her, weaving the words and guitar melody to create something sad and beautiful. The breeze carries away some of the notes, and I'm glad. The song is sad, conjuring loneliness and times past. Things that can't be undone, and as I'm singing it, I wonder how I'll feel tomorrow when this night is over, and there is no going back.

Sometimes I hate looking forward to things. I hate the anticipation and the longing because I know that once I've stepped through the door of the experience that the other side will be darker and lesser. What will it be like to step into Kyla's sunshine and have to walk tomorrow without it?

Sentimentality is something I try to push aside. I'm a person who wants to live in truth, not swamp myself in thoughts of what might be or could have been. I want to dwell in what is.

And this night with Kyla is what is. What happens after won't be changed by what happens tonight. At least, that's what I tell myself.

Tonight I get a chance to show her something new. She gets to experience me, and I get to experience her. It's like a dance.

Another Civil Wars song flits into my mind: it's a cover of a Leonard Cohen song. Dance me to the end of love.

Is that how I'll feel at the end of tonight? Kyla's not a girl who'd be easy to forget. She's the kind of girl who reaches into your chest and wraps her slender fingers around your heart to cradle rather than wound.

She's the kind of girl that any one of us should have been looking to love rather than fuck.

But this game was my idea. My idea before I'd realized who and what Kyla is, before I understood what she could become.

I know my brother feels the same. I told him I didn't want to know about his night or anyone else's. I didn't want the knowledge to taint my own. But I can see that they're changed by the time they've spent with Kyla. There's warmth in their eyes when they look at her, and effort in all their interactions.

But even if we all wanted her, what good would that do any of us?

Kyla could choose, I suppose, but that wouldn't be fair. The ones who didn't get picked would spend the rest of their lives wondering what we could have done better. Maybe Kyla would regret her choice at some point too. It would end up a giant and confusing mess.

No, we're in this game, and it has an expiration date, and there is nothing I can do about it.

As the song comes to an end, I finally look up and find a single tear leaking down Kyla's soft cheek.

She uses the back of her hand to swipe it away quickly as though she's embarrassed to be so affected. But I've seen that music can touch her, and now I want her even more. To diffuse the charged atmosphere, I pick up my kebab and take a big bite. Kyla does the same, but the thoughtfulness I sense from her lingers.

So I tell her about some embarrassing stories from our

teenage years like when Carl got caught balls-deep in his neighbor by her father and had to run home without his pants and underwear. Or the time that Niall and Nash drew Noah a mustache with a permanent marker the day before his big date with the head cheerleader. And when I and Lex pretended to be each other so we could share each other's girlfriends; it backfired because they realized and dumped us both. "Justice," Kyla remarks, and I nod my agreement.

"What about Kole and Kase? I want a funny story about them too!"

"They've always been trouble," I tell her. "What about the time they met an older woman at a nightclub, went back to her place, and in the morning saw framed pictures of their momma in her house?"

"What?"

"The woman was their mom's best friend in college. She'd only just moved into town, and they hadn't been formally introduced. I still don't think their mom has found out, which is a good thing. No one wants to find out that kind of thing about their sons and their BFF."

"Oh my God. You guys are all terrible."

"Were terrible," I say. "All very past tense."

"So what is this?" she asks, waving her free hand between us. "Isn't it more of the same? Won't you all be sharing funny anecdotes about this game with each other in the future?"

"No way," I say. "This isn't anything like those stories. This is grown-up shit."

"Grown-up? How is having one-night stands grown up? Isn't this the kind of thing we should have stopped down in our teens?"

"One-night stands?" I guess I'd never seen what we're doing in that way. It's not like we're never going to see each other again. The thought of never seeing Kyla after tonight makes my stomach clench.

"Fuck buddies. Friends with benefits but just once." She smiles, but again it doesn't meet her eyes.

I know I should say something, but I don't know what. I can't deny what she's saying. Not really. But I also don't want to acknowledge that it's strictly the truth. I want it to be more, but how do I say that when I have no answers to how it could be?

"I know what I'm going to play next," I say, repeating the clean-up operation before I handle my guitar again. I choose a Brad Paisley song that's all about finding yourself. It seems to fit our situation perfectly, and halfway through, Kyla starts to sing along. She has a pretty voice that harmonizes with mine, and we create something together that is sweet and beautiful.

After we finish our food, I clean up, ready to take Kyla home. There's still the second part of our date to go.

Kyla's apartment is decorated minimally, with stark white furniture and black-framed photographs and art. Plants nestle into corners, bringing life to an otherwise surgical atmosphere, and the pops of color coming from the cushions and drapes bring brightness and personality. There isn't any clutter, which I expected. At work, Kyla is a master organizer.

"You're the first one to come in," she says, gazing around at her own open-plan living room as though she's looking at it through fresh eyes.

"I was going to take you back to my place, but then I thought you had your night with Lex there, and I wanted to keep things separate. Plus, I like the idea of this happening in your space.

"The watching?"

"Yes."

Kyla blinks, tucking her hair behind her ears as though

she needs to be free of distractions for this conversation. "What do you want to watch?"

"Everything," I say, taking a step closer. "I want you to pretend that I'm not here. Just go about doing what you would do to get ready for bed, and when you get there, I want you to touch yourself. Bring yourself to orgasm. I want to see how you make yourself feel good."

The flush that rises up Kyla's neck and cheeks is the prettiest shade of pink. I step closer and press a hand against her face, feeling the heat of embarrassment that my words have caused her.

"You want to watch? Just watch?"

"Not just watch," I say, running my thumb over her skin that's as soft as a peach.

"Will I see you?" she asks, and I'm surprised at how perceptive she is.

"No," I say. "But you'll know I'm there. Take a shower."

With a deep, slightly trembly breath, Kyla nods. She steps away and turns her back to me, walking to the kitchen area and fixing herself a glass of water. I slide the sneakers from my feet and hang my black jacket over the back of the couch. Then I creep through the hallway and into her bedroom.

It's neat and tidy, exactly as I expected it, and it smells of her perfume. There is a bathroom directly off the bedroom, and I work out where I can stand in the shadows of her room to watch her take a shower. When she returns to her bedroom, I can linger in the hallway and watch through a crack in the door.

I'm pressing my back to the wall, hidden by the thick green floor-to-ceiling drapes when Kyla enters the room.

She doesn't look for me as she eases her rings from her fingers and unhooks the hoops from her ears. Her eyes don't scan the corners of the room as she lifts her sweater over her head and slides her pants over her thighs. The sight of her in just a pretty cream bra and panties set is enough to send heat flooding between my legs. In a second, my cock is straining against my jeans, but I resist the urge to adjust myself. I have a lot of watching to enjoy before I come. Delaying sensation is part of this for me.

Kyla picks up her phone from the bed and smiles at something, tossing it back onto her comforter. I wonder if she really did receive a message or if this is all part of an elaborate act. Either way, it doesn't matter to me. It feels real, and that's what's important.

She strolls toward the bathroom, unhooking her bra on the way and switching her hips in a way that makes her ass jiggle. Oh God, she's built with just that perfect amount of softness and a few dimples across her thighs that make me want to grip the flesh with my fingers.

The sound of the shower starting is what spurs me to move forward, and I watch her drop her panties to the floor.

Bend, I think, wanting to see more, wanting to see everything, and she does, flashing her pussy in my direction so quickly that I gasp.

Shit.

I don't know if she's enjoying this, but I am. Every last bit of it. When she gets into the shower and turns to allow the water to cascade over her, I finally get a view of her pretty breasts. They're soft-looking and tipped with nipples that are drawn into tight points. Kyla takes a handful of soap and begins to rub it over herself in a way that looks natural rather than seductive. She's worked out that I don't want a show. I just want to see what's real.

The urge to yank my own clothes from my body and join her in the steam is overwhelming, but I hold back, knowing that there is more to come.

As Kyla dries herself, I back into the hallway to get

ready for the main event.

And when she's done, she gets me for dessert.

30

KYLA

Dex is watching me, but I don't know where from. He could be in the hallway, in my closet, or behind my drapes. I guess it doesn't matter where he is, only that his eyes are on me as I dry myself.

I'm guessing that he wants me to be as natural as possible. It wouldn't feel real if he could tell I'm putting on a show for him, and I'm glad about that. I'm not a good actress, and if there is one thing I vowed never to do in my life, it's to fake pleasure during sex.

I reach for my cutest nightshirt, which is made of pink satin and lace. I don't search out panties because Dex wants to watch me play with myself, and they would only get in the way. As I'm pulling the nightshirt over my head, I debate whether I should use my fingers or a toy.

If Dex wasn't here, the toy would be my go-to. It's an average-sized purple vibrator that always gets me off nice and fast. What would he prefer? Without asking, I have no way of knowing, so I decide to go with my usual.

It's in my nightstand, in a cute little makeup purse, and I find it before settling back against my comforter. If the truth is told, I would usually masturbate under the covers, but Dex wouldn't get to see much, and the idea that he can see everything has already made me hot and slippery between my legs.

When I pull out the vibrator, I listen to see if I can hear a response from him, but wherever he is, he's cool, calm, and collected. Lying back against the pillows, I twist the base of the vibrator so that it begins to hum, spread my legs, and draw up the hem of my nightshirt.

The first touch of it against my clit makes me jump. I'm already so swollen and sensitized that it's almost too much. I run it lower, dipping the tip just inside my entrance, and close my eyes at the sensation. I know it's not going to take me longer than a couple of minutes to come, and I imagine Dex behind the door to my bedroom, his eyes glued to what I'm doing, and his hand wrapped around his cock. I imagine him bursting in and replacing the vibrator with his big cock, hammering into me so hard that my head hits the headboard, and my back arches like a bow.

I imagine him coming inside me, the pulsing of his cock pushing me over the edge. I think about his teeth on my nipples, his hands gripping my flesh, the punishing force of his kiss, and that's all it takes. I come with the vibrator on my clit and my legs spread wide, knowing he'll see the contraction of my pussy. Knowing he's watching and listening to my pleasure.

I keep my eyes closed as I come down from the intensity of my orgasm, wondering if it was everything Dex hoped it would be. This fantasy of his seemed strange when he explained it, but I can see the appeal. There's something so naughty and forbidden about watching someone do the simple things that happen in private. And for me, knowing I had an audience just made the pleasure even sharper.

When his hand touches the skin on my ankle, I don't flinch. I don't open my eyes either, simply letting him begin to explore my body as though I'm asleep, and he's still a forbidden outsider to my pleasure. The trail of his finger up the inside of my leg is sweet torture. I almost shiver with pleasure, but I control my responses so I can stay inside the fantasy for as long as possible.

Is he enjoying my unresponsiveness, or does he want the fantasy to be over? I decide I don't care. This is about my pleasure too, and this is what feels good to me. I can hide behind my eyelids and let him explore my body.

The first brush of his finger against my pussy makes me want to sigh, but I bite the inside of my cheek instead. Then there's hotter, rough pressure on my clit, and I realize he's replaced his finger with his mouth.

Oh God, it feels good. The piercing in his tongue flicks against me in the same way as his brothers. I want to widen my legs and give him easier access, but I don't. I'm a puppet and he's pulling my strings. He's the one with the control, and I'm just a docile participant. He's an invader to my home, taking what he wants.

For a moment, I consider whether it's me with the kink here? The idea that a man could sneak into my bedroom and take advantage of me has my pussy squeezing between my legs. Is it wrong to be aroused by this? I guess one thing I've learned through all of this experience is that no two people experience sex the same way. We all have different triggers and fantasies, and that's okay. As long as we respect the people we're involved with and we don't hurt anyone in the process, anything goes.

My body wants to tremble with arousal, and it takes every ounce of control for me to preserve the fantasy, but then Dex adds a finger, and I'm gone. The pleasure swallows me, and my legs trap his hand inside me as wave upon wave of pure contracting heat steals my voice.

The soft kiss that Dex presses to my lips brings me

around. "That was hotter than hell," he whispers, grinning.

"It was," I whisper. "It really was, but you know what would be hotter?"

"Tell me," he says, dark brown eyes searching mine.

"If you take off your clothes and get on this bed with me right now." I grab the front of his shirt to illustrate the point.

"Yes, ma'am," he laughs. When he tugs off his shirt in one motion, I notice that he has an identical snake tattoo to his brother's, disappearing beneath the waistband of his jeans. Where Nash, Niall, and Noah have tried to create differences between them, Lex and Dex have attempted to preserve their similarity. He unfastens his hair, letting the glossy brown strands fall around his face. There's something warrior-like about Dex. Something a little more dangerous than his twin.

Maybe it's to do with what I know about his fantasy. It's darker and edgier, and that fits with his character. He's the one who started the game. The one prepared to push boundaries.

"Everything," I say, nodding at his jeans. I'm intrigued to see if he really is identical to his brother in every way.

And it turns out he is.

But only skin deep.

I guess the way we fuck isn't genetic.

Where Lex was gentle, Dex is rough. There's a bite to his grip, force behind the way he fucks into me, flipping us from one position to another until I'm dizzy with it. There's pain in the way he pulls my hair when he's fucking me from behind and heat in the speed with which he thrusts. There's desperation there that feels different too. When we're spent, he wraps me in his arms and holds me against his chest. We don't talk, just dwell in the *after*. So many words dance on the tip of my tongue, but I don't say them.

I don't tell Dex that my heart is aching. I don't tell him that I want him to stay so that we can talk more about music and start to dream about the things that could happen between us when the sun rises and a whole new day of opportunity presents itself.

I don't tell him that each of the men from Ink Factor has left an imprint on me that I can't seem to shake. Or that I lie awake at night wondering how I'm ever going to move on when the game is done.

No man is going to live up to this experience. Just the thought of being with someone else fills me with dread and disgust.

It surprises me when Dex's breathing changes, and I realize that he's fallen asleep. Apart from the first night with Lex, it hasn't happened on any of the other dates, but I guess this is the first time it's not me who has to get up to leave for the date to be over. The first time since I decided that falling asleep with each of the men would only make this experience harder.

Turning in his arms, I map his face, committing his peaceful beauty to memory. Dex is the man who saw how trapped I was in my past experiences and wanted to find a way to free me, and he has in a way.

But in another way, I feel more shackled than I ever have before.

Until I played the game, I just imagined that I'd have to kiss a whole lot of frogs before I found my prince. Now I've kissed a whole lot of princes, but they're not my live-happily-ever-after ending. They're supposed to be the beginning of a new life. A springboard for me to jump from. Except I don't want to jump anymore.

I just want to swim again, with all of them around me.

31

NASH

Kyla had moved the empty white plastic bowl that was the center of the game back into the kitchen area after she picked Dex's date from its depths. After she left last night, I placed it back on her desk with my neatly folded date in the bottom.

I wished I could see her face when she arrives in the morning, but Carl wants me to travel to one of the franchises to deal with a quality issue so I'm going to be out all day. Really bad timing, but business has to come first, at least during working hours. After, it is a different story.

I've made sure that everyone apart from Dex has cleared their schedules for the next seven nights, knowing that Kyla may not decide to go ahead with my date immediately. She may decide to forgo it altogether. It was always a risk, but one I felt was worth taking, now even more so.

I call Dex from the car to find out how his night went.

He doesn't go into details but tells me that he stayed at Kyla's overnight and left before work so he could shower and change. When I ask him if Kyla was happy with his night, he snorts. "And why the hell wouldn't she be. You think I don't know how to keep a woman happy?"

"I think this process might be more difficult for Kyla than you originally anticipated."

"She was fine…amazing even, Nash. You don't have anything to worry about there."

"So, do you think she's going to want to go ahead and finish the game?"

"I thought she'd finished. She told me there weren't any more dates in the bowl. I thought you'd decided not to go ahead."

"As if!" It's my turn to snort.

"So why the hell wasn't your date in the bowl?"

"Because I wanted her to have been with each of you already before she finds out what my date is."

"What is it?" Dex asks, his voice slow and low, suspicion coming through loud and clear.

"All of us," I say. "That's why I'm calling. I need you to keep yourself available for the next seven days so that Kyla can decide when she wants to go ahead. I don't want anyone to be left out."

"All of us?" Dex speaks slowly, as though he needs time to digest the idea.

"You told us to pick a kink. Well, mine is sharing."

"You want to ride a train over her?"

"That's a gross way of putting it. I want to show her how amazing it can be to be the center of a group of men focused only on her pleasure."

"It's a train," Dex huffs.

"With that attitude, you can sit in the back carriage."

"I don't think she's going to go for it," Dex says.

"And why the hell not? You other reprobates have got her doing some seriously 'out there' things. And she's fucked you all already. She's fucked everyone apart from me. She's already done it in public with people watching. Why would it even be a big deal?"

"I think she's struggling," Dex says. "I kept seeing this thing in her eyes…and feeling like it was sadness or regret. I don't know…I just get the feeling that it's taking it out of her."

"Physically or emotionally?"

"Maybe both."

We sit in silence for a moment, and I wonder if I've made a big mistake leaving my night until last. If she decides she won't go ahead, I will have missed my chance. It's a chance I may never get back. This could blow it, not just for me but for the whole group.

I don't tell Dex my plan to turn this game with Kyla into something more permanent. I've kept it between Carl and me because I fear that if too many people know, it could make it weird. Maybe they won't want to participate.

I need them to see how perfect it could be so that they won't need so much convincing.

"It'll be okay," I say. "More than okay. It'll be great. And Kyla will come away happy. I know she will."

"Eight men and one woman," Dex muses. "You really think she'll go for that?"

"She's friends with that popstar, Luna, isn't she? She knows that Luna has seven men. One more is kind of nothing, don't you think?"

"Just because her friend does something doesn't mean that Kyla will want to," Dex reminds me.

"We have to try," I say a little too quickly, screwing up my face at the possibility that Dex might guess what I have in mind. "We have to try because it's my kink, and I think Kyla will enjoy it."

"You're sounding selfish," Dex says, "But whatever. Let's see what Kyla says. Just make sure you try to ascertain if she's feeling pressured. She's such a good person. I worry she'd give in just because she didn't want to disappoint you. Especially since you're going last."

"It was always a risk," I say. "But I'm not worried."

I don't make it back to the shop until late afternoon. When I arrive, Kyla isn't at the reception desk, and the bowl is gone too. My heart drops in my chest like a pebble into a pool, the rippling of anxiousness a cool ache inside me. Carl hears the door and sticks his head out of his office, asking for an update.

"It's all sorted," I tell him. He wants to know more, but for once, I don't embellish. What's the point of me going to handle things if he wants to micromanage everything from afar? When he concedes, his eyes flick to the door of his office.

"She picked out your date," he whispers. "I watched her do it."

"And?"

"She folded it and slid it into the pocket of her jeans."

"Did she look for me?"

Carl nods solemnly. "I told her you wouldn't be back until later, but if she wanted to go ahead with the date tonight, it would be okay."

"What did she say?"

Carl blinks slowly as though he's delivering news that he's worried might seem good but could be bad. His hands, which are linked together, wring against the desk. "She said yes."

"That's good, right?"

"Maybe. Or maybe she just wants it all over with. I just…there was something about her expression that I couldn't read. Something that felt…"

He trails off, and I wait for him to continue, but he doesn't.

"We only get one chance," I say softly. "We can't blow it. Me and you…it all hinges on tonight."

"I know," he agrees, standing and turning to the wall, his hands linking again but this time behind his back. "This could go really wrong," he says. "The rest of them could get carried away. Maybe she won't like it at all."

"I trust them," I say. "You should too."

When Carl turns, his icy blue eyes seem to soften into a warmer tone. "I should," he says softly. "That's on me."

I guess that Carl has always been the one who's existed slightly more on the outside of our friendship. He's the only one without a brother, the only one who isn't part of a twin or triplet set. We each have a blood connection, as close or annoying as it can be. It definitely affects the strength of bonds, but I had hoped after all this time that he'd know that we have his back like a real blood brother.

"I'll leave now to get our place ready," I say. I don't make it a question, but Carl nods anyway.

"See Kyla before you leave, though. She'll need it."

When I'm done with Carl, I find Kyla in the kitchen fixing herself a glass of water. "Hey," I say softly, not wanting to make her jump.

Her head turns, finding me filling the doorway. I can't read her expression. All I can sense is some trepidation. "You picked out my date," I say, even though I already know the answer.

"I see why you saved it until last," she says. "It really will be a grand finale."

Her last word tightens around my heart, like a clinging

vine around a stem. I don't want anything about tonight to be final. I want it to be a grand beginning, if there is such a thing. The start of something amazing. The change we all need to bring us together and root us as a unit. This girl might be small. She might lack confidence in herself and need to be organized to almost crazy levels to hold herself together, but she has power. Power to love and power to bond. Power to make all of us devoted to her, and to the life we can make with her.

"It'll be great," I say. "I promise."

Her hand grips the counter as though the very thought of what's to come has her seeking stability. "I won't be enough," she says quietly.

Instinct carries me nearer until I'm close enough to touch her. Pushing her hair over one shoulder, I stroke her neck gently with my thumb, cupping the back of her neck with my palm.

"You're more than enough, Kyla," I whisper. "Trust me."

She doesn't nod, but she doesn't deny it either. Maybe I can't fully convince her with words, but we will with actions. We will later when she becomes the center of our universe, the sun we all want to orbit.

I'll show everyone how right it can be, and then the talking, the convincing, will be almost done without me saying a word.

That night, we gather in the den of the apartment I share with my brothers. Kyla's been here before with Noah, so there's no doubt in my mind that she'll find the place. There's a restlessness in the air that isn't usually present. The TV is on, and a football game is being watched with minimal attention as we make conversation that avoids any discussion of what's going to happen.

I don't want there to be any preparation. I don't want it

to feel synchronized or preempted. I wanted it to be as natural as the sea lapping against the shore. I want Kyla to feel each of us offering ourselves in our own way. It's the only way this can work.

At least, that's what I tell myself.

I can tell that Carl feels differently. He's a planner. He likes to be in control. I guess he's like Kyla in that way. He wants to know the order of things and his posture, leaning forward with a bottle of beer clutched between two hands, tells me he's struggling with the uncertainty.

But that's life.

We all have to learn how to deal with what can't be known in advance.

Right now, Kyla's on her way over here with no certainty about anything, other than the fact that we'll all be here to greet her. She called it a grand finale. At least she has high expectations of our performance.

As I look around, it hits me that she's been with every man in this room except me.

What will she expect of me? To push myself to the front of the line or hold myself back to the end. I haven't planned a thing, wanting the same fluidity for myself as for the rest of my friends.

When the doorbell rings, I almost jump out of my skin. The muted conversation in the room halts immediately, and as I rise to my feet, the rest of them do too.

Noah swears under his breath, the pressure getting to him. Dex shifts on his feet, shoving his hands into his pockets as though he needs something to contain him. Carl runs his hand over his braided hair, his eyes lowered in thought. I don't look at the rest of them.

My focus has to be on Kyla.

At the door, I take a long deep breath, needing to steady my nerves. So much rides on what happens next, and even though I'm not a control freak like Carl, the number of unknowns still tightens my chest.

When I pull open the door, I find Kyla on the doorstep looking very different to the way she usually does. Her eyes are ringed with smoky black eyeliner. Her hair is straightened, and her lips painted red. She's wearing a long black coat and high spiked heels, dressed in a way that screams power and sex.

My throat swallows involuntarily as my mind tries to process what this means.

Has she painted on make-up and chosen clothes to act as a mask or a form of armor? Or is this what she thinks we expect of her tonight? A sultry woman dressed for sex.

Although she looks beautiful, I wish she'd left herself exactly as she usually is, with soft eyes and pink lips, and clothes that are pretty and practical. I wish she'd come as Kyla, not a different woman created for us.

Her eyes are wide, her lips slightly parted as she waits for me to speak.

"Everyone's here," I say softly. "Are you okay?"

"You mean, do I want to go ahead?"

I nod. That's exactly what I need to know. If she feels in any way coerced, I'll be escorting her home.

"I want to," she says. "This is the end of a journey of exploration, isn't it? You only live once."

"We do." I take her small hand, cradling her fingers in my warm palm. As she steps over the threshold, I place a hand into her hair and kiss her softly on the lips, hoping that it's the right thing to do. This is my date, after all. It's my experience, so my responsibility to lead her through, and I want her to know that I'm her rock through it all. Our first kiss is tentative and exploratory, and gradually, she opens to me, her free hand resting on my chest over my already pounding heart. She tastes of mint and of home, and as my emotions take over, I fleetingly imagine what it would be like to just take her to my room and show her all the things that I feel. We could be alone, and it would be different; more intimate and sweeter than what I had planned.

But that wouldn't take us any closer to where I want us to be. All it would do is seal the end of her experience, and that's the opposite of what I want and what I know is best for Kyla.

I know this experience is going to push her boundaries. I know it's going to take courage and confidence that she might not naturally have. It's going to force her to lose control of the situation and relax in a way that she might never have before. And as hard as that will be, I know it's going to be good for her. We can show her that it's okay to hand over control to others as long as they are good and trustworthy.

As I draw back, I wipe her lipstick from my mouth, and she smiles shyly up at me.

"You all kiss differently," she tells me. "Before the game, I wondered if your similarities would stretch to more than just your appearance, but they don't."

"I've heard that," I say. "And it doesn't surprise me." Stroking her cheek gently, I ask her if she's ready.

Kyla takes my hand and presses it to her chest so that I can feel her racing heart. It skitters beneath my palm as fast as it would if she'd run from her apartment to mine. "I feel like I have balloons in my brain," she says. "I've never smoked a joint, but I guess this could be the sensation."

"You feel high?"

"Yeah. My knees are like jelly, and we haven't even started."

"Shall I carry you? Would that make it easier?"

Kyla blinks her eyes the color of chocolate and nods. "I think that would be good."

She's not a wisp of a girl, but she still feels light in my arms. I hold her close with her legs draped over one of my arms and her body cradled in the other. Pressing a soft kiss to her forehead, I carry her into the apartment, straight through the den and into my bedroom, giving the rest of them a nod on the way. A few moments pass before I hear the shuffling movements of my brothers and friends, and I let Kyla slide to her feet, stroking my hands down her face and neck, kissing her lips, and loosening the belt around her coat.

Beneath, I'm expecting her to be wearing a dress or top and skirt, but she isn't. As the coat falls away, she's completely naked, her skin glowing in the low light from the candles I've placed around the room.

A hiss of breath being drawn emits from the doorway as Kyla comes into the view of all the men from Ink Factor. Her brazen confidence sends a ripple through the group, but I don't give a shit about them. All I can think about is the gorgeous woman in front of me and how perfect she is. How all my worries about whether she really wanted this were misplaced. She traveled here undressed for us. She didn't want even a few clothes to get in the way.

I know I'm the only man here who hasn't seen Kyla naked, and I take the time to take in every soft curve. "You're beautiful," I say, reaching for her hand. Instinct drives me to kiss gently, wanting to show her that even though there are eight huge men in this room, that we're all going to treat her with reverence and respect. And a whole lot of passion.

My cock is already rock hard, straining for her soft, slick pussy.

"All you have to do is tell us to stop if it gets too much," I whisper against her ear. Her head jerks in a nod, and my shoulders drop just a little.

Noah, Niall, and I have had some fun before. There isn't a shortage of girls out there who enjoy being the meat in a triplet club sandwich. I know the other twin pairs have too. But Carl has always been a lone wolf, and I've never fucked a girl with so many guys before—none of us have.

We haven't coordinated an approach, so I take the lead, drawing Kyla close, kissing her cheeks and jawline, gently helping her relax. That part is pretty key for a woman who's about to take eight huge men inside her. She'll need to be wet because I don't want her walking out of here in pain. That part definitely wouldn't turn me on.

My hands drift down her back until my palms cup her ass. The sweet moan she makes when I squeeze lets me know she's feeling good. When I pick her up again, she wraps her legs around me as I climb onto the bed, releasing her onto the comforter. All around us, I can hear the rustle of clothes. Belts clatter to the floor, but I don't take my eyes from Kyla's, keeping her grounded in the moment between us. Despite my musings about Carl being the least experienced in multiple group sex, he's the first on the bed beside us, his hand taking Kyla's and kissing it too. She reaches out to stroke his face, her eyes glazed, her fingers trembling.

Drifting down her body, I kiss a path between her breasts, across her belly, and around her navel. She smells of summer flowers and evenings on the porch swing. Every kiss takes me closer to the promised land.

I've imagined the moment I'd get to taste her from the first time Dex suggested the game. Before that, I tried to keep her firmly in the "work colleague" category, knowing how crazy Carl can be about the business. As I breathe in her scent, my mind seems to melt, no longer caring about what the rest of my Inked brothers are doing or worrying that Kyla might be overwhelmed. I'm lost in her body and desperate to give her pleasure.

If I can give her an orgasm with so many onlookers, I'll know she's into this. Mind, body, and soul.

Her clit is already swollen, so she gasps at the first lap of my tongue. My eyes open, gazing up at her body, checking she's okay. I find Carl's mouth latched to one nipple and Noah's to the other, and Kyla's head turned to face Kole as he runs his cock over her lips.

It looks like I have absolutely nothing to worry about.

So I take my time. I lose myself in her softness and sweetness, playing with her until her thighs are clenching and her body is bucking.

"Fuck her," a voice whispers behind me. It's Dex, and he sounds hoarse, as though watching the action is already too much for him, and maybe not enough. Watching is his kink, after all. It wouldn't surprise me if he wanted to go last. Denying himself while others experience pleasure in the most extreme way.

I don't need to be told twice.

It takes no time for me to shrug off my clothes, and I fist my cock, needing to take the edge off the frenzied urge to bury myself in Kyla's sweet pussy in one hard thrust. Taking my time will ensure that everyone gets to share the experience.

Kyla moans around Kole's cock, and his abs flex with the exceptional restraint it's taking him not to thrust into her throat. I line my cock against Kyla's entrance, giving her time to sense what's going to happen before I lean in, sliding forward, inch by inch, until I'm deep. "Fuck," I grunt, closing my eyes at the perfection, but I don't stay that way for long because watching what my friends are doing to Kyla is like a tongue across my balls.

"That's it," Dex says. "Give it to her. Make her moan."

And I do. I roll my hips, making sure to graze her clit with each thrust until she's making sounds that don't even sound human, and Kole is crying out, his hand on Kyla's throat as he comes and she swallows.

Kase is quick to take his place on the other side, gently encouraging Kyla to turn, stroking his thumb across her lips. Her eyes flutter as she gazes up at the carbon copy of the man to her right. "Are you ready?" he asks her softly, and she nods as he brings his cock to her lips, shifting to get close enough for the depth he's seeking.

Niall is next, taking Kyla's hand and wrapping it tightly around his cock, seeking the friction of her palm as he thrusts slowly. I watch my brother's eyes roll as I hitch Kyla's leg over my shoulder and force my cock even deeper. I'm not going to be able to last long, but it doesn't matter because she's coming around my cock before I need to release, and I know I've done what I need to do.

I've given Kyla pleasure and brought us all together. Now it's up to the rest of my friends and brothers to do what needs to be done.

All I can do is slump back onto my haunches, my heart pounding, my mind thrumming, and hope that everything will work out just as I want.

32

KYLA

Eight men surround me, all naked and all gorgeous. I've never seen so many rippling abs and broad chests, so many rounded shoulders and bulging biceps. Tattoos mark every one of them, the black and colorful inked images a kaleidoscope of artistic talent exploding across the skin of men who circle me like lions around fallen prey.

And I have fallen.

I'm one orgasm down and trying my best to gather my thoughts while Kase slides his cock between my lips. Kole, his twin, has already given me a taste, and Kase is close.

One orgasm to them and two to me.

Not that keeping score should really be a thing, but this is a game after all.

A game that I want to come out of as the winner.

That sounds stupid, even in my own head. In my heart, it feels like the mutterings of a delusional fool because no matter how many orgasms I cause among the men of Ink Factor, I'm never going to win.

Winning would involve me getting to live the life that Luna gets to experience every day. It would involve me transforming myself into a person who is beautiful enough and interesting enough to be worthy of all these men. I'm not a snake who can shed skin that doesn't fit. I'm a woman who's deeply ingrained in who I am and who doesn't know how to become something brighter.

For now, I'm bright enough to offer them pleasure. I am shiny enough for them to want to lose themselves in my body. I'm new dime while the lights are low and the game is on.

But I'll go back to being tarnished after we're done.

I try to lose myself in the touches to my skin and between my thighs. Nash has moved to the side, giving way to Lex, who's taking his place. A new cock pushes inside me as Kase grips my hair, his fingers tight as he comes too, tasting just a little saltier than his brother.

"Flip her over," someone says. I think it's Dex. He's the one who likes to watch and the architect of the situation we all find ourselves in. Dex is the puppet master, pulling the strings until we're all jerking with pleasure, then dropping them so we can all go back to our lives.

For a second, I'm weightless as hands reach out to position me on my hands and knees. Noah tugs me over him, his hands on my breasts, his lips parted with arousal. "There you are," he smiles, blinking his long lashes. "Eight bananas on the menu tonight," he grins.

"That's no kind of fruit salad," I quip, and he laughs throatily.

"You think you can take two of us?" he asks.

"Haven't I just been doing that?" My eyebrows head toward my hairline, trying to work out what he means.

"DP," he says. "Double penetration. Two bananas in one sundae dish."

"Enough with the food metaphors," Lex says. "You're

making me hungry."

"I guess you can try." Even though I'm unsure, the thought of having two of these gorgeous men inside me at once makes my vagina contract with a fresh wave of arousal.

"Sit on my cock," Noah says, tugging my hips down. "Lex will do all the work. All we have to do is relax."

Relax.

I'm not sure that's a word that goes with this kind of sexual experience, although I left my insecurities at the door when it came to my body. There are too many eyes looking at me from too many different vantage points for me to suck my stomach in or worry about the dimples on my thighs.

Hands rest on my hips, but they aren't Noah's. I'm angled over his cock and forced down as another hand strokes up my spine and urges me closer to Noah.

God, he smells good. Little flickers of our night together flood my mind, and I close my eyes, wanting to slip back into the powerlessness I felt when I was with him. His strong arm anchors me to his body, his cock thick and good, spreading me open.

And he thinks I can take another man?

I think he's crazy.

The bed shifts behind me. Fingers tweak my nipples, and mouths lick over my skin. Someone trails their fingers over my taint, causing me to clench my pussy around Noah's cock. "Relax," he soothes. "Let that sweet, tight pussy relax around my cock. Let Lex in too."

His words and gentle hand on my back lull me into a place where it's warm and safe, where I can believe that it's possible for me to be enough, to be what they need.

The first press of Lex's huge cock at my entrance burns, but a finger finds my clit and strokes, and then, like a rub of Aladdin's lamp, all wishes suddenly come true.

The stretch is unbelievable, and I find myself panting fast, trying to acclimatize. "You're okay," Noah murmurs against my ear. "You're more than okay. You're perfect."

Perfect.

I know I shouldn't believe his use of the word. The man is balls deep inside me, and his mind is sex addled and stupid. I could be anyone right now, and he'd be feeling like it was perfect.

As Lex begins to move and his hands trail over my skin, I'm crushed against Noah's chest. "She's taking it," Dex says, his eyes alight with excitement. "She's taking them both."

"She's perfect," Carl says, his voice gravelly and slow, as though he can't quite believe it either.

And there's that word again.

Perfect.

"Fuck," I whimper, the press of my clit against Noah almost too much.

"That's what we're trying to do," Noah says, his voice light.

"Oh God," I pant, so close I can almost touch the sweetness on the horizon.

"That's kind, sweetie, but I'm just a man," Noah quips, earning a "shut up" from somewhere in the room. He can talk all he wants because his voice is low and sexy, and I'm coming hard around his cock and Lex's. There's a growl from behind me, and Lex thrusts faster, his fingers biting into my hips. "Shit," Noah mutters, the laughter wiped from his face as everything gets real. I know he's close to coming. I can feel they both are from the swelling of their cocks and the urgency of their movements. It's a frenzy of desire that sears me from the inside out.

"Fuck," Lex says again as he bottoms out, spasming as he fills me. Noah follows, his hand in my hair, his fingers wrapped around my wrist, trapping me in place until he's done.

"That was..." someone says, not finishing their sentence but leaving behind a sense of awe in their tone.

"It was," I whisper as Noah brings his lips to mine, kissing with passion and happiness.

I'm rolled onto my back, sprawled out like a starfish, and in a flash, Carl is between my legs. His hand rubs the fleshy part of my hip, that harsh palm searching out willing skin. If we were alone, I know he'd turn me over and tell me I've been a bad girl. He'd make my ass pink and my lips tremble before he'd make me come. But we're not alone. We're surrounded.

Instead of spanking, his fingers grip my flesh harshly, his tongue circling the shell of my ear. "You like fucking my friends?" he asks, sounding angry.

"Yes," I gasp as his cock pushes an inch inside me.

"You like it when two men fuck you at the same time?"

"Yes," I whisper, the shame and the arousal heating my cheeks.

Gripping even harder, he yanks my hips so that he's buried deep. I stare up into his icy blue eyes, not knowing if he's really mad or if this is part of the game. "This body," he hisses through gritted teeth. "This body is ours to use, ours to tease, ours to please."

"Yes," I say.

"This body is ours to chain. Ours to punish. Ours to soothe."

"Yes," I agree again.

Because it is. I've surrendered to them. I belong to them.

Carl fucks into me so hard that I'm shunted up the bed until my head tips over the edge of the mattress. I look up into Niall's soft eyes, my gaze drifting down his tanned, ripped torso to the cock he's gripping like a weapon. It's so hard it looks almost painful. Carl's hand rests over my throat, his thumb sliding into my mouth. "You see this mouth," he growls. "This mouth is for our pleasure. Use it."

Niall takes a moment to react, but he follows Carl's fierce instruction, bending his knees to bring his cock to my lips. It's an awkward angle, the top of his cock sliding over my tongue, but I manage it. My body is stretched, my breasts angled high, nipples tight and ready for the fingertips of whoever is closest. Carl's hand remains on my throat, as though he wants to feel Niall there and witness an aspect of the experience for himself. Or maybe it's a possessive thing? He offered my mouth to Niall, and by holding me, he's asserting his ownership of that part of me.

My mind spins, aware but unaware. My eyes flutter and snapshots of the room around me, the men moving in and out of my vision, enter my consciousness like old-fashioned flicker movies. Nothing feels real. Even my body feels disconnected, the pleasure I'm feeling so distant. It's as though everything is happening to someone else. The perfect me. The one who's brave enough to seize the day and experience life through the you-only-live-once mantra.

The other me is different. Cautious. Controlled. Shy. Worried that I'll be a disappointment.

This game, this experience, hasn't made me into something I'm not. It's split me into two warring essences and left me unsure which is the real me.

When Niall is close, he pulls out and comes in his fist, and I watch it all like a voyeur, a bystander, not the person responsible for the pleasure that drives his jerky movements and the relief in his face when he's done.

Carl isn't far behind, his cock jerking inside me as his thumb brushes my clit, once, twice, three times, and I'm lost, spinning and whirling, lights flashing and heart banging so hard against my ribcage that it feels as though it could shatter.

Lips find mine, kissing softly. Hands stroke my body, focusing on places like my arms and legs, my fingers, and my ankles. I keep my eyes closed, needing the solitude and worrying that if I catch anyone's gaze, I might break open.

Eventually, Carl leaves the cradle of my thighs, and another voice begins to whisper in my ear.

"Have you had enough, Kyla?" It's Dex. I know his touch, his scent, the husk in his voice. He's the one who started the game, so it seems fitting that he'd be the one to end it too. "If you've had enough, that's okay. I can take you home and tuck you in. If you need water, we can fetch it. If you need food, Lex can rustle you something up." I hear the smile in his voice, and my lips draw into a reluctant smile. "Is he seriously the only one who can cook?" I ask.

"Lex cooks. The rest of us eat. It's the perfect arrangement," Noah says from somewhere in the room. They're all still there, watching, waiting. They're around me and inside me. In my pussy and in my heart. They're buried so deep in my mind that I don't know up from down, left from right, front from back. Have I had enough? It's a question I can't answer. Nothing will be enough, but what I've had is too much.

I've tasted perfection, and now I'm going to have to deal with the fact that no man could ever live up to any of these inked gods. No Mr. Right is going to come along and give me more than they have given me.

"You think I'd leave you out?" I ask, in awe of his sensitivity and selflessness.

"It's not about that," he says, stroking back my sweat-slicked hair from my forehead. "It's about your wellbeing. That will always come first."

Tears burn like white fire in my throat, but I swallow

against them, forcing a smile.

"My wellbeing is intact, even though your friends have done their best to dislodge it."

There's a grumbling murmur around us, and Dex shakes his head. "Tell me what you want, sweetie. This whole thing has been about us giving you experiences that we enjoy, but what about you? I can do anything for you. What would you like?"

His words are kind and sweet, but they cut like a blade. He's trying to make the last time as good for me as possible but reminding me that we're so close to the end hurts so bad.

"Just hold me," I whisper. "Let me lose myself in you."

"Okay," Dex says.

As he wraps his arms around me, I wonder if this is hard for him. He likes to watch, but now he's the center of attention. Seven men flank us like guards around royalty. Seven men get to witness the sweet way Dex fucks me, the tender way he touches me, the emotional way he kisses me. Seven men, if they're looking close enough, will see my chest hitch with unshed tears, will notice the single tear that leaks from each of my eyes when I come in Dex's arms, and he comes too.

I bite my lip to suppress my moans, the pain pushing back my tears.

And after, when our sweat has cooled and the night has crept closer, Dex helps me find my coat, and he drives me home, leaving me at the door with a soft kiss, and a whispered goodnight, and a heart that feels like an anchor dropped to the bottom of a foreign sea.

33

CARL

I don't even get a chance to think about the amazing experience with Kyla or consider what Nash might be planning for the next stage, now that the game is over.

At 6 am, I get a call from two of my franchisees, warning me that the cops have raided their shops searching for drugs. I'm out of bed in a flash, throwing on jeans and a hoodie and sliding my feet into my workout sneakers. The drive to the store is quick at this early hour, but all the while, my heart is pounding.

I know I shouldn't take this so seriously. It's work, at the end of the day. No one's life is in danger. It's just business, but we've all worked so hard to make Ink Factor a brand with a good reputation. If news of the raid gets out, the local news could pick up on it. There's no way I want us to be sullied with any connection to drugs.

I'm unlocking the shutters to the store when I hear footsteps behind me.

I don't need to turn to know the cops are turning their

sights on our shop now.

"Carl Fury?" The voice is deep and fits the big muscular cop who's taking the lead. With an overhanging brow like a Neanderthal, and huge arms hanging by his sides, he looks like he could play a mafia hitman in a Hollywood movie.

"That's me."

"We have a warrant to search your premises. Do you usually come to work this early?"

"I do when I hear my business is in jeopardy," I say.

The noise of the shutters sliding upward makes the cop squint. I feel awkward unlocking the door, as though I'm about to expose myself. It's stupid because there's nothing to expose. We're up to date with taxes, and I would stake my life on my boys being one hundred percent clean.

I'm not so sure about the cops. "Can I see the warrant and your badges?" I say.

The look the main cop gives me could wither grapes on a vine, but he hands over the paper. It looks legit, and although I wouldn't know a genuine cop badge from a fake, I let them in.

I immediately call Noah, who agrees to mobilize the rest. It'll take them around twenty minutes to get here, and although they can't prevent the search, I'll be glad to have their support.

It takes over two hours for the cops to complete their searches. They're not tidy either, so Lex takes on the job of rescheduling the first couple of hours of appointments to give us time to get the shop back to a functional standard. By the time Kyla arrives, the cops are gone, but my stress levels are through the roof.

"Did something happen?" she asks, looking around at everyone tidying their workstations. Noah's sweeping the whole shop, something we always do at night. Her eyes scan me from head to toe, and her face twitches at the sight of my jeans and hoodie. She's never seen me in this kind of outfit before, and my hair must be unkempt.

"Police raid," I say, turning my back and storming into the office. I can't talk to her like nothing's happened when my nerves are frayed this way. My phone rings and it's another franchisee who's just been approached by cops with a warrant. I yell to get the attention of the boys, and when they crowd into the office, I give them each a franchise to attend to and send them off to minimize the collateral damage.

"You need to cancel the entire day of bookings," I snap at Kyla. "We can't be bringing people in for tattoos under these circumstances."

"The whole day?" she says.

"That's what I said."

Her cheeks flush with color, but I turn and storm back into the office before I have a chance to see any more. I don't need her asking me questions. I just need her to listen when I tell her to do something. Why the fuck can't she see that? Doesn't she understand me at all?

From the office, I can hear Kyla apologizing to customers and trying to find spaces to rebook their appointments. We're pretty much fully booked for months in advance, so it won't be easy. The shop is so quiet that even from the office, I can hear how irate some of the customers are. Kyla handles it well, but she must be feeling the pressure.

It's her job. I tell myself as I bury my head in my hands. Calls start coming in as each of the boys reaches the other stores. Noah's the first to report bad news, as he arrives to find the store owner being led away in handcuffs. "Fuck!" I yell, tossing the stapler at the wall. The plastic top splinters against the exposed brickwork, and staples fly like shrapnel across the room. That's two. How many of these fuckers have been using our brand as a front for illegal operations? One more, and it's going to look like something organized, and if it does, will it come to our doorstep? Will we be dragged into a case against our franchisees?

I don't know what to do.

None of this is within my control, and I can't stand it. My fists are clenched so hard that my palms begin to hurt. When I release them, my nails have cut crescent shapes into the skin. I rest my head in my hands, trying to breathe deeply and evenly, needing to find a way to settle the raging uncertainty that's spinning my mind out of control.

When there's a soft tap on the door, I snap my head up, finding Kyla standing nervously in the doorway. "I've called everyone," she says. "Is there anything else I can do?"

"Just go," I say. I don't mean it to sound so dismissive, but I don't have anything left in me to soften my words or tone. She's done what she needs to do. No point in her staying around to witness my unraveling.

Her face falls, her eyes dropping to the floor. Her shoulders lower, too, as she turns and walks away.

Last night, Kyla was our everything. She was the glue that brought us all together—the one woman we've all desired equally and who seemed to desire us equally, too. But everything's coming apart at the seams. Without our business, I can't even contemplate what the rest of our life would look like. Kyla deserves men with their shit together, not ones that are fighting for their survival. She deserves to work in a place where she's not risking getting dragged to the police station at any moment, or worse, getting accused of being complicit in something she knows nothing about.

I don't trust the justice system. There are too many wrongful convictions and too many lawyers more interested in lining their own pockets than helping the clients who desperately need them.

I know I don't look like a traditional businessman. I look more like an extra from the Sons of Anarchy, a man more comfortable on the back of a Harley than behind the wheels of a successful business.

Maybe I'm jumping to conclusions.

Maybe everything will be fine. Closing a couple of dirty franchises wouldn't be too hard. They're in breach of contract for their conduct. Dealing with it will mean hiring lawyers, but at least they can sort out the technicalities.

Maybe we can get back to running this business and being the kind of men who could make the kind of proposition that Nash was talking about to a girl as great as Kyla. Maybe she'll still see us as decent men. Maybe there's a chance.

But even as I think it, it doesn't feel real. The images of that future are watery in my mind.

I hear the shop doorbell ring, and the door slam closed as Kyla leaves.

I don't want her to go. I want to wrap my arms around her and tell her that everything will be alright. I want to be the kind of man who doesn't retreat inside himself whenever there's trouble. But I'm not. And Kyla's better off without me.

34

KYLA

Crying is stupid. It doesn't achieve anything except make me blotchy and smudge my mascara in a very unattractive way. I can't even hold it in until I get home, so I have to suffer the indignity of passers-by shooting me sympathetic looks as I try to stifle my sobs.

I'm an idiot.

An absolutely huge, gargantuan, monolithic idiot for letting myself imagine that the men at Ink Factor see me as anything more than a colleague they've all fucked. I'm an idiot for thinking that the way they kissed me and touched me when we were all together was anything more than the final part of a game.

I agreed to the terms of the game. I agreed to all of it and told myself that I wouldn't let my heart get involved. It was about living in the moment and discovering things about myself that I didn't know. It was about shrugging off some of the shackles of my past.

But who was I kidding?

The men of Ink Factor are not men you can turn into fuck buddies without risking your heart. They're too awesome, too funny, too caring, and too hot. They've looked out for me through the process and made every moment that we were together feel special.

And in the process, I've lost my heart.

And not just to one of them.

To all eight of them.

This game was supposed to make things clearer to me. It was supposed to help me work out what kind of man I want so that dating in the future would be less about stumbling into a relationship and more about me only accepting the kind of love that I want. Instead, rather than settling on one type of man who would be my Mr. Right, I'm not stuck with feeling that all eight of them are perfect for me.

Before Nash's date, I could never have truly comprehended what a relationship like Luna's could be like. The girls of the Reverse Harem Ladies Club all seem so happy and content in their poly relationships, and I guess a small part of me was starting to wonder if it could happen for me too.

I'm so stupid to take Luna's flippant comments and start to create a fantasy life out of them.

I'm so stupid to look at my eight colleagues and imagine that they could ever be happy with just one woman.

Forget one woman. That they could ever be happy with just me.

Who the fuck do I think I am?

I'm no supermodel. I'm not special enough to gather a harem around me. I'm not the kind of woman with the strength of character to be a queen bee amongst so many kings.

Because they are.

They're kings, and all I should ever have hoped for is that I could get to worship at their feet just once.

And that's what I got. Well, twice, really.

And now it's all over.

The way Carl spoke to me tells me everything about my status for the men of Ink factor now. They all threw their names into the bowl, had their fun, and now the respect has gone. Before we fucked, there was a mutual understanding between us. Now, Carl's treating me like I'm nothing and the rest of them are avoiding me. I know the game is over, but they haven't sent me a single message. Not even a smiley faced emoji, or something short to check how I am.

Carl's discarding me. They all are.

And I don't think I can take it.

My heart has been bruised too many times before.

It's been ripped out of my chest, and I've had to take my time to put it back and try to heal it, and now it feels torn all over again.

When I'm home, I take a washcloth and clean my face, but it's only a temporary fix. The tears fall again, and this time, I don't have a reason to stifle them.

In my comfy pajamas, I slump onto the sofa and sob my heart out. I try to push away all the amazing memories I've made with the eight men of Ink Factor. I convince myself that all their tenderness and care was just part of the game and nothing more. I tell myself that I shouldn't feel hurt. They're not doing anything wrong. Not really. If my expectations were of something bigger than they promised, then my disappointment is my own fault.

I watch a murder mystery on TV because anything with love it in would be too much for me. Losing myself in a fictional drama is the only thing that takes my mind off my aching heart.

Dawn calls me, but I don't pick up. When I message

her to tell her I have a migraine, she sends me a hug emoji and asks if I'll call her tomorrow. Maybe by then, I'll have stuffed down all this emotion and sadness, packing it tight into the box containing all my other heart-shattering moments. Maybe I'll be able to tell my friend brightly that the game was awesome, and You Only Live Once is the best mantra to live by. I can convince her that I'm forever changed for the better.

By morning, my skin has recovered its usual glow, and my eyes have lost their swollenness. I dress all in a bright red sweater and tight black pants, needing to feel powerful and in control when I face whatever is going on at work.

My heart is skittering as I arrive outside Ink Factor. I can hear music from inside, which is a good sign. It feels odd to open the door and step inside as though I'm trespassing. This is my place of work, but I'm not comfortable here anymore.

When I rest my purse under the reception desk, I notice that the white plastic bowl that held eight dates with eight men has gone. It was empty anyway, but its removal really underlines the end of a chapter.

"Hey, Kyla," Lex says as he passes. "Things have been crazy around here."

"Yeah," I say, even though I'm not a party to what's been going on. No one has told me why everyone left, and I had to cancel a whole day of appointments. No one told me why the shop was turned over so badly or why Carl was throwing things at the wall.

I may work here, but I'm not in the inner circle.

Customers begin to arrive, and everyone keeps their head down, trying to clear the backlog of people wanting permanent marks made to their skin.

It's almost lunchtime when the bell over the door sounds, and I look up, finding a man entering the shop who looks familiar.

The moment he sees me, his eyes blink with recognition, and a smile eases over his handsome face. I know that smile, even though I saw it from across a crowded nightclub. It's etched into my memory because of all the frantic and overwhelming sensations I was feeling while I was watching this man watching me.

How the hell did he find me?

"Now, this is a happy coincidence," he says. "What are the chances that I'd book in for a tattoo and stumble across the woman of my dreams?"

To the background of a thudding heart, I contemplate that this isn't just happening by chance. Is there a way he could have tracked me down? Not really. I didn't leave my name or number anywhere at the club. Kase and I were just two random strangers in a nightclub.

Or were we?

Kase has been there before. Maybe he spoke to someone before about what he does. Maybe he mentioned Ink Factor by name. With a little light investigation, maybe that's enough for this man to find me. But who am I kidding? I'm no one special that such a gorgeous man would go to so much trouble to try and find me.

"You have a booking?" I stutter.

"Yeah. It's under the name Daimon Swan."

I scan over the screen in front of me, finding that he's booked in as Dex's next customer.

"You'll be with Dex. He's just finishing up. You can take a seat over there." I point to the customer lounge area. "Can I get you a drink? Coffee? Water?"

"A coffee would be great."

The coffee machine is in the back, and as I leave the reception, Kase is returning from the men's room. His eyes scan reception, probably to see if his next customer has arrived. When his gaze lands on the man from the club, his whole body freezes. I don't stop for long enough for him to say anything about it. It'll be embarrassing to recall the reason we both know the customer, and in my current state of mind, I just don't want to go there.

When I return with the coffee, Kase is nowhere to be seen.

"Here."

"Thanks. Hey, I was wondering if you'd consider coming out for a drink with me. It seems we like to hang out in the same kind of places, and I'd love a chance to get to know you." He rests his arm along the back of the purple couch, oozing confidence. I open my mouth to reply as Carl appears from the back. His eyes flick between us, his face like a thunderous mask. Who knows what he's pissed about? It could be about yesterday's drama or maybe that he's caught me flirting with someone else. If it's the latter, he has no right to say a thing.

There are no rules about dating customers. I know that from the number of stories I've overheard about the shenanigans that happened in this place before I started. I'm a free agent, and I can do what the hell I want.

Daimon is sexy and interested in me, and I'm all about living in the moment these days. If I've learned anything from my experience with the Ink Factor men, it's that there is a whole world out there of experiences just waiting for me.

Fuck Carl and his moodiness. Fuck him if he's jealous too. He's made it clear where I stand, and that's out in the cold.

But not for long. "I'd love that," I say with a wide flirtatious grin.

"Tonight?"

Damn, he's keen.

"Tonight would be perfect. I've got nothing else

planned."

The last part is for Carl's benefit, and it seems to work. For a moment, his ethereal blue eyes flick between Daimon and me, filled with what looks like panic. He doesn't want me to go on a date with another man, but if that's how he feels, he's gone the wrong way about expressing it.

I'm not a toy. He doesn't get to discard me and then get jealous when another man wants to play with me.

"I'll meet you outside the club," Daimon says. "Eight pm sharp."

Footsteps and laughter behind me drag my attention. Dex has finished his client and is ready to see Daimon.

"This is Dex," I tell Diamon, relieved for a reason for our conversation to end. With Carl looming, it's far from comfortable.

"Great. I'm ready." Daimon sips some more coffee and then rests the cup on the table. "I'll see you later." As he passes me, his hand trails to touch my fingers fleetingly. The memory of the way he watched me with Kase in the club floods through me, setting my pussy fluttering, but I'm confused. Is it Daimon watching that has me aroused, or the recollection of how it felt to be with Kase?

Everything is tangled and confused; my memories like a string of lights that have been left in a drawer because they're too knotted to use. It's pointless to carry forward any feelings about my colleagues. I have to do what they're expecting and just let all the memories settle into the past. The future is yet to be written. Mr. Right is out there somewhere. The men of Ink Factor have made it clear that they're not interested in taking that place in my life.

Carl watches Daimon disappear into Dex's booth and then sets his gaze onto me like a blue flame, hot and cool at the same time.

"I need you to reconcile these," he says, handing me a

pile of papers.

"Sure."

I hold my breath, waiting for him to say something, but he doesn't.

When he turns, his huge hands flex into fists as though he's imagining breaking a skull, and I spend the rest of the afternoon arguing with myself about whether I'm doing the right thing. But isn't that how I felt when Dex proposed the game, and pretty much every time I picked a new date out of the bowl? Isn't it the way I always feel?

Will I ever have the inner confidence to feel secure in the decisions I make? I mean, what's the worst that could happen? I won't have a good time with the guy, and I can just leave. Is that really what's making me feel so stressed?

When I'm ready to leave that evening, everyone is still working. They're open later than usual to try and work through some of the cancellations. I call out my goodbye, and a few voices return the same, drowned out by the constant whirring noises of the tattoo guns.

All the way home, I'm trying to imagine myself having a good time with Daimon. In my mind, the club plays some great music, and the drinks are awesome. The atmosphere is really buzzing, and he seems like a really friendly person.

Even after all that positive thinking, I still send Dawn a message to let her know where I'm going and with whom. I tell her that I'll confirm when I'm home safe and sound. It's a routine we have, to alleviate some of the stress of dating new people.

I choose a blue satin camisole and pair it with black faux-leather leggings and some black spiked-heel shoes. It's an edgy look for a night I'm hoping will take me out of myself just a little. I've gotten used to pushing the boundaries, and it's become kind of addictive.

But even as I line my lips, I wish that it was Kase who was meeting me at the club. I'm wishing it was Dex who'd be waiting to watch me. I imagine all my men waiting to escort me into the venue for a night of fun and dancing. My heart sinks in my chest like a deflated balloon, and my eyes look haunted when I apply my mascara. Even if Daimon turned out to be the best date ever, he'd never match up to the men of Ink Factor.

The truth is, they were supposed to expose me to all the things that are out there in the world, but all they did was make me want to stay in the warm glow of their part of it. They were supposed to broaden my horizons, but all they made me realize is that I'm happiest when I'm with them.

I used to believe there was a Mr. Right out there for me, but now I feel like there are eight. The world is cruel to hold so many juicy carrots in front of me and then tear them away after only one bite.

I take a cab to the club, and to his credit, Daimon is waiting outside for me, looking slick and sexy. If this was a few weeks ago, and I'd never met Carl, Lex, Dex, Kase, Cole, Nash, Niall, and Noah, I'd be so excited. My heart would skitter, and my palms would sweat. I'd be hoping so much that he'd like me and that maybe the evening could lead to something more. But now, all I can think of is that he's not them. He's not the men I want.

I paint on a bright smile as he opens the cab door and holds out his hand to help me alight. There's a wolfishness to the way he looks at me, as though he's already imagining eating me all up. "You look stunning," he says in his smooth voice, already leading me to the club's entrance. The doorman doesn't even blink before letting us in, and that tells me Daimon must come here a lot.

Inside, the bright flashing lights seem to signal danger rather than excitement. The intermittent darkness feels sinister rather than comforting, but I follow Daimon through the crowd to the bar and I let him buy me a cocktail.

I sip the drink while he talks about his business, worried that finishing it too fast will leave my senses dulled.

He's not a boring man, but I'm bored because my heart is just not in it.

It doesn't matter how much I try to force myself to smile.

The Ink Factor men have ruined me.

35

KASE

"Tell me that again," I hiss at Carl and Dex.

"He's taking Kyla out tonight. He asked, and she said yes," Carl says.

Dex scowls. "How the fuck has this happened? I mean, the game only ended a couple of days ago, and she's already looking for someone else."

Carl kicks the empty trash can, and it skitters noisily across the floor, thumping against the bare brick wall and rebounding. "I told you this thing was a bad idea from the start. What we needed was a great administrator, and we found one. Now there is a whole heap of shit piling up between us. She's not going to want to work here anymore. We're going to lose her."

"Sounds like you care more about her shuffling your piles of papers than you do about keeping her in our lives."

"That's not what I'm saying," Carl snorts. "I want her. I've never wanted a girl so bad. But I'm thinking about *her* too. We've messed this up for her. She quit her other job, and I can see it in her eyes. She's not comfortable working here anymore."

"She's comfortable enough to go out on a date with another man," Dex growls.

"A man that I don't trust," I say. "You know how he knows her? Because he watched me fuck her at the club."

"What the fuck?" Carl turns and stomps two paces away, as though he's afraid he's going to blow up and wants to minimize the fallout.

"He's a watcher," I say. "That means he's going to want her to fuck someone else before he fucks her…if he fucks her. She doesn't realize what she's letting herself in for."

"You serious?" Carl says, turning back to us in a flash.

"As a heart attack," I say. "We need to get down there. We need to make sure she's okay."

"Did you ever stop to think that maybe she wants that?" Dex says. "Wasn't the whole idea of the game to expose her to lots of different kinks so that she can be more confident sexually? Well we showed her, and maybe she's picked her favorite. Maybe she's gone on this date because she wants to relive the date that she had with you. Maybe she's picked her favorite kink."

"Or maybe she's the Kyla we know, who's innocently stumbled into a situation that she might regret or could even be dangerous. Are you willing to take that risk?"

"What right do we have to turn up to her date and disrupt it? We're not her boyfriends. We never told her that we have feelings for her. She is off out there living her best life. We don't have a right to act like possessive stalker ex-boyfriends. I'm not sure I want to," Dex says. "But on the other hand, if she's in danger…"

"It's my fault," Carl says. "I've been off with her because of what's been going on. We've all been distracted. Maybe she's taken that as rejection."

"Storming in there isn't going to make any of this

better," Dex says.

"But I can't sit here and worry about what might be happening. I can't stand thinking about her with another man, not even just talking and having a drink with him. Forget about the rest," I say.

"Fuck," Carl says, slapping his hand against the reception desk so hard that the vase containing the funky flowers that Kyla bought wobbles. "We need to get down there. I don't care if she's mad. She's our girl, and we need to protect her."

"Except she's not our girl," I say. "We're eight men, and she's just one woman. We can't share her like she's a sweatshirt we all like to wear every so often."

"This isn't a discussion for now. We need to get moving." I'm already in motion, not caring if the rest don't agree.

"My truck's out back," Carl says. "Let's go."

It takes us a few minutes to close the shop. While we're dropping the shutters, Kole arrives back from the local takeaway with a box of burgers, but all of us have lost our appetites. We jump into Carl's truck while we fill Kole in, and then drive in silence, weaving through the streets until we pull up outside the club. None of us is dressed for this kind of establishment, a thought that only crosses my mind when I see everyone waiting outside in smarter attire. Carl, in particular, is wearing torn jeans, which definitely won't fly. "You'll have to stay here," I tell him. "The jeans…they won't let you in, but can you give me your jacket?"

We switch my hoodie for Carl's smarter black collared jacket, and I guess all we can do is hope for the best.

The doorman knows me, but even so, he's never seen me dressed this casually. There's a moment where he hesitates, but I distract him by clapping him on the upper arm and saying, "Good to see you." He blinks, then nods, but I don't release my held breath until Dex, Kole and I are through the doors into the club beyond.

"You bought her to this place?" Dex yells over the pounding music.

"This fucking game was your idea," I shout back as I scan the dancefloor for Kyla's glossy chestnut hair and her pretty smiling face. Where's my girl? Where is she?

"Fuck," Dex growls.

"What, do you see her?"

"Over there," Kole says.

I follow the direction of my twin's index finger, finding Kyla at the bar, crowded in by two men. The guy who got a tattoo is sitting on a barstool. The other has his arm around Kyla, his fingers playing with her hair. I can tell by the way she's holding her eyes wide and the stiffness of her body that she's uncomfortable. This guy is doing exactly what I thought he would do. He's found someone to fuck Kyla so he can watch again.

"Shit," Dex says. I know this is probably tough for him because Daimon's kink is his kink too. But he'd never be this way with Kyla. He'd never wheel out a stranger for her to be with. He was gentle in his proposition, not forceful.

What's happening to Kyla right now is coercion. We begin to cross the dancefloor, getting buffeted all the way by drunk dancing people who are more concerned about having a good time than making room for us. We're only around fifteen feet away when I watch the guy slide his hand up Kyla's top, and her flinch and try to move it down.

And that's it.

I shove the last people out of the way, a red mist descending over my vision. I hear my twin shout and feel the rumble of their thudding feet behind me.

"Get your sleazy hands off her," Kole shouts. "Do you

hear me?"

He's the first to get close enough to shove the guy away, but I'm not far behind. Kyla's eyes are wide with surprise and fear. She brings her hands across her chest like she's trying to protect herself from what's going on.

The guy, who's big and meaty, recovers from the surprise attack and spins, his hands already balled into fists. Daimon slides off his stool and begins to back away, holding his hands up with palms facing forward. "Listen, she told me she's single. She agreed to come on a date with me. I didn't know she was with someone."

"I'm not," Kyla shouts. "But I agreed to come out with you, not to fuck someone else. This isn't what I signed up for."

"You knew the deal," Daimon laughs, shaking his head, and I want to knock it off his shoulders. No one makes my girl feel stupid. No one.

Before I have a chance to tell him that, Daimon's huge friend is heading for Kole like he wants to tear him apart.

Behind us, I can already hear the shouts of the security team mobilizing to disperse the fight that hasn't even started yet. Kole already has his fists raised, and all I can think is that this guy doesn't know who he's messing with. I've seen Kole knock out huge guys before. He fights like a pro, and he doesn't seem to give a shit about self-protection. It's how he got his nose broken and the scars on his cheek and brow. They're the only things that make us look different; the rage he suppresses most of the time surging like a volcano. I go to step in between them but Kole shoves me out of the way, not because he wants to take the credit but because he wants to protect me. He'd suffer horrific pain as long as he could keep it away from me. He's always been that way.

The first crunch to the man's jaw echoes, even though the music is loud enough to make the floor vibrate. Kyla winces, cowering back against the bar as Kole lets loose.

The guy doesn't stand a chance. He's too slow and lumbering to even respond. Dex steps in as if he's going to try and pull Kole back, but he realizes there's a chance that the guy will take that moment to get the upper hand. There's no stopping Kole now. Not until security take hold of them both.

"You fucking asshole," he screams. "You put your hands on that woman. You could see she didn't want you to. What the fuck were you doing?"

The man laughs through another punch to his jaw. "Your girl was cheating on you," he says, and it's like a red rag to a bull. Kole hits him so hard on the side of his head that his head jolts on his neck, and his eyes droop momentarily. Even slightly harder, and he would drop like a sack of potatoes but he's still standing. Daimon is already far enough away to not get dragged into the situation, and Dex has turned his attention to Kyla, wrapping his arm around her shoulders and pulling her away. Just before the security team arrives, I grab Kole and pull him back. For a moment, it seems as though he hasn't registered that it's me. "We need to get the fuck out of here," I say, dragging him into the dancing crowd. I scan for Dex, and he's already ahead of us, leading Kyla out of the place that I exposed her to. The place where she could have been badly hurt.

The shame that burns inside me is hotter than lava. I shouldn't have done it. I shouldn't have brought her into my sick fucking fantasies. I could have chosen something less extreme. I should have chosen something less extreme.

"Hey!" A shout from behind spurs me faster. A man staggers into my path and I have to bump him out of the way with my shoulder, spilling his drink all over a girl in front of him. The security team are close on our heels but we're going to get out of here without getting caught. Carl is just outside. We need to reach that vehicle, drive away from this place, and not look back. I need to tell Kyla to never come here again.

Dex is the first to burst through the door, but we're not far behind. He breaks into a run, with Kyla struggling on her high heel shoes behind him. "You shouldn't have stopped me," Kole says. "I wanted to break that guy's head open."

"'Cause that's just what we need. You arrested for smashing someone to pieces."

"Hurry up!" Dex shouts as he waits for Kyla to slide across the seats. As I'm closing the door of the truck, there's a shout behind us, and Carl just manages to pull away before the club security has their feet on the sidewalk.

I exhale a massive breath, turning to get a good look at Kyla sandwiched between Dex and Kole in the backseat. "Are you okay?" I ask her before I have a chance to register the furious scowl that's twisted her pretty face.

"No, I'm not fucking okay," she spits. "Just take me home."

"What the fuck were you doing in that place?" Kole says, cradling his bruised and bloody right fist in his left. "What the fuck were you doing with those two guys?"

"Why the fuck is it any of your business?" Kyla shouts. "We're not dating. I wasn't cheating on anyone. If I want to go out on a date, I will."

"That wasn't a date. That was a fucking setup," Kole yells. "Don't you realize what that guy was about? He didn't give a fuck about you. He just wanted to use you to get off."

"Sounds like some other people I can think of," Kyla spits gritting her teeth as though she's daring one of us to deny her words.

But it's like they knock everything out of us because she's right in a way. What we all did with Kyla was supposed to be about her, but we were all in it for maxing out our enjoyment. We did nothing to show her that the further we got into the game, the more we wanted from her. We've been so wrapped up in the problems with the business that she's gone out in search of another man.

We should have battled it out between us so that at least one of us could ask Kyla out on a date. Yeah, we all want her, but we'd step aside so that one of us could have her. We'd do that for Kyla and for our friend or brother. We'd make that sacrifice so that she could be happy and protected.

"Please just take me home," she whispers. "I can't do this."

I wish I was in the backseat so I could throw my arm around her shoulders and tell her how much I care about her. I wish she'd hear how everything that happened between us meant so much more than just sex. But we don't even know what to do about this situation. We're not clear on how to make it better. How the hell can we communicate it to Kyla?

The silence in the car is deafening. None of us knows what to say to make things better.

Thank goodness it doesn't take long to get to Kyla's place. Dex steps out of the car to help Kyla, but she doesn't say thank you or goodbye. Her retreating form stomps toward the door and then disappears inside, and we're left to deal with the fallout between us.

"What the fuck happened?" Carl asks when Dex has gotten back in and slammed the door behind him.

"We fucked it all up," Dex says.

Five words sum up our situation.

The question is, what do we do now to make it better, or is it too late to fix?

36

KYLA

I don't think I've ever felt angrier or more ashamed.

And stupid. Don't forget stupid, Kyla. How could I forget *stupid?*

Was I seriously standing at my mirror imagining a nice date with Daimon only a couple of hours ago? What was the worst that could happen? I thought.

My imagination obviously wasn't capable of fathoming the worst.

That sweet-talking asshole didn't want me. He wanted to watch his huge, meaty-fingered friend fuck me. He wanted a repeat performance of what I did with Kase.

And if that wasn't bad enough, I had to be rescued by the man who took me to that club in the first place and his three friends. I had to face down the men who played a game with me and left me feeling broken.

Shit.

Tears stream down my cheeks like liquid shame and

heartache. I should have known that this YOLO thing was only going to go wrong for me. I'm not a live-in-the-moment kind of person. I'm a planner. I'm cautious, and I like to think things through. I need to take my time to work out how I feel. I need to shelter my heart against pain because I know myself. I can't take another fractured heart. I can't cope with any more rejection. My tolerance for emotional hurt has been used up, and now the only way to get through is to shield myself from any possible repeat of what I've been through in the past.

I knew all this about myself, but I wanted to try to let go of the barriers I've put up to protect myself from trauma. I wanted to heal myself by being different. Dawn always seems so happy and free, and I was envious. I wanted that for myself, but what did I end up with?

More hurt.

An ache in my chest that doubles me over.

Panting, I swipe at my cheeks and unstrap my stupid sexy shoes. Daimon didn't deserve them. He didn't deserve an ounce of me, let alone the whole thing.

As I'm swiping off my eye make-up, I get a message from Dawn.

How's it going, you sex goddess. Is he hot? Are you having fun?

What do I tell her? It's a blowout, and I'm already home?

I'm so embarrassed, but she's my best friend, and I can't leave her worrying about me. I made an arrangement to tell her when I'm safely back in my apartment. And I can't lie to her about the date. We don't lie to each other, ever.

My fingers are trembling, so I decide to call her instead.

"There's my girl. Why are you calling me on your hot date?"

"Can you come over?" I mumble, my voice hitching with more tears that are threatening to break through my tight-throated resolve.

"What is it? What happened?"

"Nothing. I'm okay. I just really need you."

"I'm on my way," she says, clicking off the phone.

By the time my bestie arrives, I'm dressed in my comfiest pajamas, my feet warm in fluffy slippers, and my face scrubbed clean. As soon as I see her, I burst into tears, and Dawn throws her arms around me, patting my back and making the kind of soothing noises that mamas reserve for babies.

"It's okay," she says. "Oh my God, Kyla. Just tell me you're okay because if that guy did anything to hurt you, I swear they're going to find pieces of him all over town. I've watched CSI. I know how to dispose of a body."

"He didn't hurt me," I say. "Well, not physically. I just feel like an idiot."

Dawn draws back and places her hands on my cheeks, using her thumbs to wipe away my tears. "Take a deep breath and tell me everything."

So I do. We flop onto my squishy beige cord couch, and I share the whole mortifying story, and all the way through Dawn keeps her hand on my knee and tells me to keep going. There's no judgment in her expression, just empathy. And when I'm done, she hands me a tissue and pulls me into a huge hug.

"You're not an idiot," she says. "Not at all. You're just a hopeful and good person who judges others by your own standards. You would never treat another person like that, so you don't expect someone to do it to you. It was naïve but not stupid."

"I should never have played the game," I tell her. "It was all a terrible mistake. I was trying to be someone that I'm not and now everything is ruined. I really enjoyed the job, and I was doing well. I like everyone I work with…I mean, how often does that happen?"

Dawn shakes her head. "Like never, sweetie. My boss is a toad and most of my coworkers wouldn't spit on me if I was on fire."

"Exactly. And now I have to quit." Another tear falls from my eye, and Dawn passes me yet another tissue.

"I don't think you have to quit, honey. Those men came to find you when they thought you were in danger. They wanted to make sure you were okay. They went out of their way to keep you safe. That doesn't sound like men who want you to leave. It sounds a lot like men who care."

"Or men who feel guilty. If I wasn't an idiot for going to the club, I was for agreeing to the game in the first place."

"You weren't an idiot for that either," Dawn snaps. "You were just a girl who wanted some fun and interesting experiences. I bet none of those men are kicking themselves for enjoying sex with you. There's such a hideous double standard about sex that keeps women feeling guilty while men get to have all the fun. What's the difference between a woman's body count and a man's? Are we seriously still looking at life through an ancient patriarchal lens that holds us in a subservient position forever? A woman's vagina doesn't get any more affected by sex than a man's stupid penis, but we have to listen to all these ridiculous bros on social media spouting off about women losing their value. I'm sick of it.

"You had fun, and that's it, sweetie. Give yourself a break. You lived in the moment, and you enjoyed it. Life goes on. Your job is still there. All you need to do is hold your head up high and get on with it."

"It's not that easy," I reply, frustrated that she's not getting it.

"Why not? Explain to me."

"Because I have feelings for them. Because they're the

best men I've ever met, and I can't just go back to seeing them as fun work friends when I want more."

"You have feelings for them? Like more than one of them?"

I hang my head, rubbing my hands over my face, feeling so weary right through to my bones.

"All of them," I admit.

"You have feelings for eight men? Like, seriously?"

I nod, and Dawn's shocked face begins to expand into a grin. "They must have all really been something special. I think they've fucked the sense out of your head."

"Are you serious?" I say, raising my eyebrows and shaking my head. "You've just spouted all this stuff about women being emancipated enough to have sex without feeling guilty, and here you are suggesting it wouldn't be possible for me to have genuine feelings for more than one man at a time. I mean, Luna's done it. The other women who came to the Daily Grind were doing it. Why not me?"

Dawn rests her hand on my knee and squeezes. "I'm sorry, honey. You're right. Why the hell not you! If you have feelings for them, then maybe instead of running away, you should tell them."

I stand, needing to pace up and down while I contemplate what she's telling me. "I can't tell them," I say. "Have you seen them? As if they're going to want me…all of them, and just one of me."

"Why not? You're beautiful inside and out. You have a soft and kind heart and always treat others with respect—you're funny and loyal and interesting and daring. You've had tough times, but you've never resorted to trying to hurt anyone. You're a great person, Kyla, and any and all of those men would be lucky to have you in their lives."

"Men like that don't share," I say.

"Except they did, didn't they? On the last night, you were all together."

"Only because that's Nash's fantasy. They all stepped in to complete the game."

"And did they seem uncomfortable?"

"No, not at all," I say, recalling just how comfortable they seemed with the whole evening. There was a synchronicity that I hadn't expected from eight very different men. It might not have fulfilled all of their fantasies, but it was electric.

"Well then. They're men who live together, work together and fuck together. Who's to say they couldn't love together?"

"Anyone with some sense in their heads. If they wanted me, they would have told me already. They wouldn't have gone back to treating me like someone they barely know."

Dawn rises from the couch and crosses the room to where I'm standing. Her hands grip my upper arms. "In life, you will never know the answer until you ask the question. Our ability to create the reality we want is directly determined by our willingness to face its opposite. You have to be brave and ask for what you want, or you'll go the rest of your life wondering if there could have been a chance that all of your dreams could come true, and regret that you never took it."

"Or the rest of my life facing up to the fact that I just wasn't enough to deserve my dreams," I say. "You know, I love you, Dawn. I know everything that you're saying to me is based in love and friendship, but I know myself, and I can't fight who I am. It's just making me even more miserable."

Dawn pulls me into a fierce hug, and we stand like that for what feels like several minutes. She's always been there for me, through thick and thin, and I know she always will be, as long as we're on this godforsaken planet. We'll be two white-haired women one day, and I'll still be calculating the risk in everything, and she'll be jumping off buildings attached to a bungee cord. We're just different people. But that's okay. I've realized that it takes all kinds of people to make the world go round.

When my friend eventually draws back, she sighs and pats my shoulder. "So, what's your plan, then? 'Cause, I know you have one!"

"I'm going to quit and try to find something else. Something closer to home."

"Closer to here?"

As I shake my head, the thought that was just dust in my mind begins to crystallize into something more solid. "My lease is up soon. I'm going to move home for a while. See what opportunities come up. Maybe save to try and buy a place so that I have some roots."

"You're going to move home?" Dawn throws her hands in the air and then brings her palms to her cheeks. "You can't be serious. I mean, I love your mom, but she drives everyone crazy. That small town…you were desperate to escape it. You really want to leave all this behind so you can turn back into Kyla one-point-zero…you remember what she was like?"

I do. She was frustrated and lost. The girl who settled for anyone who expressed an interest in her because she didn't ever want to be alone, because she was so desperate not to end up like her momma, because she was desperate to escape a life that felt like it was wrapping its fingers around her neck and squeezing. My dad left us because mom was so crazy with him all the time. I know that my fear of being alone comes from past trauma that I might never be able to face. All I can do is protect myself from more. "I'm not that person anymore," I say, but my voice sounds weak and pleading rather than confident.

"It's a mistake," Dawn says. "But I can't tell you how to live your life. I've tried…maybe that was an error on my part. I might sound like a parent, but maybe you have to make your own mistakes to realize where you're going wrong. I just hope you'll see it and come back."

Her words catch at my heart like fishhooks, and although something whispers in my mind that I'm being stupid, that I don't have to run back to a place that never made me happy, I can't deal with the alternative. So, instead of facing up to my fears and insecurities, I change the subject, knowing that Dawn will never be the first to let it go.

"Are you going to stay over?" I ask her.

"Of course. But only if you have another pair of pajamas like those."

Luckily, they came in a two-pack.

So, for the rest of the evening, we eat ice cream from tubs and watch terrible reality shows about people that neither of us cares about. We laugh like it's the last evening we're going to have together, even though it's not.

My mom's place isn't a quick cab ride away though. There won't be drinks after work or sneaked lunch breaks together. It'll be different.

Everything will be different.

And as much as I know that I'm doing the only thing that I'm capable of, the creep of regret is already seeping in at the edges.

37

NASH

The whole day passes like I'm wading through water in a fast-flowing stream, the current tugging at my ankles and threatening to pull me under.

Carl got a message from Kyla, handing in her notice, and the news is like a knife to the heart.

Everything that I thought we were building toward is crumbling. I'm not the only one who's taking it hard. Although we've been too busy to even discuss it, I can see from the dark expression and hunched shoulders that the rest of my Ink Factor brothers are as messed up about it as me.

The difference is that apart from me and Carl, they're all thinking about it from their own perspective. They might have had ideas about what the days and weeks after the game had ended might be like. Secretly, they may have thought they had a chance with Kyla if they just kept showing her that their relationship could be more.

Maybe they're just pissed that we're losing a friend and

a great administrator. I don't know for sure, but I'm going to find out.

It can't wait any longer. I need to tell them that I want Kyla, and I want us to share her. I need to help them understand how good it could be and ask them to join me and Carl in fighting for her to stay.

My hands flex, the ring I wear on my finger feeling too tight.

As the last customers leave, Carl locks the front door, and our eyes meet.

"It's now or never," he says, his jaw ticking with tension.

"I know." Looking around, I find Noah and Niall emerging from their work areas, Noah wiping his hands on a cloth that he tosses into the laundry bin.

His eyes drift over the empty reception desk, and for the first time in a long time there's no smile playing at his lips or laughter dancing in his eyes. Even my most lighthearted brother seems to have the weight of the world on his shoulders.

"It won't be the same without her," Niall says mournfully.

"It's my fault," Dex says, appearing from the back, closely followed by Lex. "If I hadn't come up with the stupid game, none of this would have happened."

Kole slumps down onto the customer couch, throwing his hands along the back and spreading his legs wide. "If you hadn't come up with the game, we wouldn't be feeling this way about Kyla leaving."

"That's true," Kase says. "We were worried about her getting attached to us, but it turns out the opposite has happened. She was so quick to move on, and now she's leaving."

"It's my fault," Carl says. "I've been snappy with her. With everything going on with the cops...I wasn't a good person to be around. I think she took it to heart."

"It's all our faults for being preoccupied at work at a time when she needed the extra reassurance," Lex says, shoving his hands into his pockets, defeated.

"It's all our fault for not being honest about what we want," I say firmly. We can sit here all night blaming ourselves and each other, but in the end, it's not going to make a damned bit of difference.

"But what would the point be?" Noah says. "We can all want to be with her, but only one of us can take that role. Maybe that's why she's leaving. She doesn't want to become the person who drives a wedge between us."

"She doesn't have to drive a wedge, though," I say. "She could have us all."

Quiet settles across the group as my words drop into the space between us and spill out like ink in a bowl of water. Carl catches my eye and nods once, giving me reassurance that I'm doing the right thing.

"You mean like Luna Evans and her bodyguards?" Lex asks, his eyes flitting from man to man, trying to gauge reactions.

"That's exactly what I mean, and before you say anything, just take some time to think about the next ten years and the life changes that are heading our way. Girlfriends, wives, kids, houses, cars that fit baby-seats and crazy volumes of luggage, people that might want to lead us in different directions. We can't fight that. Life is a journey with some fixed stops on the way, stops that we don't want to miss. But if we had Kyla…if we all had Kyla…things wouldn't need to change so much. We'd be walking the same path, investing in the same future. We'd share all the good times and bad times. What we have now will stay the same."

"You want us all to share one woman," Dex asks, his eyebrows drawn up in confusion. Of all of us, I would have thought he'd get it. He's the adventurer in the group. He's the one I would have expected to have the fewest reservations about my proposal.

"Yes. But not just any woman. I want us to share Kyla because we've shown that we can. We've shown that we can handle being with her separately and as a unit. We work well together, and we play well together. She's become a friend as well as a lover. She's perfect for all of us. That shit won't happen again. It's hard enough to find one good woman, let alone a good woman who all your friends love."

There are a few nods around the room at that because we've all had our fair share of difficult relationships. We've all had to walk away from women who didn't want to play second fiddle to our work passion or our friendships. We've all wondered how our lives will develop and what our futures will look like. It's part of being a human being, this desire to try to see ahead, if only in our own minds.

"But she doesn't want us," Kase says softly. "She proved that by going out with that asshole from the club the first chance she got."

"She wants us," I say softly. "It's been there in every soft glance she's given, every tray of brownies, every erotic touch. It's been there throughout this game as the backdrop to every experience. We just didn't acknowledge it, and so she doubted herself. She's pushing us away before we have a chance to hurt her. What we need to do now is fight for our girl. We need to tell her that she belongs to us and that we're never going to let her go. She needs to know that we won't let her run away. We won't let her retreat back into the life she had before she joined Ink Factor."

"It was fate," Carl says softly. Everyone swiftly turns, their eyes wide with surprise. Carl doesn't believe in things like fate. He's a pragmatist, a realist. He likes to be in control because he doesn't trust that there's anything else out there that can make his life better. And here he is talking about the abstract concept of fate. "I felt it from the moment she walked in the door. I felt it in all the decisions I made to bring her in, even though the way she was introduced was so random. There's been something nudging us in the background. Something that's brought us all to this place and is forcing us to look at this situation. Forcing us to focus on what's important to us." He runs his hand over his braids, his face relaxing as though revealing his thoughts has eased a burden that he didn't realize he was carrying. "I want Kyla in my life, and I want you guys too. I can't imagine a life without you all, so if sharing one woman is what I need to do to achieve the life I want, then I'm in."

I nod, exhaling a long breath at getting the agreement of just one of the group. My eyes drift to Noah, and he nods, the flicker of a smile playing at the corners of his mouth. "Fuck yeah, I'm in," he says.

"Me too," Niall jumps in, nodding at me with an expression of pride in his eyes. Only four more men need to agree.

"We're in," Dex says softly, his hand resting on his brother's shoulder. Lex nods in agreement, glancing at his twin and smiling. I never doubted that they would be of the same mind.

"Only you two left," I say to Kase and Kole.

They share a look, Kole dropping his arms from the back of the sofa and leaning forward, "I'm in," he says, "If Kase is. I know seeing Kyla with that guy at the club messed you up."

"If she wants us, I'm in," he says softly.

"Okay then." My hand slaps the reception desk to punctuate the decision, but I can't allow myself to be too relieved. I've climbed some of the hill, but there is still a very difficult part of the journey to overcome.

We might want to share Kyla, but now we have to convince her to want to be with us.

I won't relax until I hear her say yes, no matter how long it might take.

38

KYLA

Dawn is on box-assembly duty, and she isn't happy. I'm not happy either. My throat burns with tears that I keep swallowing so that Dawn doesn't see my wavering. My heart is beating too fast, sending way too much oxygen to my brain. Everything about me is fluttery and nervous. I'm a bundle of stress because my life is out of control. The roots I've put down that have given me a sense of stability are being torn up.

I've quit my job, given notice on my apartment. I'm relocating back home, but that doesn't fill me with any feelings of security. Instead, I'm swaying like a ship in a choppy sea, taking hold of the edge of my dresser to try and gain some equilibrium.

"I know I told you that I'm going to help you, but I really don't want to," Dawn grumbles.

"You told me you wouldn't tell me that I'm doing the wrong thing again," I say, reaching for the first pile of clothes to stack in the first box.

"Well, sometimes I say things that I don't mean," she says, scowling.

"That's not fair," I protest. "I have enough doubts on my own without you adding to them."

"Haven't I told you before that you need to listen to your gut? Your gut knows that you're making a mistake. It's trying to tell you."

"My gut is constantly telling me that I'm making a mistake about almost everything I do. Seriously, I constantly feel as though I'm going to be sick."

Dawn's hand rests on my shoulder, a calming weight that triggers me to release a long exhale of tense breath. "I don't want to make things harder, Kyla," she says softly. "I never want that. I don't know what to do to help you. Telling you that you're making a mistake is hurting you. Letting you make that mistake will hurt you. I'm stuck between a rock and a hard place."

"Don't you think I know that?" I say. "I know that because it's how I feel. I've had to weigh up two lots of hurt, two possible paths, and take the one that less terrible."

"Sometimes we have to travel the difficult path to get to the beautiful open meadow," Dawn says, her eyes taking on a soft and spiritual quality. "Sometimes, the slightly less difficult path is longer and leads to a place that is dull and lonely. I know it's hard to face the pain head-on. I know it's hard to feel out of control, but it's the difficult times we face in life…the hurt that we experience…that makes happiness and joy taste sweet. Those gorgeous men from Ink Factor won't want you to leave like this."

"You don't know that," I say. "They're probably grateful that I won't be hanging around while they're trying to find other women to have fun with. Maybe I'm not the first woman they've played the game with. Maybe I'm just one in a long line of administrators who have played their kinky game. How awkward would it be to watch that happening in front of me?"

"They thought you were in danger, and they came running to rescue you. Does that sound like men who don't care? Does that sound like men who'd want you to leave? Or men who are looking to replace you?"

I flop to the edge of the bed, holding my face in my hands. "I can't face them again, Dawn. Not after everything that has happened. I can't deal with their pitying stares and their embarrassed expressions. I can't deal with seeing them with other women, knowing what it felt like to be the center of their worlds for just a few weeks."

"So, tell them that. Tell them how you feel."

"Tell eight men that I've fallen in love with them? How pathetic will I sound? How unhinged? Who falls in love with eight men at the same time? They'll never believe me. They'll think I'm a pathetic woman who can't tell the difference between lust and love. Who wants to cling onto men she's had sex with because of some pathetic sense of emotional connection?"

"Or maybe they'll understand. Maybe they'll feel the same."

"All of them?"

Dawn sinks to the bed, throwing her arm around my shoulder. "I don't know, hon. I wish I did. Maybe all of them. Maybe some of them. Maybe one of them. If it was one of them, would you want to stay?"

"And spend the rest of my life looking at the rest of them falling in love with other people?" I shake my head, the hopelessness only growing in my chest. "I couldn't do that. I'd spend my life craving what I couldn't have. It wouldn't be fair to any of them."

"So, it's all or nothing," Dawn says.

"All is ridiculous. Nothing is hopeless," I say, repeating the argument that I've been having in my own head and heart since the start of the game.

"Luna doesn't think so," Dawn reminds me. "She's ecstatic with her arrangement."

"Luna's a superstar. Her men surround her like seven stars around a moon."

"You're a superstar, too," Dawn says. "I just wish you could see what a great person you are. I want you to believe in yourself."

"Believe that I'd be enough woman for eight amazing, sexy, gorgeous, kind, funny men? Who has that much confidence?"

"Me," Dawn says. "Luna. Those other girls you told me about from the Reverse Harem Ladies Club. They all have that much confidence."

I raise my hands and hold my face, allowing my hair to hang down and cover my frustration. Why don't I feel enough? Why can't I find that confidence?

As Dawn squeezes my shoulders, there's a loud knock on my front door. "Are you expecting someone?" she asks.

"No."

"A delivery?"

"Nope."

"I'll go and see who it is."

She rises and disappears into the hallway, leaving me feeling as though I've been hit by a train. My heart aches so much that my body feels like it wants to slump onto the bed and never get up. There's no hope inside me that it'll ever feel any better, either.

I hear Dawn's voice and the muted sound of a man. Maybe it's a neighbor looking for a missing package. The sound of many feet on the hardwood flooring has me swiping at my face. Who's she let into the apartment when I'm feeling so low?

"Kyla."

Nash is the first to enter my bedroom, followed by his

brothers, Kole and Kase, Dex and Lex, and last of all, Carl. They stand at the end of my bed, a wall of men taking in the disarray of boxes and unpacked clothes, their faces grave.

"What are you doing?" Noah asks.

I can't answer. My tongue feels desert dry and is stuck to the roof of my mouth. My cheeks heat with the embarrassment of being caught out. All the shame from the night at the club, Carl's dismissiveness and their apathy washes over me, hurting all over again. This is mortifying. All I wanted was to be able to leave without having to face them.

Too much has happened between us.

Too much that was good and too much that hurts.

"She's packing," Carl says. "She's packing up and leaving."

"What?" Kole says. "You can't be serious."

"Oh, she's serious," Dawn says from the hallway. She's too small to be seen behind the men, but she's big enough to be heard. "I keep telling her that she's making a mistake."

"She is," Kase says.

"I keep telling her that she just needs to tell you how she feels," Dawn continues. Oh my God. Is she seriously going to put me in this position?

"How does she feel?" Dex asks, turning to look at Dawn.

"She loves you," Dawn says. "She loves you all, and she doesn't know how to tell you so she's running away."

Dex swivels quickly, his eyes wide, fixed on me. "She loves us?"

"Yeah. All of you."

"DAWN!" I yell. "Can you just stop?"

"No," she says, "Because I love your stupid ass, and

you're never going to do it for yourself. Are you seriously thinking about just walking away from these men? Look at them. Are you crazy?"

"They don't want me," I say, exasperated.

"Who the fuck told you that?" Carl says, his voice matching his angry expression.

I straighten my back, shocked at his fierceness and reeling that I don't have an answer. Nobody told me directly. It's all just feelings and sensations—a look here and a sharp tone there.

"We want you," Nash says softly. He takes a step forward and then kneels on the floor in front, his hand reaching out to cup my cheek the way he did the night of his date, before we were all together. "We all want you, Kyla. We're sorry if we didn't show you. We're sorry that you ever felt uncertain about what was going on between us."

"But...but..." I look around the room at Carl's blue eyes that today seem more like melted ice, Kole's and Kase's eyes that are like the softest clouds, and Dex and Lex, who gaze at me with warmth. I find Noah, whose mouth is turned up into its usual grin, and Niall, who winks to show me that his triplet is right.

"But nothing, Kyla," Nash says firmly. "From the moment you walked into Ink Factor, you walked into our hearts. And when Dex came up with the idea of the game, we knew we couldn't pass up the chance of being with you. It's not something we planned. We weren't looking for one woman to walk into our lives and bowl us over. We weren't looking, but you came anyway."

"But..."

"Is that all you can say? We're pledging ourselves to you. All eight of us." There are nods around the room, confirming everything that Nash is saying, and a tear escapes my eye, trickling down my cheek.

"She doesn't know how to accept it," Dawn says softly. "She doesn't know how to believe that she's enough."

"Believe it," Carl says. "Believe it and accept it." His right-hand flexes as though he imagines himself slapping my ass in chastisement, and a bubble of laughter forces its way through me.

"Believe it," Nash says softly. "We love you. We want you. We're not going to let you leave us."

I exhale a long breath that I didn't know had been building in my chest, through pursed lips. All the tension of the past few weeks pushes to escape me. Laughter and tears wage war inside me, but Nash wipes it all away with a soft kiss to my parted lips.

"Now that's what I'm talking about," Dawn says with a whoop. "And it's also my cue to leave."

I don't draw back from Nash's kiss to say goodbye to Dawn, but I manage a flap of my hand in an uncoordinated wave.

Happiness surges, and my hands move to draw Nash closer until my legs are wrapped around his back and he's holding me so tightly I almost can't breathe.

"Do you want to let someone else take a turn?" Noah says from above us, and I feel Nash's lips quirk with amusement. Even though he's reluctant, he steps aside for his brother to take his place. And that's how it goes. I'm passed from man to man, sinking into loving kisses and tight embraces, being shared by brothers and friends without jealousy.

Tears stream down my cheeks that are a mix of relief and jubilation. Even in my sweetest of fantasies, I could never believe that this would happen. I could never hope that I'd find even an eighth of the happiness that is fizzing around my heart like champagne bubbles.

"You love us?" Lex asks softly, kissing away my tears and stroking my damp hair back from my face.

"I love you. I love you all. So much."

"Then what the fuck are we waiting for?" Noah says.

"What do you mean?" I ask, glancing around to see if I can read the expressions on the faces of the men who've spent the past ten minutes showing me just how much they feel for me.

"Forget packing up your stuff. We need to clear this bed right now."

I snort with laughter, and while the room is filled with the rumbling of eight men chuckling, I stand quickly and swipe at the box on the bed, not caring that it clatters to the floor and spills my clothes onto the rug. I don't care that I'm a blotchy disheveled mess because they love me. They all love me, and it's enough to put clouds under my feet and star-bright light in my chest. It's enough to drive away all the uncertainty and worry that I've been carrying since James cheated on me and stole my confidence.

"As much as having amazing sex right now is exactly what we all want to do, I think we need to clear up some stuff first," Carl says.

The rest of the men groan, but I lift my hand to let him know I'm listening.

"We don't accept your resignation," he says softly. "We need you at Ink Factor, and we want you to come back and work with us."

I nod because that's an easy fix. I love my job, and I love working with them all.

Carl smiles, relieved, then looks around at the chaos of my apartment. "What's happening with your apartment?"

"I gave notice," I say. "I need to move out by tomorrow. They have new renters lined up."

"So, you'll come to stay with me," Carl says. "Until we work out something permanent."

"Permanent?" I ask.

"Until we can move into one place," he says.

My imagination explodes in that moment, weaving images of a pretty house with enough chairs around a table for us to all eat together and enough beds for us to sleep in. It's like the three bears' cottage on steroids, but I don't envisage the men surrounding me tucking into porridge any time soon.

Tucking into *me*? Well, that's a whole other matter.

"Sounds good," I say, eager to move on from practical matters to physical and emotional ones.

"Wait a minute," Noah says. "Why does she have to stay with you?"

"Because I'm the only one living on my own," Carl says. "And because I thought of it first. You snooze, you lose."

"Is this what it's going to be like?" I ask, shaking my head. "Am I going to spend most of my time when we're altogether defusing squabbles?"

"You're going to spend most of your time when we're together on your back," Noah says, immediately grabbing me and tossing me onto the bed. I bounce a little, but he's climbing over me before I have a chance to complain. "Or on your front." He flips me over without any effort, so my face is mashed into the comforter. Tugging beneath my hips, he yanks me up until I'm on my hands and knees. "Or just like this." His hips push against my ass, the rigid bar of his cock resting along the seam.

"I think she likes being manhandled," Niall says with a smile in his voice.

"She does," Carl says. "Kyla likes a lot of things."

"She's perfect," Lex agrees, climbing onto the bed, followed closely by his brother.

"You guys still haven't thanked me for setting up the game," Dex says, resting his hand on my back.

I turn and smile as Noah yanks my yoga pants over my hips. "Thank you, baby," I say. "But I know a better way to show you than with words." I incline my head, motioning for him to take a position in front of me. When he retrieves his cock, I don't hesitate to take it into my mouth, knowing how good he tastes, and how big and powerful he feels.

What happens next feels different from the first time we all came together. The intensity is still there, but in front of it is laughter and affection, bubbling happiness, and relief that this won't be the last time I'm with them and they're with me.

There's so much tenderness in their touch and so much awe in their eyes. We move like our bodies were always meant to find each other. We slip into another time where kink and experimentation are set aside for something greater.

Love.

It's the start of something amazing—the start of a new life.

The one where Kyla, two-point-zero, gets a harem of eight men who want her, who love her and will be there to keep all the dark shadows at bay.

I don't know what I've done in a past life to deserve it. All I know is I'm going to spend the rest of *this* life working to make our relationship the best it can be.

And as I bask in the afterglow of our reunion, surrounded by eight gorgeous, inked men, sticky and exhausted from our passion, I know they will do the same.

EPILOGUE

KYLA

I arrange to meet Luna at the Daily Grind for a drink before she braves her first tattoo appointment. She's left her baby at home with his fathers, except for Asher. He's accompanied her, along with six huge bodyguards who take up the two tables on either side of us and stand like two sentries outside the door. Asher stays outside, respecting the fact that Luna needs time to catch up with girlfriends every so often. The fact that Luna refers to me as her girlfriend has me blushing with happiness.

My old boss doesn't look happy to see me, or to have half her coffee shop taken up by nonpaying customers, but I couldn't care less. It feels satisfyingly like a small payback for the months I suffered working here.

When I tell Luna everything that's happened over the past few months, she slaps the table with the flat of her palm, disrupting the pot holding paper packets of sweetener and sugar. "What did I tell you? I knew it was going to happen. I just knew it. All you had to do was manifest what you wanted."

"I don't think I was very good at that part," I say. "I mean, I thought about what I wanted, but then spent most of my time telling myself that it could never happen.

"Mmmm." Luna rests her chin in her hands and gazes at me across the table. With her wide green eyes and super-long lashes, it's like being stared at by a mythical creature. I guess she is, in a way—a girl who used to be ordinary but is now part of the celebrity world. "I still think you played a part in it. If you hadn't have agreed to the game, none of it would have happened."

"That sounds kind of passive for involvement," I smile. "I wish I could say that I'm a seize-the-day kind of person, but I'm just not."

"Maybe you are sometimes," Luna says. "What about how you got the job at Ink Factor in the first place? You seized that day."

"Out of desperation! I mean, look at the face on that woman. She could wither a new bloom with one stare."

"But you still took an opportunity that started it all."

"I guess. You know, maybe this wasn't my situation to manifest. Maybe, that was the role of my inked eight?"

"You could be right. I mean, it was Dex who came up with the idea and Nash who saw how happy everyone was and came up with a plan to make it permanent. They saw the girl they wanted, and they made it happen. That's manifestation alright."

"So, what are you manifesting right now?" I ask her, expecting to hear a ton of really dynamic goals.

"Just happiness in my day-to-day life, and time to have another baby. I love being a mom, and I love the simplicity of our everyday lives. All I ever wanted when I was growing up was a happy family, and I'll never lose sight of that, no matter how many other opportunities come my way."

"That's awesome," I say. "I'm not ready for the

children part just yet, but one day, I know all my men will make great fathers."

"How are you going to work out the procreating situation?" she asks as the new waitress places our cups on the table.

"We've talked about it. They want to take it in turns so that they can each guarantee a child," I say. "But I've told them that there is no way I could manage to have eight children, and anyway, there could be multiples, and that scares the living daylights out of me."

Luna's eyes flick to the ceiling. "So, four babies at least?"

"If each of the sets of twins and triplets has one each, then yeah. Four still seems crazy, but manageable."

"Don't forget you're going to have an unbelievable amount of help. Just trying to get a hold of Jacqueline can be a challenge. There is always another daddy who wants a cuddle."

We laugh and finish our hot drinks until it's five minutes to Luna's appointment. The walk to Ink Factor is short, but I soak in the sunshine and the soft breeze that ruffles our hair. People pass us, staring at the men in black who accompany us and trying to work out who we were behind the sunglasses. For a short time, I get to feel what it's like to be Luna, trying to do everyday things as an extraordinary person.

"Are you ready?" Asher asks, gazing down at his girl with warm eyes.

"As I'll ever be," she says.

There's a nervousness about her today, which I wasn't expecting. She's a person who believes that thinking about the things you want can make them a reality. Getting a small tattoo should be easy. But beneath it all, she's a human just like the rest of us.

"I'll tell you what," I say. "I'm going to get one done at the same time," I say.

"What? Are you serious?"

"Yeah. I've been meaning to for a while. I know that Carl is free now, so he can fit me in."

"What are you going to get? Have you even thought about it?"

"I have. You know the symbol for infinity?"

"Yeah. It's like a figure of eight." As soon as Luna says the words, realization dawns across her face. "Wow…that is so cool."

"It will be if I can be brave enough."

"I think you're a rockstar," she grins. "The girl with the biggest harem in the Reverse Harem Ladies Club. To be honest, I thought I was going to hold that title for longer than I managed to."

We both laugh, and Asher shakes his head. "Don't even think about trying to add any more men to your harem, Luna."

"Well, Elijah does have those two cute brothers," she jokes.

When Luna is settled into Noah's station with her tattoo design outline pressed onto her skin, I give her a little wave and make my way to the back, where I'm pretty sure I'm going to find Carl. He's looking scruffy today and is rubbing his beard thoughtfully as he stares at a document. Despite getting this place organized, Carl still has too much to do. I make a mental note to tell Dex that it's time for him to shoulder his way into some of the responsibility. I know that Carl will resist at first, but eventually, when he's delegated a little, he'll be grateful.

By loving them all, I've realized that sometimes we do need a push to be different.

When I knock at the door, he raises his beautiful blue eyes, and when he sees it's me, the frown softens from his forehead. "Is Noah working on Luna?"

"Yeah. He's all set."

"So what can I do for you? I thought you'd be in there watching."

"She has Asher to hold her hand," I say. "And I wanted to ask you something."

"Sure."

"Will you pop my cherry?" I grin as he blinks, not getting what I'm asking.

"I'm working, baby, and anyway, I think that ship has sailed."

"Not that cherry," I snort. "My tattoo cherry."

Now *that* has him sitting up straighter. "You want me to ink you?"

"I do."

"Me?" With his eyes open wide, he seems almost innocent in his surprise, which doesn't fit with the Carl I know and love. Is her seriously so surprised?

"You. I know what I want, but I'm sure you'll have some ideas to bring it to life."

He rests his palms on the table and pushes himself up to standing. The room suddenly feels smaller, and I get the same rush of heat between my legs that I always do when I get close to my men. My pussy is like Pavlov's dog. It's ridiculous.

"Tell me what you're thinking."

As we stroll to his booth, I explain my idea, and Carl nods with a flicker of a smile at the edges of his lips. He gets how big this is for me. He understands that this is me marking myself with my love for them. It's about showing the permanence of our relationship.

I know I'll be with them until I take my last breath. My

eight men, to infinity and beyond.

Now I've finished my ridiculous Buzz Lightyear thoughts, I lie back on the bed while Carl searches books for inspiration and begins to pull together lots of ideas into a unique tattoo for me.

Dex sticks his head around the booth and immediately straightens. "What? You're getting a tattoo?"

"Yep."

"And you asked Carl."

I raise my hand and shake my head, knowing that with seven other men who could all have fulfilled this request, this could get crazily competitive. "I asked Carl, and that's it. He's free to do it now, and I want it now."

Dex nods, and I'm glad that he's heard me and is not going to ask any more questions. This is a hard enough step for me to take without it being questioned. "I'll show you when it's done, okay?"

"Do it well," Dex orders Carl before retreating to find his next customer.

"You're learning fast," Carl says with a twitch of a smile. "A woman with eight men needs to know how to defuse them without anger."

"Lucky I'm not an angry person then."

When he shows me the design that he's created, tears spring to my eyes. It's an intricate and feminine combination of the infinity symbol with a single open flower on one side and eight tiny swallows lined up around the other curve in various stages of spreading their wings. It's our love represented in a single tattoo.

It's perfect.

"What do you think?"

"I think, if I didn't already love you with everything that I am, I'd love you more."

Carl's eyes lower for a second, and he inhales deeply as

though he can draw the sentiment into his lungs. His fingers find the edge of my shirt, sliding slowly up the center of my abdomen. I don't stop him from exposing me because, although it feels completely sexual, I know he's thinking about where to place the tattoo. I break out in gooseflesh, and I have to stifle a moan as his fingers explore my skin.

"Are you sure you want to mark yourself?" he asks. "Your skin is so beautiful."

"I'm sure," I whisper, taking hold of his tender hand. It's a hand that can touch me with gentleness but also a hand that needs to deliver pain. My Carl is a beautiful quandary.

"Then here?" he asks, stroking a place beneath the wire of my bra at the side over my rib. "Or here?" Moving his hand, he strokes over the top of my left breast.

"Over my heart?" I ask.

Carl nods, touching that place again. It's a place where I feel him and the rest of my boys every day. A place that was cold before they came into my life but is now filled with soft warmth, day, and night.

"There," I say. It's perfect.

"Okay."

It takes him a while to convert his drawing into a format that can be transferred to my skin, and for all that time, I watch him silently working, knowing this won't be easy for him.

Pain without pleasure doesn't come naturally to Carl, but it'll be worth it.

That evening, with my beautiful tattoo completed and wrapped to keep it sanitary, I sit on the back porch and watch the sun go down. The boys are late home. Work has been crazy, but I don't mind waiting for them. It builds anticipation, and the rewards are something else.

When I eventually hear the front door opening, it only takes two seconds for someone to call my name.

"Kyla, where are you, baby?"

"Out back," I yell.

The stomping of eight sets of feet through the house is like a herd of elephants. They don't have a chance of creeping up on me, that's for sure.

"There she is," Nash says, beaming. He's the first to bend to kiss me, his eyes drifting to the place he knows I've been inked. "I can't believe you did it," he says.

"Ha, you thought I was too chicken?"

"Nah. I just thought it wasn't your thing."

"Carl better have done his best work," Noah says, kissing my lips a little harder than his brother.

The rest take turns in greeting me, the smell of something delicious filling the air. "We bought burgers," Dex says. "Lex didn't feel like cooking tonight."

"Well, he's allowed a day off once in a while," I laugh.

"It wouldn't hurt you guys to learn to do more than boil an egg," Lex grumbles.

"Isn't the whole benefit of having a household with so many people that each of us takes on a role?" Niall asks.

"What's yours?" Lex begins unwrapping burgers as Carl returns with plates.

"Who do you think makes sure the clothes are clean?" Niall says. "Are you enjoying the fresh underwear you're wearing right now? That was me."

"Well, I guess my ass should thank you," Lex laughs.

"Yes, it should."

"I feel like I'm slacking," I say, realizing just how much my men are doing to keep our household functioning.

"Your job is the most physically taxing in the house," Kole says. "We only have to fuck once each. You have to times that by eight every time."

"I know," I say, rolling my eyes theatrically. "My life is so hard."

Lex snorts with laughter. "I bought you two burgers. You're starting to waste away."

He's right. The demands on my body have been crazy since we all moved in together. I think I've dropped ten pounds in the past three months just from having sex. I'm not complaining, but it would seem the boys like me with more meat on my bones.

"Well, I'm glad you're all appreciative of what I do," I say, rising from my chair and walking with a seductive sway to my place at our long table.

"Oh, we do," Kase says, tipping his head and watching me pass like a hungry man watching a plate of Thanksgiving dinner get carried to the table.

"We really do," Dex smiles as he takes his seat opposite me. Beneath the table, his foot strokes against my ankle, and just that small touch is enough to prime me for more.

It's a miracle that anyone is getting anything done in this house that doesn't involve being naked. Maybe all the enthusiasm will wear off, but somehow, I doubt it.

The men of Ink Factor have shown me that love can come in all shapes and sizes. What started as a kinky inky game has become the life that I never had the bravery to dream could be mine.

And I'll be forever grateful that I took that chance to experience something new.

ABOUT THE AUTHOR

International bestselling author Stephanie Brother writes high heat love stories with a hint of the forbidden. Since 2015, she's been bringing to life handsome, flawed heroes who know how to treat their women. If you enjoy stories involving multiple lovers, including twins, triplets, stepbrothers, and their friends, you're in the right place. When it comes to books and men, Stephanie truly believes it's the more, the merrier.

She spends most of her day typing, drinking coffee, and interacting with readers.

Her books have been translated into German, French, and Spanish, and she has hit the Amazon bestseller list in seven countries.

Printed in Great Britain
by Amazon